A DELICATE DECEPTION

By Cat Sebastian

The Regency Impostors Series
Unmasked by the Marquess
A Duke in Disguise
A Delicate Deception

The Turner Series
The Soldier's Scoundrel
The Lawrence Browne Affair
The Ruin of a Rake
A Little Light Mischief (novella)

The Seducing the Sedgwicks Series
It Takes Two to Tumble
A Gentleman Never Keeps Score

Coming Soon
Two Rogues Make a Right

A DELICATE DECEPTION

A Regency Impostors Novel

CAT SEBASTIAN

AVONIMPULSE
An Imprint of HarperCollinsPublishers

A DELICATE DECEPTION. Copyright © 2019 by Cat Sebastian. All rights reserved. Printed in the United States of America. No part of this book may be used or reproduced in any manner whatsoever without written permission except in the case of brief quotations embodied in critical articles and reviews. For information, address HarperCollins Publishers, 195 Broadway, New York, NY 10007.

Digital Edition DECEMBER 2019 ISBN: 978-0-06-282067-9

Print Edition ISBN: 978-0-06-282162-1

Cover design by Patricia Barrow
Cover illustration by Christine Ruhnke
Cover photographs © Period Images (couple); © PinkyWinky/Shutterstock (background)

Avon Impulse and the Avon Impulse logo are registered trademarks of HarperCollins Publishers in the United States of America.

Avon and HarperCollins are registered trademarks of HarperCollins Publishers in the United States of America and other countries.

FIRST EDITION

19 20 21 22 23   HDC   10 9 8 7 6 5 4 3 2 1

To internet friends

ACKNOWLEDGMENTS

Many thanks to my editor, Elle Keck, for her endless patience with this book, and to Margrethe Martin for reading more drafts than I care to count and also for gently persuading me that I did not need to launch this manuscript directly into the sun. Felicia Davin kindly fixed my French; any errors and anachronisms are entirely my own. As always I'm grateful to my agent, Deidre Knight, as well as to everyone at Avon for their support and enthusiasm.

CHAPTER ONE

Derbyshire, 1824

After only a year of living at Crossbrook Cottage, Amelia had worn a path along the perimeter of the property, a comforting length of bare earth she had trod hundreds of times before, tracing the boundaries of her small, self-contained universe. Here, in a part of Derbyshire sufficiently remote that she could depend upon never being invited to a gathering larger or grander than a card party at the vicarage, but not so far from good roads that her friends and family would be deterred from making brief visits, she felt safe.

Safe, but also ready to weep from boredom.

She hadn't meant to stay away this long, but the thought of returning to London made her heart race and dread pool in her belly. She was not by nature a quiet and retiring person, but if this isolation was the price of her sanity, she would pay it. Despite the assurances of well-meaning friends, she did not even think this was hyperbole: that last year in town, leading up to . . . the incident, she had feared herself to be on the verge of something very much like madness.

To keep herself from clawing the cottage walls from sheer boredom, she kept to a routine. Nothing too precise, just a knowledge that she would leave the house as soon as it was light enough to see the path before her, and that she would return home in time for a late breakfast. At this hour she could be certain of running into nobody at all, not the gardener, not the vicar's officious wife, not so much as a stray dairymaid.

At least that was what she had supposed before she saw the giant. He lumbered along the path she had worn with her own feet as if he weren't intruding on her property, her quiet, her peace of mind. And then, with God as her witness, he tipped his hat as he passed her by. The next day he did the same, and accompanied his hat tip with what sounded like an oddly old-fashioned "good day to thee." Infuriating.

By the third day she begrudgingly concluded that he was not a proper giant, merely a large man with a fondness for trespass. Surely he was twice as large as any man needed to be. Worse—because he could not be held responsible for the breadth of his shoulders or the length of his legs—was the fact that he persisted in tipping his hat to her and murmuring a greeting. She would have thought that from her demeanor (eyes unwaveringly set on the path before her, shoulders back, face unsmiling) he might have gathered that she did not wish to acknowledge his presence. She had the rules of etiquette all but etched into her skin, and knew to a certainty that even in the country, ladies were under no obligation to acknowledge any man to whom they had not been properly introduced. That precept was firmly implanted in her mind, along with all the rest of her mother's teachings, and which rural solitude had for the most part rendered blessedly irrelevant. But still the giant tipped his hat, and did it with such cool courtesy that Amelia felt the fury down to her bones.

"Why not take your walk at another hour?" Georgiana asked when Amelia returned to the cottage, snarling and hissing like an outraged badger.

Amelia flopped into the well-worn chintz chair and glared at her friend. "That would be letting him win."

"Do you suppose he's aware that you're engaged in a contest?" Georgiana asked without looking up from the latest *Ladies' Register*. She lounged on the sofa, her head on one end and her feet on the other, a cat wedged between her face and the armrest. If for Amelia the country promised solitude, for Georgiana it allowed a degree of idleness that Amelia found frankly inspiring. After over a decade of working as a governess, Georgiana had taken the notion of retiring to the country very literally. She was one of the few people on the planet whose company Amelia felt equal to bearing, partly because most days she was as still and silent as a piece of furniture.

Amelia sniffed. "That hardly matters. I know it is, and that's enough."

Georgiana turned a page. "Ooh, Amelia, this would suit you." She held up a page featuring a fashion plate. "Green velvet, with a pelisse and bonnet to match, I should think."

"It's nearly August. Why are you thinking of green velvet?"

"Fine, green satin, have it your way."

"I didn't agree to any such thing," Amelia protested,

laughing. "Besides, where on earth would you have me wear a satin gown of any color?" She gestured at their surroundings, indicating the parlor with its plain white curtains and its shabby rug, its single sofa and the table where they took their meals. Looking around, she felt a sense of relief. No stifling gowns. No audience eagerly awaiting her next misstep. Only this little room and the other equally neat and tidy rooms in this cottage. It was a refuge, a sanctuary, the first place on earth she had ever felt that she could rest.

"You can have nice things without needing them," Georgiana said. "We dine from china when I daresay tin cups or slabs of tree bark would do just as well." She turned the page of her magazine. "Where do you think your giant lives? Heaven knows he can't live nearby or we would have heard about it."

Amelia had wondered the same. The nearest village was a mile away, but it was little more than a hamlet. If he were a visitor who had come to enjoy Derbyshire's scenic vistas, he would hardly walk the same route each morning. If he were a newcomer, Amelia would have already heard of his arrival ten times over from her maid and manservant, and Georgiana would have had the news from every neighbor in the parish.

There was another possibility, which was that Pelham Hall had been let. Amelia strongly preferred not to think of that. The entire appeal of this place was its isolation, and a neighbor within walking distance would ruin that. When she had taken this house, the Pelham Hall land agent who handled the transaction in the owner's absence assured her that the manor was half ruined: quite picturesque but sadly unfit for human habitation. There had been a fire some years earlier, and the place had stood empty and crumbling ever since.

Still, the next day she took a walk up to Pelham Hall to put her mind at ease. The east half of the house stood a blackened ruin, its windows gaping ominously. The west half appeared to be intact, but still desolate. Weeds obscured the gravel drive and ivy grew over the door. There was no sign of anybody having been there recently: no cart tracks, no windows opened for airing, not a single sound other than the birds chirping and the leaves rustling in the wind. Beside her, Nan growled.

"I quite agree," she told the dog. "Highly unpleasant and unfit for humanity. Thank heavens."

She returned home, her heart lighter in her chest.

Sadly, morning strolls turned out to be less enjoyable when they were part of a one-sided war of attrition. Amelia considered walking in the evening instead, but it was the summer, and farmers and cottagers were out and about until the sun finally set at nine. Just about the last thing Amelia needed was to stumble upon a courting couple. Roaming about the countryside before dawn or after dusk seemed a good way to break an ankle, not to mention give Georgiana fits from worry. So every morning at her appointed hour, Amelia took her old-fashioned wide-brimmed rush hat off the peg by the door, wrapped herself in a shawl she could remove once the sun began to warm the hillsides, and headed off for a walk as if it weren't all about to be ruined by the stranger.

Nan, as per her habit, materialized from the stables and began trotting hopefully a few paces behind Amelia. Nan was a mongrel who had liberated herself from the thankless drudgery of herding sheep in order to live off the land. Except that Amelia was almost certain Keating, her manservant, slipped the beast some table scraps, and she wouldn't be shocked to discover that the dog bedded down by the fire in Keating's rooms.

As Amelia made her way down the familiar lane, Nan drew closer. While she liked to think that Nan joined her either as protection or out of a sense of adventure, she suspected that the dog thought Amelia was a sheep. Well: fluffy hair, general roundness of form, she supposed she could not blame the dog. Nan seemed to believe that every living creature who got within ten yards of Amelia was a potential sheep rustler.

"I haven't any bread today," she said to the dog, who had developed a bizarre fancy for the stale bread Amelia fed to the ducks who gathered at the bend in the brook. "You're only going to be disappointed later when you realize you've wasted your time on me." Nan looked up at her hopefully. "Fine, then. Don't say I didn't warn you."

Nan barked, startling her out of her thoughts. Amelia looked up, expecting to see that a goose or duck had strayed into the path. But no, it was the giant. And he was standing right in front of her.

Sydney could not quite see the woman's face beneath the wide brim of her straw hat, but he could see enough to know he was being scowled at. The scowl was in the clench of her fists and the set of her shoulders; the very air around her was thick with her annoyance. Of more pressing concern was the woman's dog: its hackles were up and it looked about to go for his throat. He had seen her with the dog often enough to know that this seemed to be the dog's way of letting the world know his mistress was spoken for. Sydney approved in theory, even if in practice he did not much care for the prospect of being eaten. If young women had to walk about the countryside on their own, they ought to have excessively mean dogs with them. There was probably a charitable foundation somewhere whose aim was to pair every snarling cur with a wandering maiden. He would be certain to ask the next time he had to make pained conversation with one of the railway shareholders' wives. If he ever got back to Manchester, that was.

To that end, he was headed for the village to post a letter. With an aim to dispatching his errand as quickly as possible, he made to step around the woman and her dog, and brought his hand up to tip his hat.

"Don't you dare," she snapped. It was the first time he had heard her speak, and he was appalled to hear a plummy English accent. He had thought her a village girl, wearing that plain dress and raggedy hat. But instead she opened her mouth and *that* came out. Good Lord. He tried not to recoil.

"I beg your pardon?" he asked stiffly, unsure as to what he dare not do.

"Don't you tip your hat to me. Not on my own property. Don't even think about it. Not even once."

Was hat tipping a lewd gesture now? He was sufficiently unacquainted with the great and good of the land not to be sure it wasn't. He would have to ask Lex, presuming the man weren't lying dead in a ditch somewhere. "This isn't your property," he said instead. That much he knew to a certainty. He could see the boundaries of this part of the country as clearly as if his map were spread out before him.

He thought he saw her flush under the brim of her hat. "Technically, it belongs to an absentee landlord"—she pronounced this as the vilest epithet—"as does most of this part of the countryside, but I hired Crossbrook Cottage for a full three years. I have all rights to the land from this lane to the canal."

So, this was the tenant of Crossbrook Cottage. His own tenant, he supposed. The Pelham land steward had mentioned such a circumstance. "No, you don't," he said. "This is a cattle path. There's a right of way along this lane as far as—"

"I've never seen a cow on this path nor any sign a cow has ever been here," she protested, her chin in the air. "Nor a sheep, nor any person other than you. Besides, you aren't a cow. How can you claim a right to a cattle path?"

He shrugged. He had reached the end of his knowledge of both rights of way and of cattle. "Couldn't tell you," he said.

"And who are you to lecture strangers on cattle paths, anyway? Obsolete and probably fictitious cattle paths, I may add."

Sydney opened his mouth to speak the truth but he couldn't do it, couldn't say that he owned this land without reckoning with what that meant. A shadow of grief lurked at the edges of his vision on even the brightest days here, and he found that he was too weary to fight it all the time; sometimes he had to pretend it wasn't there, following him about. "I'm a land surveyor," he said, and maybe that wasn't such a bad lie, because it had been true once upon a time.

From the hillock where Sydney stood, the countryside looked much the same as ever. The place seemed to have gotten on swimmingly even with an absentee landlord, or as swimmingly as it ever had, which was probably not saying much. He badly wanted to return to the railway, where he could turn his attention to the future and rid himself of the moldering past. There, he could keep his mind busy and free of old ghosts.

He turned and faced the woman again. Oh, she was definitely scowling now. He sighed. Sydney didn't actually enjoy making people cross with him, but it seemed to be something he achieved with effortless grace.

"Excuse me," he said in his best attempt at cordiality, which probably fell several degrees short of whatever this fine lady was accustomed to. Too bad for her. "I apologize for disturbing you." That, he thought, was quite a magnanimous concession, considering that it was she who had interrupted him, not the other way around. "Good day." He stepped past her, staying well clear of the dog, and made his way to the village.

Chapter Two

It had been nearly a week, and still there was no sign of Lex.

After the fire, Sydney had written no fewer than half a dozen letters to Lex, all of which had been answered in an unfamiliar hand, none of which contained more than a bland sentence or two: his lordship sends his condolences, his lordship is recovering from his injuries, his lordship returned to London and has no plans to return to the North. Mortified that it had taken him six such letters to grasp that his correspondence was unwanted, Sydney had given up writing altogether. After all, they had only known one another for a year—a year during which they had become brothers-in-law, lovers, and then—Sydney had thought—friends. If Lex considered Sydney a reminder of the inferno and catastrophe with which that year had ended, Sydney could hardly blame him.

So when two weeks ago, Sydney had received a letter from Lex's secretary, indicating that the Duke of Hereford required Sydney's presence at Pelham Hall, post haste,

Sydney had been puzzled. He had thought it odd that Lex would summon him to what was, technically at least, Sydney's own house, and a ruin to boot. But Lex had always been peculiar and imperious, and had likely grown even more so since inheriting the title, so Sydney hadn't dwelt on it overmuch. When he arrived at Pelham Hall and found it empty, he thought Lex had perhaps been delayed, but nearly a week had passed and there was still no sign of his old friend. He asked in the village and no message had been left for him. Had something dreadful happened to Lex? Had he simply forgotten that he had sent for Sydney? Sydney did not know which prospect bothered him more.

He had a week before he had to get back to Manchester, so he took a room at the village's tiny inn and spent his days roaming the countryside, which was troublingly unchanged from two years earlier. He remembered every path, every lane, every stream and boundary line which he and Andrew had surveyed and mapped with their own tools, walked with their own feet. He could almost conjure up the image of the first map they had drafted, see where *Pelham Hall* was written in Andrew's bold scrawl, before they had known the toll that place and its inhabitants would take on their lives.

A week, and then he would return to the city, to a world of building and creation and progress. The prospect of returning to a life of usefulness, of solving problems that most people didn't even realize existed, made him wish he hadn't paid Lex's summons any mind. But he and Lex had been something like family once, and he owed the man this much. Then he could leave the charred ruins of this manor house, and with it he could bid a final and relieved farewell to a part of his life he wished had never happened.

He avoided the scowling woman's property line. He had no wish to trouble women with his presence, and the countryside held an almost infinite number of paths he could choose instead of the one that traced the property line between Pelham Hall and Crossbrook Cottage. He knew that if he followed the brook for about an hour, he'd come across a circle of standing stones, so he packed a flask of ale, bought a loaf of bread from the baker, and set off. It was still early, but the day was already hot, so by the time he reached the stones, he had stripped to his shirtsleeves and tucked his hat under his arm.

The first thing he saw was the dog, asleep at her mistress's feet. If it hadn't been for the presence of the dog—unmistakable with those gangly legs and peculiar black-and-white markings, like a child's clumsy sketch of a shepherd's dog—he might have convinced himself that this was not the woman with the border dispute, but some other person. The woman herself was seated on the grass, her back resting against one of the standing stones. She had a book open in her lap, and bare feet stretched before her. Her ease contrasted so sharply with the straight spine and upturned nose of their previous encounter that he felt almost ashamed to see her so lax and unguarded. This was Susannah at her bath, but instead of seeing her in a state of undress, he had a sense of seeing her without armor.

For a moment Sydney considered retreating. Perhaps he

could slip away and she'd never know he had been there. But if she did happen to look up and see his retreating form, she might think he had followed her and was lying in wait. So there was nothing for it but to keep walking towards her.

"I do beg your pardon," he said by way of greeting once he was close enough to be heard. Too late he realized he ought to have donned his coat and hat.

"Oh!" She looked up with a start, but then immediately recovered herself, transforming into the woman he had previously encountered. She jumped to her feet and snapped her fingers for the dog, who promptly positioned herself between Sydney and the woman.

He raised his hands, palms out, and took a step backward. "I didn't mean to intrude upon you. I only—" He stopped, acutely aware that telling her he did not mean to attack her would be the opposite of reassuring. "I'll be on my way now," he said, taking another step backward.

She was still looking up at him with an unreadable expression when the dog sprang at him, its teeth sinking into his calf. Sydney remained utterly still, partly because he was stunned, and partly to avoid further provoking the dog.

"Nan! Heel, you bad dog," the woman said. "Heel right this minute." The dog gave a confused whimper and slunk off behind the woman's skirts, darting betrayed looks over her shoulder at her mistress.

"She did her job," Sydney said, striving to sound normal despite the pain shooting up his leg. He looked down to assess the damage. His calf had been protected by the sturdy leather of his boot, but he suspected he was bleeding anyway. "Don't scold her." He fully resented whatever antiquated feudal instinct led him to want to reassure this woman.

"I'll scold her as much as I please, thank you," the woman said with acid sharpness. "She's not supposed to attack every man she dislikes. She's not supposed to attack anyone. She probably thought you were a goose out to steal her sandwiches. She's not even my dog."

Sydney did not try to make sense of any of this, but instead pulled his boot off and dumped the contents of his flask on the bite, wincing. Then he unwrapped his neck cloth and tied it around the small wound before replacing the boot. "There," he said. "I'll be off." He started to tip his hat and then remembered she objected to that gesture. He stuck his hands in his pockets instead.

"You will not," the woman said in a tone Sydney generally heard from foremen commanding their workers. "You'll sit down until you're certain your leg isn't too badly off. Then you'll give me the address of your bootmaker so I can arrange for a new pair to be sent to you."

His bootmaker? Sydney didn't have a bootmaker. When his boots started to look shabby, he had them repaired. When absolutely necessary, he demoted his old boots to the status of second-best and bought a new pair at whichever bootmaker happened to look most sensible in whatever town he happened to be at that moment.

"I'm afraid I'm in between bootmakers," he said gravely, suppressing a mad urge to laugh.

"Then tell me where to send money. Two pounds?"

Two pounds? Two *pounds*? Did she think his boots were made from cloth of gold? "I assure you that won't be necessary," he said, reminding himself that guillotines were against his principles. "These boots are fine, you see." He indicated his leg.

She peered doubtfully at the marred but unbroken leather. "Regardless," she said, waving an airy hand, "sit."

Quite before he realized what he was doing, Sydney sat. "I really don't wish to bother you," he said.

"What would bother me would be if you came to harm on your way home. It would be my responsibility and I'd spend the rest of my days feeling guilty. I have quite enough of that already, so I'd like to spare my future self the trouble, thank you."

Sydney opened his mouth and snapped it shut again, knowing that whatever came out would be uncivil; he might not have the knack for making himself agreeable, but even he knew that he should not deliver a lecture on how women of at most five-and-twenty who thought boots cost two pounds couldn't possibly have anything of substance to be troubled about.

"Come, Nan," the woman said, "be a good girl and show the man that you aren't a ravening beast." The dog snarled. "I'm afraid her poor brain is a mass of confusion. She thinks you're a sheep rustler intent on stealing me. Here, give her a morsel of cake." She produced a cloth-wrapped bundle from her basket and handed it to him.

And that was just too much. It was utterly typical of a woman of her class not to have the sense to keep herself alive.

"No," he said, realizing a moment too late that it had come out rather gruff. "You mustn't train your dog to befriend me. I could be any variety of villain." *I might tip my hat to you,* he thought.

She narrowed her eyes, something like approval flashing in their gray depths. "True. You eat the cake." He began to protest—he was not going to sit here and have a picnic with a woman who not three days earlier had expressed in no uncertain terms a desire never to share so much as a cattle path with him. But she made a disapproving sound, cutting him off. "Eat the cake. What if you go into shock? However would I get you back to Heatherby? I would have to leave you here while I got help, which I assure you I would find tedious in the extreme. It would take three strong men to carry you, and I wouldn't know where to find two strong men, let alone three. So eat the cake."

He ate the cake, if only because it would keep his mouth too busy to tell her what he really thought. It tasted lemony and rich and exactly like the sort of cake a woman who thought boots cost two pounds would have on her person. He didn't even want to think about where the sugar came from. Meanwhile, the woman had turned back to her book and was ignoring him. Since the moment he stepped into this clearing he was reminded of the time Andrew had convinced him to ride in one of the Durham tram cars as it went down a slope—confused as to his destination and then regretting everything that had led him to agree to such a venture in the first place.

Their positions, she with her back against a standing stone, he sitting on the ground a few feet away, gave him an unobstructed view of her profile. She appeared younger than he might have supposed from the way she ordered him about. And not just ordered him about, but did it competently, as if tending to dog bites and replacing boots and bossing about strange men were all part of her ordinary day. This, he reminded himself, was a regrettable result of class distinctions and not a quality he admired.

The hair that escaped her bonnet was curly, a rusty shade too red to be called auburn, too dark to be called copper. She had no small quantity of freckles, which stood to reason if she spent her mornings out of doors. She was plump in a way that suggested softness, and beneath the cotton of her gown he could see the roundness of her stomach and the heaviness of her breasts. He dragged his gaze away.

"How did you know I'm staying in Heatherby?" he asked when he finished the last bite of cake. He wasn't surprised that she knew where he was staying. He had enough experience with country life to know that word of new arrivals traveled fast. But he wanted to learn how much of his identity was common knowledge.

She blinked at him, as if she had forgotten he was there, and he wished he had remained silent. She closed the book, but kept her place with her finger. "You're in the county on business, so it's unlikely that you would be staying in the home of a friend. Therefore you're staying at an inn, and probably one very near to my house because your path took you past my lane at an hour too early for you to have walked very far. The nearest inn to my house is the Swan in Heatherby."

She was right that he was staying at the Swan in Heatherby, but wrong about everything else. Correcting her would entail forcing his entire biography onto a stranger. It would mean speaking aloud the truths he preferred not to even voice within his own mind. He rose to his feet, dusting the cake crumbs off his trousers. "Thank you for your courtesy. I had no intention of bothering you today—"

"I know you didn't," she answered, tilting back the brim of her hat as if to get a good look at him. "I'm aware that after I spoke to you, you altered your path to avoid meeting me. Why? You said yourself that you believe you have every right to walk there." She spoke those words bold as can be, no trace of hesitation or a blush, as if he owed her an answer.

"Common decency," he said, vaguely affronted that she thought him the sort of man to force his presence on a woman.

"Piffle," she retorted. "Many people take a positive delight in doing things they believe they have a right to, especially if it annoys someone else. Don't pretend not to know that. You don't seem like you've led a sheltered life." Her gaze raked up and down his form, as if she could read his years of experience in the length and breadth of him. His face heated.

Of all the times to form an ill-advised attraction. But, heaven help him, he had always had a weakness for people with sharp tongues and a tendency towards imperiousness. Speaking of which: when he got back to the inn he would need to ask the ostlers if they had heard of any carriage accidents, or perhaps bad weather to the south, or any mishap that might explain Lex's delay.

"You're a young woman alone in the countryside," he said, striving for patience. "I have about ten inches and five stone on you. I try to be conscious of that sort of thing." Not only was he large and tall, but had frequently been told that he looked perpetually cross, that in particular his eyebrows gave him a look of grave disappointment and imminent anger. His clothing was serviceable but not fine, his hair was always in need of a cut, and he seized upon any excuse to avoid shaving. All told, he did not look much like a person any right-thinking woman would relish the prospect of meeting on a secluded lane. He tried to present a less threatening aspect by tipping his hat and wishing her good day, but he was very much afraid this had produced the opposite result.

He had thought it entirely reasonable for her to be wary of his presence, yet now when he thought of it, she hadn't seemed precisely afraid. She certainly didn't seem afraid of him now, even with her dog asleep in the sunshine. Her reaction to him that day she scolded him on the path had been one of frustration, he now thought. Not fear.

"All right, then," she said, closing her book and rising to her feet. As she stepped into her boots, he caught himself trying to get a glimpse of what a two-pound pair of boots looked like, but they seemed a perfectly ordinary pair of stout brown half boots. He looked away as she tied them. "Let's get you back to your inn."

He shrugged into his coat and slung his satchel across his chest. As they walked along a path that hewed close to the brook, he resisted the urge to give her his arm or to insist on carrying her basket. She was only being fastidious in walking him back to the village, and he knew she walked these hills daily. She didn't need his assistance. He forbore from making any conversation, not wanting to presume on her, and also not having the faintest idea what to talk about.

"What are you surveying?" she asked after they had walked in silence for some distance.

It took him a moment to remember that he had told her he was in the area as a land surveyor. A decent man would inform her that she was speaking to her landlord, that he owned the land they stood on, Crossbrook Cottage, and the ruins of Pelham Hall. After two years he surely should be used to Andrew being gone and all Andrew's worldly goods now being Sydney's own. But he hadn't, and was vaguely ashamed of this failure on his part. So he grit his teeth and told another lie. "A tramway," he said, because that was what he and Andrew had been mapping out three years ago when they had first been assigned to Derbyshire. And, true to the nature of these projects, the first rail on that line hadn't yet been laid and perhaps never would; he and Andrew needn't have come here in the first place. "I plan routes and I design engines," he added, almost desperate to say something honest.

She blinked, and he had the impression that she was riffling through her mind for another conversational gambit; surely young ladies with expensive taste in footwear did not care to hear about hydraulics or steam engines. She would steer away from engines and instead ask where his people came from, whether he knew some cousin's wife's vicar, or how he found the weather. But instead her eyes flicked up to meet his. "What kind of engines?" she asked. Across her face flitted the same expression Andrew used to have when sneaking a lemon drop out of their father's pocket. It was a look of barely concealed longing. It was, to say the least, not the expression that usually accompanied polite inquiries about engines.

Granted, he had been out of civilized society for some time, living in a make-do sort of way among engineers and tinkerers, occasionally making reluctant forays into more refined company to curry the favor of railway shareholders and promoters. Perhaps at some point in the past few years engines and tramways had become all the rage among whatever rarified circles this lady traveled in. He doubted it, though.

"Steam engines," he said.

"Well, obviously," she said with undisguised frustration. "I hardly thought you were building siege engines. I meant what are you doing with them? Where are these engines going? Looms? Pumps? Ships?"

"Well, yes," he said, flustered.

She stared and made a prompting *on with it* sort of gesture with her hand.

"Mostly railways and tramways at the moment," he added, not certain why she was staring at him but finding it disconcerting.

She licked her lips. His face flushed with mortifying promptitude. He stumbled over a tree root and only barely regained his footing. Served him right for looking at young women's lips like he had never seen a pair of them before. He tried to get some control of himself.

"I beg your pardon," he said, thinking that if she could be frank and forthright about their previous meeting then so could he, "but three days ago you didn't want me on your property. Now you seem eager to hear about steam engines. On the one hand I feel certain I ought to remain silent so as to spare you the burden of conversing with me, but on the other I don't want to be silent and churlish. I'm afraid I'm quite at a loss." This, he knew, was too much honesty. People didn't care for that. He expected a chilly silence, perhaps even a rebuke. Maybe he even wanted that, just to get it over with, just so he'd know where he stood.

To his surprise, she let out a ripple of laughter that might have been deemed a snort in someone with any other accent. "Believe me, sir, if I could begin to explain the inner workings of my mind I'd be a very happy woman. The fact is that I'm—" She hesitated long enough for Sydney to turn his head, seeing her furrowed brow and pursed lips. "I don't do well with people," she said slowly, as if weighing each word. "I'm something of a recluse." The hesitation in her voice reminded him of the way he thought about being the owner of Pelham Hall—a reluctance to give voice to an unwanted truth. "So it came as an unpleasant surprise to see you at a time when I wished to see nobody. But when my dog—excuse me, a dog who thinks she's my dog—attacks a man, I rise to the occasion. And when I have the chance to learn about something that's unknown to me, I can't resist."

She spoke those last three words as if speaking of a pleasure more carnal than machinery. Sydney ran a finger under his collar and kept his attention on the path before him until they reached the place where the lane diverged towards Heatherby and the inn in one direction, and Crossbrook Cottage in the other.

"Good day, sir," she said, her face tilted up towards his. "I wouldn't object to seeing you on my walk in the future." With that, she nodded her head at him and walked away.

Really, he shouldn't be so flattered by a person announcing that she wouldn't dread encountering him. He watched her progress along the lane to her cottage for a full minute before he realized that if things went reasonably well, there would be some message from Lex waiting for him at the inn, and he wouldn't ever see this woman again.

That would be for the best. Sydney remembered what happened the last time he had met a young lady with a moneyed accent on these hills.

"Georgiana!" Amelia cried upon entering the cottage. "I met a person unexpectedly, spoke to him, and it wasn't terrible!"

She already knew she was able to make sufficiently unremarkable conversation. Her years in London had been nothing if not proof that she could talk to virtually anyone without disgracing herself, regardless of how she felt about it. Occasionally, when she had been able to talk to people who had ideas and learning, she had been able to lose her self-consciousness in the thrill of actually talking about something interesting. Those moments had been rarer and rarer with every season she spent in London, as the weight of apprehension crushed any joy she might have once felt.

Furthermore, she was far from unused to men. Amelia's mother had firmly believed in demystifying the entire gender, and had therefore allowed her daughters to attend dinners and salons far in advance of their official debuts. Amelia had been making conversation with gentlemen since she could string together a sentence. And even though she was far from a sparkling conversationalist, she could get the job done.

"Georgiana?" she called again. "I think I've discovered the solution to all that ails me. The trick to graceful social intercourse is to wait until after one's dog has attempted to murder one's interlocutor. Do you think they'd let me do that at Almack's?" She knew she was being absurd, but the fact that she had managed to comport herself in a somewhat social situation, without wanting to run screaming away made her think there might be an end in sight. Perhaps her mind was reverting to something like normal. "We'll be in London before Christmas, or as soon as I've trained up a pack of dogs to do my evil bidding. Georgiana?" But there came no response. She remembered belatedly that Georgiana had taken the pony cart into Bakewell to purchase some things for the house.

Georgiana had been the Allenbys' governess until the girls no longer required one. The daughter of an impoverished but respectable family, she was an unobjectionable choice as a lady's companion. That, however, was not why Amelia had asked her to come to Derbyshire. Georgiana

had been a perfectly responsible and respectable governess, but after—well, Georgiana had always been game for
what Amelia's father had once indulgently referred to as
her pranks. When Amelia smuggled a kitten into church,
Georgiana covered up the animal's mewls with a feigned
coughing fit. When Amelia slipped out of ballrooms to flirt
with red-coated officers and moustached fortune hunters
and bejeweled widows of ill repute, Georgiana aided and
abetted her at every step. When Amelia anonymously
published a novel so obscene that it would have sent her to
prison if her identity had been discovered, Georgiana demanded an annotated copy. And then when Amelia began
publishing much less objectionable novels, Georgiana insisted that all the best villains be named after her.

So after that final incident, when Amelia decided becoming a hermit in the Peak District was preferable to
watching her mind come apart at the seams, of course
Georgiana had declared herself delighted to come along. It
was not meant to be permanent, only a holiday from the
circumstances that were quite literally driving Amelia mad.
Amelia had thought a few months would do the trick, and
then Georgiana could return to town and get another post
as governess or finally accept Amelia's offer of an annuity.
But a year had passed, and still Amelia was no closer to
feeling ready to return to London. She couldn't keep Georgiana here indefinitely, nor could she face a future of total
solitude. It was no wonder that she had greeted that day's
painless interaction with the stranger as a good omen.

"There was a letter for us at the inn," Georgiana said

when she burst into the parlor later that afternoon. Her face was alight with barely checked mischief.

Amelia glanced up from the book she was reading. Georgiana waved a folded sheet of expensive stationery. At least, Amelia assumed it was expensive. All previous letters from Mr. Marcus Lexington had arrived on paper so fine that Amelia hadn't been able to resist looking up her correspondent in *Debrett's*, but to no avail. "Give it over," Amelia cried, making a grabbing gesture with her hand.

Georgiana plopped down beside her on the sofa. "Shall we?" she asked as she broke the seal.

This bizarre correspondence had begun six months and twelve letters ago, in the middle of a harsh winter. For several days Amelia had been unable to leave the cottage for so much as a stroll around the grounds, and Georgiana hadn't even been able to call on the vicar's wife. Huddled around the fire, Amelia had read aloud Mr. Lexington's defense of Richard III in one of the historical publications she subscribed to. A bottle of wine and some righteous indignation later, they had penned the first letter together. Amelia hadn't expected the man to write back. She has assumed anyone who could be so devotedly ignorant about history would also be the sort of chauvinist who did not condescend to engage with ladies on the merits of his theses. But he had written, and—wonder of wonders—seemed to enjoy quarreling with them as much as they enjoyed quarreling with him. Now she and Georgiana looked forward to new letters from Mr. Lexington, Georgiana because she thought the letter writer very droll, and Amelia because perhaps she enjoyed getting herself riled up more than she cared to admit.

"'My dear Miss Russell,'" Georgiana began to read aloud from over Amelia's shoulder.

This letter, as always, was addressed to Miss Georgiana Russell, care of the Swan in Heatherby. This small subterfuge had seemed a reasonable precaution: Allenby was not only a more unusual surname than Russell, but Amelia had achieved some notoriety as the writer of three historical novels. Meanwhile, calling for letters addressed to a totally fictitious name would have created unwanted gossip in the village. Perhaps the wisest course of action would have been simply not to engage with lunatic historians, but that would have required a degree of restraint that Amelia had never possessed.

"'My dear Miss Russell,'" Georgiana repeated, elbowing her for attention. "'Regarding the future queen's ladies-in-waiting and their possible loyalties to continental powers—'"

"Ha!" Amelia interjected.

"'I advise you to consult the transcript of Sir Reginald Howard's 1797 address to the Society for the Advancement of—'"

"Does he think that his Sir Reginald is some kind of seer? A mystic? A man with a unique line of connection with someone in Richard III's court? Because unless Sir Reginald had access to papers the rest of us don't, I don't give a fig what conclusions he draws about anybody, past or present."

"I'd bet this plate of biscuits he's having you on, and that there's no Reginald Howard and never has been." This wager might seem inconsequential to anyone who did not know Georgiana. She clutched the biscuits to her bosom like a newborn baby. "He goes on to say that surely you don't mean to impugn Elizabeth of York's character—"

"That's precisely what I mean to do, and he knows it! He's being deliberately obtuse. I'm accusing the woman of cold-bloodedly killing her little brothers and framing Richard III for it. Does he think I'm paying her a compliment?"

"Well, it's probably the most interesting thing anyone has ever suggested about her. She really is such a bore. The next time we decide to defame a historical figure, let's pick somebody more interesting."

"There's no challenge in that," Amelia argued.

Instead of continuing, Georgiana paused, her brow furrowed. "Amelia," she began, and pointed at the final paragraph. "He means to visit."

"Impossible," Amelia said. But she looked at the lines beneath her friend's fingertip. "He says he'll be at Pelham Hall for the month of August into the autumn. That's—it's a ruin, Georgiana. I was there only the other day. He's having us on."

"It gets worse. Look at the postscript."

Amelia squinted. "'Forgive me for deceiving you, madam, but Marcus Lexington is a pseudonym and my true identity is the Duke of Hereford.'" She shook her head and thrust the paper at Georgiana, not wanting to see it again. "This has to be a prank. And not even a very good one. Pretending to be a duke is laying it on a bit thick. A bishop or even an earl would be more plausible." Still, her heart raced.

"I don't think so," Georgiana said slowly. "I know you don't really talk to many people, but it's common knowledge around here that Pelham Hall belonged to the Duke of Hereford's sister before she died. Do you remember who signed your lease?"

"Only the land agent and solicitor," Amelia said.

"Amelia, what's the courtesy title of the Duke of Hereford's eldest son?"

"Lexington," Amelia said promptly, this having been one of the many facts drilled into her brain by her mother. "You can't mean—"

Georgiana was already at the bookcase, paging through the *Debrett's*. "This is an old copy, but it lists the duke's oldest son as Marcus. And we both know the duke died last year."

"You cannot mean to suggest the man we've been haranguing in these letters is the Duke of Hereford." This was too close to what had happened in London—insulting rich and powerful men and drawing more attention than she could handle. "And he's coming to stay in an abandoned ruin not two leagues from our house?" She did not want to have anything to do with a duke, nor an earl, nor so much as a well-heeled country gentleman. Even on her walks, she took pains to avoid any of the grander homes. This duke would bring his London ways and his judgmental eye and Amelia would turn once again into the frightened and ashamed child hiding behind her mother's skirts. "We'll pretend this has nothing to do with us," she said, feeling the creamy paper crumple in her hands.

Georgiana was silent for a moment. "That might work, but if he returns to town with tales of how Miss Georgiana

Russell of Derbyshire snubbed him, that might not bode well for my future."

Amelia buried her face in her hands. "We ought to have used an entirely false name rather than borrowed yours." It probably said no fine things about her character that her remorse was over the insufficiency of her lies rather than the existence of them in the first place. But Portia Allenby had raised her daughters according to the principle that the truth was both useless and inadequate in any situation involving the aristocracy. Amelia felt the walls of the room start to close in on her, combined with the horribly familiar sense that her skin was a size too small. She caught herself worrying at some imaginary mark on her forearm, as if trying to dig out a foreign object.

"There's an easy solution," Georgiana said. "I'll go to Pelham Hall and meet with the duke, if that's even what and who he is. You needn't have anything to do with him."

This was wildly optimistic on Georgiana's part. First, she doubted her friend's ability to make conversation about Richard III, even with a man whose knowledge of the monarch bordered on hallucinatory wrongness. Second, if a duke truly were to arrive at Pelham Hall, that would mean balls and parties and a steady stream of visitors. Amelia would not be able to set foot outside her cottage without encountering someone. There would be people she knew, people who remembered her and her disgrace. Amelia forbore from mentioning any of this to Georgiana. There was, after all, nothing her friend could do.

Her house felt stifling for the first time ever. It was as if the pressures of the outside world had crept inside. And she did not know how she would ever be rid of them.

It had been over a week now and still Sydney had received no word from Lex. He found himself checking Pelham Hall every day, in case Lex arrived unannounced. As if such a thing were possible. During the year he had been close with Lex, he had never heard of the man doing anything without the maximum amount of fanfare.

But each morning he found the house as desolate and un-occupied as it had been the previous day. And every morning he noticed something else about the structure. The windows of the surviving wing were mainly unbroken. The chimneys seemed sound, from the outside at least. Ivy had crept over doors and windows but cutting it back would be the work of a single day. And while his glimpses through the windows showed the interior of the ground floor to be in bad condition, it was in no way as bad as it might have been if the roof had failed. Finally he could put off his curiosity no longer, and shouldered his way into the house.

There would always be a part of Sydney that saw a struc-turally unsound pile of stones and greeted it as a welcome challenge. Even seeing the house where his brother had died, even knowing it to be little better than a hulking monument to his own grief, he speculated that the roof probably wasn't beyond salvation. He heard the wind whistling through the chimneys, felt the floorboards creak and shift under his feet, smelled the pervasive damp, and could not help but calculate the number of hands and the cost of supplies it would take to make the place right, to make it better than it had ever been.

The other part of him remembered what he had lost here, what this place had cost him, and wanted to watch the entire blasted edifice sink into the earth.

He walked the halls with a miner's lamp, surveying the peeling paper, the warped paneling, the broken glass, but also seeing the beams that remained whole and solid. The newer half of the house—where the parties had been, where Penny had dragged him onto the floor for reels while Lex laughed from the shadows and Andrew played the fiddle—was all but gone, thank the merciful Lord. By the eerie light of his lamp, he saw a curling piece of flowered wallpaper and remembered it like a punch to the gut. He could almost hear the music, smell Lex's cigarillo. They had all been so reckless and stupid, so foolishly caught up in the moment and so heedless of what could come. Sydney had never been like that before, had never wanted to be. What use was fun when there were bridges to be built, roads to be leveled. But Andrew had been so happy, happy in a way that had made Sydney wonder if he even knew what the word meant. And Penny and Lex had been carefree in a way that Sydney had never dreamed of. He ought to have distrusted it—the recklessness, the joy, all of it.

He shoved aside a broken french door and stepped onto the terrace, filling his lungs with clean summer air. He had to get away. He set off along the first path he came to, not caring which direction it led. He couldn't get lost in these hills if he tried. Their topography was burnt into his mind no matter how much he'd like to forget it.

A felled tree formed a convenient footbridge over a brook, so he used it, aware that he was no longer on an actual path, but blundering oafishly through the woods. He followed the brook with a half-formed notion of seeing where it met the River Wye.

And then he saw her, sitting against a tree, a book once again open in her lap.

Sydney, who never swore, not in the company of laborers, not even in the company of his mother, who had a mouth like a sailor, ground out a hoarse "bollocks."

"Well," the woman said. "This time you're definitely on my property." But she didn't seem cross about it. "You have twigs in your hair. And you seem quite out of breath. Are you running from some danger I ought to be apprised of?"

There was no way, not even the faintest possibility, that his current state of mind wasn't visible on his face. He looked grim and forbidding in the best of moods. Now he probably looked like an ogre.

"Only my own demons," he said, opting for honesty over platitudes.

"Those are the worst," she said promptly, closing her book and looking up at him. "Do you want to tell me about them?"

"God, no."

"Then have some cake." Out of seemingly thin air, she produced a square of what looked like plum cake.

"Do you always carry cake around and offer it to injured or weary travelers?"

"That sounds very high-minded of me. No, I carry it in case I get hungry. Now, are you going to take it?"

"No," he said. "I don't eat sweets."

"What?" she asked, as if he had confessed to cannibalism. "Why ever not?"

Not wanting to get into the issue of sugar boycotts and Quakerism and his parents, he waved his hand dismissively and she tucked the cake away into a tea towel. He shoved his hands in his pockets and continued to loom over her. Now was when he ought to take his leave, to retreat to the forest like some kind of feral creature.

"You can sit and rest for a moment before outrunning your demons again," she said, and patted the ground beside her.

He sat down, letting his head knock again the tree trunk behind him. She smelled like lemons, and he didn't know if it was from the cake or her soap, or if it was something else that rich ladies used and he had never heard of. It didn't matter. He breathed the scent in and let his head fill with it.

"What are you reading?" he asked, because her book remained closed in her lap.

"Oh, haunted castles and imprisoned heirs, the usual."

Of course she was reading a novel. What had he expected? A treatise on steam engines?

"You probably think it's very frivolous," she said. And before he could figure out how to respond, because the truth was that he indeed thought novels were terribly frivolous, but also that it was none of his business what she read nor her business what his opinion was—she continued. "And it is," she said gleefully. "It's appalling. It came in the morning post and I absconded with it so Georgiana couldn't get it first."

"Very cunning," he said, not entirely sure whether he meant it as condemnation, praise, or—a jest? Was he joking?

He distantly remembered doing such a thing ages ago, in another lifetime, when his heart had been stupidly unguarded.

She leaned forward and turned towards him, glancing at him from around the trunk of the tree. "You can borrow it afterwards."

"I, er, don't think Georgiana would thank you for that." Whoever Georgiana was.

"I meant after Georgiana, of course. I'm not a monster. And you look like you could use a diverting book to read, if you'll pardon my saying so."

"That's just what my eyebrows do," he said.

She rose onto her knees and peered at him, and he blushed under her scrutiny. "No, it has nothing to do with your eyebrows. It's the way you carry yourself. As if you're dragging a great weight." With that, she resumed her position against the trunk, just out of his sight. On the grass beside him, he could see the folds of her faded muslin gown, and out of the corner of his eye he could make out a glint of red hair.

"It's not actual demons," he said, before he could think too much about it.

She let out a puff of air that might have been the beginning of a laugh. "I didn't think you were actually being chased by demons onto my property. I would not have offered you cake. I'm not certain what I would have done, but cake would not have been my first recourse."

He could hear the smile in her voice, but he couldn't see her face, didn't even know her name, and maybe that was why he continued to speak. "It's my brother. He died."

"Oh, I'm so—"

"It was two years ago. Condolences are unnecessary at this point."

She fell silent for long enough that he wondered if she had resumed reading. Then she cleared her throat. "Naturally, I'm not going to force unwanted sympathies on you. But I have two sisters, and if I lost either of them I might well grieve to some extent for the rest of my life. My mother wore mourning for my father for years after his death." She paused, and he could see one bare hand smooth the fabric of her skirts. "Then again, it really did suit her. The grays and blacks, I mean."

And then—oh no, he laughed. It was so inappropriate, and that knowledge only made him laugh harder. He dug his fingers into his thighs and bit the inside of his cheek in a futile attempt at composure. She was talking about the death of one parent and the grief of another, and was appallingly unserious enough to jest about it, and he *laughed*. "I beg your pardon," he choked out. "I didn't mean to—" Didn't mean to what?

"It's quite all right. You were meant to laugh."

He regained some control over himself, tried to summon up some dignified disapproval of her levity. But before he could quite manage it, she went on.

"The truth is that she was devastated by my father's death. It was very sudden and of course nobody was sending her funeral wreaths or condolence letters, given the circumstances." Before he could ask what that could possibly mean, she continued. "I had never seen her cry before. It occurred to me that I ought to have died instead of him. Which is a very useless thought, because it's not like one can choose, and there's probably something sinful about questioning God's plan, I suppose." There it was again, that levity where it didn't belong, and he should not be so charmed by it. "But at the time I knew I was the least valuable member of the household—my younger sisters are prettier and more bid-dable and in general more marriageable, and it would have been eminently convenient if I were simply out of the way." A pause. "I was sixteen, and very dramatic."

Now, that was simply too much. He rose to his knees and turned so he could see her. "First of all, that is—you are wrong on all counts. Entirely wrong. Even assuming your sisters are unparalleled beauties of sterling character, you can't measure worth in such a way. I daresay your mother would have been horrified if she knew you had harbored such thoughts."

She blinked at him, wide gray eyes unflustered by his harangue. "Oh, she was. It made her cry even more, which made us both feel worse."

"You *told* her?"

"As I said, I was sixteen and a consummate idiot. And I had a very bad case of spots." She tilted her chin, presum-ably to show him the resulting scars, but he could not detect any in the dappled shade. "My sisters really do have steadier characters."

He scrubbed his hand across his face. "I don't find that at all hard to believe." And then he realized what he had said, and he went still. "I beg your pardon—I didn't mean—"

"Yes you did, and I'm taking it as a compliment. I will

write it in my diary. Today a very large stranger laughed at my jokes and praised my talents as a comedienne—"

"That is not—"

"—but he does not like cake, and I'm therefore inclined to disregard his opinions on all important matters."

He buried his face in his hands, both to muffle his laugh and to cover the blush he knew had spread across his face.

CHAPTER THREE

As if the imminent prospect of a duke in the neighborhood weren't alarming enough, the next day brought Amelia's quarterly parcel from her mother.

"Oooh," Georgiana said, coming in from the garden with an armful of chrysanthemums. "Is that what I think it is?"

Amelia already knew what was in the parcel, but she tore it open anyway. Out tumbled three gowns: russet merino, emerald-green watered silk, and pearl-gray muslin. The muslin, at least, she might wear. She recognized her youngest sister's hand in that last gown—something practical, something Amelia might actually use. Amelia had long since given up trying to explain to her mother that she had no use for fine clothes, seeing as how she had retired to the country with the express purpose of avoiding the kind of society where such attire would be required. But Amelia's mother had always expressed her love in yards of silk and cashmere, and Amelia tried to receive the gesture as it was meant. Still, whenever she opened the clothes press she'd see those gowns silently judging her and finding her wanting.

Rationally, she knew she could have Janet, the housemaid, sell them and donate the proceeds to some worthy charity, or she could figure out a way to slip the funds into Georgiana's bank account. Breathing the scent of the sachets her mother's maid had laid between the layers of fabric made her heart race, but it also made her homesick.

She remembered years of similar gowns, and how by the end they had felt like stage costumes; every time she slipped one over her head, she assumed a role. At first that role hadn't been a bad thing—she was used to the idea that being in polite society required a certain degree of performance, and was well aware that anything like her authentic self was grossly insufficient for most social situations. But by the end, the role had crowded out whatever was left of Amelia's actual identity. That was the problem with being schooled from one's earliest age to mask one's emotions in favor of playing a role: it left one with no doubt as to the inadequacy of one's true self. Mother would no doubt be horrified to hear Amelia say such a thing. She had always been generous with praise whenever Amelia behaved as she ought, and had never understood that this praise only confirmed that Amelia, as she truly was, warts and all, was unfit for human society.

With a shudder, she remembered the night of the incident, standing in the middle of a ballroom, crammed into that ghastly gown, and simply deciding that she was done, that she couldn't endure one more minute of it. As she moved through the steps with her partner, she overheard the conversation of another couple on the dance floor. It had been a variation on a theme she had heard since she could remember being talked about, since she could remember even existing. The man had said to his partner that Amelia seemed ladylike, all things considered; the woman had responded that Amelia was harmless, and could be relied upon to make up one's numbers at a dinner table at the last moment. And it had struck Amelia that this was the most she could hope for: all her mother's work, all her half brother's connections, day after day, year after year of checking every movement and weighing every word, and she had achieved harmlessness. At that moment, halfway through a gavotte that seemed like it would never end, she realized it wasn't worth it.

Once she knew it, there was no unknowing it. As soon as she saw that she had nothing to lose—or nothing that she didn't heartily wish to lose—she took a glance at her dance partner, who happened to be the Russian ambassador. She was on her best behavior, because the man had titles and medals and she was supposed to be very gratified that he wished to dance with her. If she made a mess of this, there would be disastrous consequences. And so, she made a mess of it. She turned, walked off the dance floor, out of the house, and directly home.

There had been a time when she had enjoyed things. Little things, like sneaking the kitten into church, and big things, like seeing her friends happy. But that last year in London, joy had been permanently out of reach, and the next-best thing—the absence of panic—she could only achieve with her bedroom door bolted and her eyes shut. She had tried to figure out where things went wrong, when the town she had loved began to close its walls in on her. Above all, she wanted to know when the simple act of being around people made her feel like an especially grotesque insect pinned to a board.

As her mother and sisters and friends had pointed out many times, she was, objectively, an unremarkable woman of four-and-twenty, not an eldritch creature from one of those novels she and Georgiana read. Sometimes she thought her perception had been skewed by those first few years of her life, when it had been Amelia and her mother, trying their hardest to appear what they decidedly were not, and having scorn heaped upon them whenever they fell short. A fallen woman, her illegitimate daughter, and everyone's judgment landing squarely on them. Perhaps that was why she now needed to be spared the gaze of anyone who might see her and find her lacking. That was the only explanation she could think of for her present condition, unless she were to admit the possibility of madness.

Her heart pounded against her ribs, and she realized she was still clutching the gowns. She glared at the silks and satins in her arms. She was starting to think it was possible for inanimate objects to judge her. This could not be a good sign.

"So lovely," Georgiana said, stroking a length of braid on the russet gown.

"You can have it," Amelia said hastily. "Janet could take it in."

"A perfect ninny I'd look in russet," Georgiana said. And she was right, of course: the faded muslins and colorless round gowns Georgiana wore suited her pale coloring and white-blond hair.

"As if you could be anything other than stunning," Amelia said, rising to her feet. "I was just heading out for a walk."

"Now?" Georgiana asked. It was not the time for Amelia's walk, and Georgiana was no more accustomed to Amelia doing things out of order than she was for the hands of the clock to start spinning backward.

"I'm feeling bold and daring," Amelia announced. She was feeling penned in and increasingly hysterical, but she could do that out of doors as well as she could in the sitting room.

She swept up her shawl and bonnet and exchanged her slippers for a pair of sturdy boots and all but fled the house. It was a sunny day, a rare cloudless August afternoon. She drifted towards the stables, trying to look casual about the direction she was taking.

"No," Keating said without looking up from the horse he was currying. Dash it. There was no getting anything past Keating.

"You don't even know what I was going to ask," Amelia said, trying and failing to keep the petulance from her voice.

"If you don't think I know by now what a young person with a bad idea looks like, you can guess again. What was it going to be? Swimming in the pond? Learning to box? Setting something on fire? Doesn't matter, leave me out of it."

Amelia suppressed a smile. Thank goodness Keating had come with her to Derbyshire. Amelia and Keating had sort of inherited one another when his employer embarked on a tour of the continent with Amelia's half brother, Alistair, Marquess of Pembroke. Keating would lie, steal, and perjure himself for Robin, but drew the line at going to France. He had remained in England, nominally to be Amelia's general factotum, but, Amelia increasingly suspected, to keep an eye on her. He didn't seem to think it was at all unusual for a pair of youngish ladies to live as recluses, or if he did, he didn't talk about it. Amelia supposed that his years working for Robin had gotten him used to people who strayed from the beaten path.

Contrast that with the vicar, who seemed to think that Amelia belonged either in Bedlam or a home for wayward girls, and that Georgiana had come to Derbyshire to tempt men into wickedness by performing such risqué acts as existing while being pretty.

"Maybe I wanted the pleasure of your company," Amelia suggested. She had been hoping she could sit on an overturned crate and watch him tend the horses, knowing that in his better moods he was capable of going hours without talking. Today Keating did not seem to be in one of his better moods.

"I'm not here to amuse you," Keating grumbled. "You're not here to be amused at all. You're supposed to be in that room"—he pointed to the house—"writing books no decent man ought to know about. Fact is that you're too young to be left on your own and I don't know what your mother was thinking in letting you out of her sight."

Amelia wrinkled her nose. She knew Keating was only trying to provoke her. She was hardly too young to be left alone. Her mother had already had three children at this age. But Amelia never came out well when she compared herself to her mother. It only made her feel inadequate, and then guilty because her mother would be the first to tell her she was merely different, not lacking. Her mother probably even believed it. She ought to be grateful to have this time and this space, but it seemed yet another way Amelia fell short of everyone's expectations and needs, including her own.

"That was only the first book," Amelia pointed out. "The rest have been quite respectable, as well you know. I was going to ask if I could watch you curry the horses."

"And I was going to suggest that you bugg—run off. No, you can't watch me. I'm not putting on a show."

"You are in an exceptionally foul mood," Amelia said. This probably meant he had suffered a falling-out with the ostler at the Swan or the curate or the traveling china mender or whoever his latest bedmate had been. She made up her mind to ensure that Janet sent over a slab of the treacle tart she was making, as long as the thing could be done without alerting Keating to anything that looked like solicitude. "Robin said you were pleasant company," Amelia said with an exaggerated pout. Although, now that Amelia thought about it, what Robin had actually said was that Keating was a good man to have around in a pinch, which could mean a lot of things.

"You believe anything that yellow-haired slip of mischief says, you're a fool," he said with unmistakable fondness. "In fact," he said, pointing the currying brush at her menacingly, "I've done my time putting up with shiftless young lunatics and I'm supposed to be enjoying a quiet retirement."

"Ha! Is that what you're calling it? And at your age," she murmured.

"You know," Keating said, shaking his head sadly, "I don't think you're quite a nice sort of girl."

"I've been trying to tell you all that for years."

"Figures, with the company you keep." He gave her the Keating equivalent of a smile—one corner of his mouth hitched up in a grizzled cheek.

Well, if Keating wouldn't let her hide in the stable, she had no choice but to go for a walk. The sun was in the wrong place in the sky. Very disconcerting. She paced along the shrubbery at the side of the house for a few minutes, but walking back and forth felt pointless. She followed her usual path along the edge of the property, and when it reached the lane she headed uphill, away from the village. There was a risk that she'd run into someone, most likely the vicar's wife, who seemed to turn up precisely where one didn't want her.

Usually she confined her walks to the perimeter of her property, sometimes completing two turns around it if the weather was especially fine. Other days—especially if she had Nan for company and nominal protection—she ventured further, exploring the countryside. That was what she had been doing when she ran into the land surveyor—she wished she knew his name—at the standing stones. And that was what she wanted to do today. She thought she might head in the direction of a ruined chapel she had once seen.

The branches were heavy with summer leaves, the air thick with the scent of blooming flowers. Bird calls and the sound of woodpeckers made an almost soothing rhythm until they started to take the shape of the sounds that would drift into her bedroom window in London, a hum of voices, hoofbeats, cart wheels. She quickened her pace.

Then the sounds changed again, resembling footsteps, loud enough that she turned her head to see a man approaching on foot, as if she had conjured the sight out of her fancy. It was, however, only the land surveyor.

"Oh, bother," he said, his expression comically dismayed, his eyebrows knitting together with stern disapproval.

"A good afternoon to you too, sir," she said, suppressing a laugh.

"I only meant— Now you're definitely going to think I'm following you."

Anyone who actually wanted to see Amelia would know she wasn't usually abroad in the middle of the day. "I think nothing of the sort. However, if you're heading up this path, I wonder if I might impose upon you to walk with me so as to protect me from the vicar's wife."

"For a minute I thought you wanted my protection from brigands, and I was afraid I'd have to disoblige you by telling you I wouldn't know the first thing to do."

"I don't think you'd need to do anything. Just stand

there looking all large and cross. Besides, who cares about brigands? They would be unlikely to try and foist off their maiden aunt as my chaperone."

"Ah, so that's the fate you wish to escape. Most under-standable."

This was, by any standard, an actual conversation. And Amelia did not know why it was not burdensome to her, whereas the prospect of mere pleasantries with a duke made her mind fray at the edges. Perhaps it was because this man in his plain coat and worn trousers, his jaw dusted with the beginnings of a beard, his hair uncombed, seemed as far from her former life as she was likely to get.

"She means well, which only makes it worse. So will you walk with me?" she asked, hoping that she didn't sound too eager. But she *was* eager, and for reasons she preferred to ignore—something to do with the breadth of his shoulders and his ready blush, the way his laugh sounded rusty and seemed to come as a shock to him. Even as she glanced up at him, she saw color spread across his cheekbones, and she bit her lip.

"I very nearly called on you to ask your name," Sydney ad-mitted.

When thinking of her—which he realized he was doing with inexplicable frequency—there was a blankness where her name belonged. But with names came explanations, per-sonal histories, family background, and right now he enjoyed the sense that they were just two people, sharing sunshine and scenery, nothing tying them to this world except what they did and said. Still, it seemed vaguely inappropriate to have met a person three times without knowing their name.

"Call on me?" she said. "How drastic. You could have asked anyone in the neighborhood."

With a start, he realized she was right—he need only have asked the Pelham land steward the name of his new tenant. He was not accustomed to overlooking obvious solutions; he would not have the career he did if he weren't in the habit of solving problems efficiently and automatically. The fact that he hadn't done something so obvious made him suspicious of his own mind, and he had to acknowledge that he had avoided learning her name for the simple reason that he wished to withhold his own: she would hear Goddard, and know him to be the owner of Pelham Hall. The truth was that he feared that this friendship—even though it was probably presumptuous to call it so—would be crushed by anything so solid as names and identities, anything as weighty as his complicated grief and his reasons for being here. Friendship, as far as Sydney could tell, was rare and fragile, not a naturally occurring substance, and he wasn't quite certain what he had to do to preserve it. He steeled himself for some minor dishonesty—not actual lying, only a bit of delicate evasion.

"My name is Sydney," he said.

"Mr. Sydney." She nodded and gave him a wintry little smile that he supposed was what ladies did upon introductions. He hated it and already regretted broaching this topic.

"No, that's my given name," he said. "I thought—well—

since we've already progressed beyond dog attacks and border disputes, perhaps we could simply use first names." Like most Friends his age, Sydney adopted a fairly flexible approach: he used titles when he had to, usually with shareholders in the railway who needed to be cosseted and cajoled, and he hated it every time. Otherwise, when speaking with a person with whom he wasn't intimate enough to use a first name, he used their full name. Or, as in this case, he could presume a little and skip right to using given names.

Besides, it was true that he didn't want to use Mrs. or Miss or—heaven forbid—Lady, with this woman. Every time he used a title it felt like a lie, a denial of a belief he held close to his heart. Perhaps being at Pelham Hall made him want to fight tooth and nail against hierarchy. Perhaps he sensed that he was forging something like a friendship with her and didn't want to start off with the taste of a title in his mouth.

"I see," she said lightly. "You wait until you very nearly have me on a mountaintop to tell me that you refuse to call me by my proper name. How shocking." A smile lurked behind the edges of her words, as if she were trying and failing to suppress a smile.

"It was part of my dastardly plan. Also I'm a Friend—a Quaker—and I don't use titles if I can help it."

"Well, my name is Amelia." They had reached a clearing and she sat on a fallen tree. "I haven't so much as a husk of bread with me today. I all but fled my house."

"Oh, I see. You wait until you have me on a mountaintop to deliver the killing blow." He was rewarded for this, his second attempt at humor in as many years, by hearing her huff of laughter. He knelt beside her. "No matter. I have bread and cheese and ale enough for us both."

She regarded him for a moment and he felt the back of his neck heat in awareness. "Sydney, you aren't surveying anything at the moment. I meant to ask you about that last time. You don't have tools."

This, Sydney knew, was where he ought to tell the truth, explain that he wasn't in Derbyshire on surveying business at all. "I already did that part of the job," he said instead. "Why did you flee your house this afternoon?" he asked in an attempt to change the topic. "It must have been dire for you not to even pause for cake."

"It's too tedious to go into. If I complain about having received a parcel of gowns I don't want or need, and resenting the prospect of attending parties with the great and good of the land, I'll sound perfectly spoiled, which is neither more nor less than the truth."

Sydney would certainly consider superfluous gowns and costly entertainments to be just the sort of indulgence he might expect from a person in Amelia's station in life. But he also saw the tightness around her eyes when she spoke of these gowns and parties. "On the contrary," he said. "I've never wanted to attend a social gathering in my life and would heartily resent being obligated to do so. Besides," he said, not knowing whether this would be going too far, "you've said that you have a hard time with people." He did not know what that meant or what it entailed, but supposed he did not need to. "In that case, gowns and invitations are precisely designed to discompose one's mind."

"Yes," she said, looking so grateful that Sydney wanted to bask in her approval. "That's exactly it." She chafed her arm with the palm of one hand, then abruptly stopped and tucked her hands behind her back. "The fact is that I have too many friends and connections, and I care too much about what they think to properly divorce myself from expectations."

She seemed nervy and distressed, and Sydney did not know what to do. He remembered how she had reacted when he had been in low spirits. "If you don't mind my saying so, you're making a terribly poor fist of being a recluse." He hoped to God that his clumsy attempt at humor carried itself off. "Extremely low quality reclusivity," he said, shaking his head sadly. "Friends, spoken of in the plural, no less." He watched her out of the corner of his eye for any sign his joke had misfired. To his immense relief, she smiled.

"You have no idea. I have a mother, two sisters, two half brothers, my brothers' spouses, and a couple of other people I acquired without even the excuse of family ties."

There was not, he noticed, a husband on that long list. "I fear that you ought to have done some cursory research into the bare minimum requirements of being a recluse before attempting such a thing."

She waved this away. "Even if I lived in the Outer Hebrides or the surface of the moon, my mother and friends would figure out a way to send me letters. Which, I realize, is something I ought to be grateful for. And I am! But one wants to make one's friends happy, and one doesn't know how to go about doing it. Meanwhile they want to make you happy, and they manifestly don't know how to do so. The result is that everyone dances around one another pretending to be quite satisfied with everyone else and secretly wanting to tear one's hair out."

"I suppose actually talking about one's needs with one's friends is out of the question."

"Of course it is," she said in tones of exaggerated outrage. "Don't be absurd. Sometimes the problem is that you don't even quite know what you need yourself."

"And sometimes the problem is that one's friends give one ulcers from the worry," Sydney added, thinking of Lex.

"Most definitely," she said.

They sat for some time in the shade, chatting in this idle and inconsequential manner. Sydney thought he should not be nearly as entertained as he was. They were only interrupted when a gust of wind whipped through the clearing, blowing Amelia's shawl off her shoulders.

"Oh no!" she cried, leaping to her feet and running after it. He was behind her in an instant, watching the wisp of fabric flutter through the air before landing on a branch about five yards from the ground. "Rats," she said. "I liked that shawl."

He laid down his satchel and took off his coat. "Stand back in case any branches fall."

"That's not necessary, Mr.—Sydney."

"It's no trouble." At some point he was going to think long and hard about why he was performing acts of gallantry for this woman. But for now, he swung himself onto the lowest branch, thanked the Creator that it was solid enough to hold his substantial weight, and then began to climb. An advantage to height was that he didn't have far to go before he was within reach of the shawl. It was a flimsy, silky thing; worldly nonsense, he told himself. Still, he took his time unpicking it from the branch, trying not to let it snag. It smelled of rosewater. When he got it loose, he leaned against the trunk of the tree and folded it into a neat triangle, then tossed it down to her.

"Thank you," she called.

When he landed on the ground, he brushed some leaves and moss off his sleeves.

"You're going to have to do better than that," she said, indicating his shoulders. "No, not there. Hold still." She deftly flicked the debris from his shirt. There was nothing coy or sensual about her touch—she was only sparing his shirt damage, just as he had spared her shawl. Her hands didn't linger, she didn't stand too near, and still his heart raced at her touch. He looked at her out of the corner of his eye and saw that she was biting her lip in concentration. He drew in a sharp breath at the surge of ill-timed desire that raced through him.

"There you go," she said, stepping back.

"Thank you." His voice sounded strange. "Now I believe I promised you bread and cheese."

"And ale," she said. "Watching you perform feats of strength is thirsty work." She opened her eyes wide for the merest instant, as if realizing that she had made an arguably personal remark and thinking better of it. But just as soon, her expression returned to its usual steadiness.

He opened his satchel and handed her the flask, then placed the bread and cheese on a flat part of the log. "Thank you," she said, handing the flask back as she wiped her mouth on the back of her hand. The wind picked up again and she clutched at her shawl.

"Come here," he said. "The way you have that thing, it's a wonder it hasn't blown away yet."

"This is my fourth shawl this year," she admitted. "I daresay the previous three are being used to line songbird nests."

Later on he would be sure to reflect on how wasteful that was, just as he would reflect on how the levity of her manner was surely a sign of poor character, a sign of precisely the sort of carelessness and irresponsibility he expected from people of her class. For now, he wrapped the shawl around her shoulders, careful not to touch her. "Arms up and turn around," he said. He knotted the tails of the shawl at the small of her back, the way his mother had always done. "There. That'll stay put."

"Thank you," she said, turning back around to face him. They were very close now, but she made no move to step away. Instead she looked at his lips, then back up to his eyes, then to his lips again.

His thoughts stuttered to a halt. There was no mistaking what she had done and what it meant. She was letting him see this, letting him know that she was—attracted? Interested in something more? She usually kept her expression so neutral, so composed, but she was choosing to let him see this. He could turn away, pretend none of this was happening. That would be safe. That was what he ought to do.

Instead he hitched an eyebrow. A corner of her mouth quirked up in acknowledgment.

He stood there a moment, not moving, neither touching her nor stepping away, but letting himself sit with the knowledge that he could ask to press his lips to that asymmetrical smile, that he could maybe rest his hand on the nip of her waist. Sydney really hadn't expected to get seduced in a woodland clearing this afternoon. Not that he was opposed on principle, not to the location or the act. But neither was he looking for an anonymous tumble in the grass. "Amelia," he said, pitching his voice low. "I think I'd better tell you about steam engines."

She let out that gurgle of laughter that made him think of bells and running streams and everything bright and clean in the world. "Sydney," she said, leaning in fractionally, "it would be my pleasure."

Amelia was fairly certain that nothing could be less relevant than physical attraction. The world was filled with people for whom she had vague longings to drag into dimly lit passageways and do regrettable things with and upon. But as she had never met someone for whom she was willing to endure the sad tedium of afterwards, her amorous experiments had not yet progressed beyond kissing. She had kissed Richard Davenheim at the Grantham Ball and Justine Broissard everywhere and every time she had an opportunity for the duration of an entire season. She had

found both Mr. Davenheim and Miss Broissard pleasant to
look at and enjoyable to talk to; miracle of miracles, they
seemed to return the compliment; so she had kissed them.
Those kisses had been pleasant, and she could have imagined things progressing. But it had never seemed worth the
bother.

Kissing Sydney seemed like it would be very much worth
any bother she could name. To start, there was his beard.
He had plainly not shaved at any point since she had first
encountered him, and now his jaw was covered in stubble.
Then there was his accent. It was, she supposed, a perfectly
straightforward northern accent, but his voice was so low
and rumbly that it sent shivers down her spine. Those qualities she could have disregarded, perhaps. What she could not
disregard was the way his cheeks reddened at the slightest
provocation. He didn't even seem aware he was doing it. She
caught herself trying to coax a blush out of him. His eyebrows
might be grim slashes across his forehead; his mouth might
set itself into a grim and stern line; but when he blushed he
seemed . . . sweet.

For his part, he did not seem averse to kissing her. She
saw the way he looked at her mouth, the way he leaned close
before startling himself back to a safe distance.

Some would argue that Amelia had been raised according to no principles whatsoever, given the fact that she was
even considering kissing strange men. But the truth was that
Amelia's mother had tried to balance the pragmatic need
for maidenly innocence with the utter demystification of

everything to do with sex. The result was that Amelia was not under the impression that going to bed with a lover was either blissful or depraved. It was merely a thing that most people did, for varying reasons and with varying results.

As Sydney crouched in the grass, using sticks to show her the path of a railway, Amelia watched the fabric of his trousers strain across his thighs, watched the muscles of his arms and shoulders move under the thin linen of his shirt.

She was very aware of wanting to touch him. But she also had the sense that he was a safe person to be around. Maybe it was that he had tied her shawl around her without so much as touching her, maybe it was that he had acted like her dog's attack was a matter of course.

Now he added a few stones to the railway map he was laying out before her. "This here, Amelia, is a bog—a pit that leads straight to hell—" He looked up at her with wide brown eyes. "I beg your pardon."

"I've heard worse," she assured him. "In any event, pits that lead straight to hell don't sound like sound foundations for pylons or what have you."

"Exactly," he said, pointing triumphantly at her with a stick. When he talked about railways and engines and bottomless bogs, his expression transformed from stern dismay or reluctant amusement to radiant delight. "The problem is that routing the railway around the bog increases the cost by nearly twenty percent. And they won't hire me on as head of engineering without some way of getting over that bog."

Sydney looked up and scrubbed his hands across his jaw. Something about his beard made his lips look especially soft.

She wanted to run her thumb across them, an urge she was quite certain she had never felt before. "And you really want that post, do you?"

"I do." His voice was gravelly and low. "I've worked on other railway projects but this would be mine. It would be a chance to make sure things got done right." He passed a hand over his jaw. "The railway is going to be built one way or another, you see? But it might be a small, inconsequential operation. Or it could change everything." He leaned forward, his eyes sparkling, his hands moving animatedly as he spoke. "Imagine how different life would be if we could move things—and people!—around cheaply and safely. People could purchase goods for fair prices, or could seek work and experiences that suits them. People could see *one another*." He swallowed, and she could see his throat work above the collar of his hastily tied neck cloth. "I apologize for boring you."

"You're not boring me," she said, and her voice came out higher and more breathless than she had intended. "Far from it." She cleared her throat. Amelia was a lot of things, but bashful wasn't one of them. "Are you married, Sydney? Or promised to anyone?"

He looked at her for a long moment, and she knew he understood what she really was asking. "No, I'm free. And you, Amelia?"

"Decidedly unattached." She crossed her legs at the ankle and saw his gaze flicker to the hem of her skirt. Good. "Very well, then."

"But nor am I looking for a dalliance." He spoke softly,

with the hint of a rueful smile, and Amelia was left uncertain about whether she had been rejected or asked to make her intentions clear.

Maybe it hadn't been either. Maybe he had just spoken the truth, without hidden layers of nuance or misdirection. That possibility was one of the reasons he was a relief to be around.

He went back to telling her about railways, and she watched his big hands and listened to his rumbling northern voice, and reveled in the feeling of having an entire afternoon of conversation without feeling like she needed to claw her way out of her own skin.

CHAPTER FOUR

Driven by sheer boredom and restlessness, Sydney began exploring Pelham Hall, seeing how deep the damage ran. At first it was just prodding a bruise, deliberately stirring up grief and regret. But then he started to see the building not as a ruin but as a thing to be fixed. He was increasingly certain that the roof was solid, the structure sound. He hauled out debris, found tools, bought lumber and nails, and set about repairing a handful of rooms. The east wing would need to be taken down, but the west wing could be preserved. He told himself he did not care about the structure of Pelham Hall except insofar as he could not resist poking about at the inner workings of things, seeing how they were broken and how they might be made whole again. It didn't matter: all he knew was that he was no good at sitting idle, and pulling down rotten woodwork and measuring window openings kept his mind and his body busy. He gave up his room at the inn, instead bedding down before a smoking fire.

During a trip up the rickety attic steps, his arms laden

with mousetraps, his foot plunged through a rotten floorboard, and he cursed himself for not having tested the stairs.
This was the sort of thing he had used to scold Andrew
for doing: testing staircases by climbing them, figuring out
whether a bog was solid or quicksand by means of attempting to walk across it. Andrew had always taken the risks,
charmed the investors, and figured how to explain their
plans and inventions in a way that made people care. Sydney
had been the voice of reason and caution, the one who made
sure every measurement was correct to the last decimal point
and that the survey had been checked and rechecked to a
certainty. Maybe after years of trying and failing to embody
both halves of the partnership, something of Andrew's in-
fluence had finally penetrated Sydney's skull. Naturally it
would result in his boot being stuck in the attic steps and
not, say, actually becoming likable.

He dropped the mousetraps, listening to them clat-
ter down the steps. Then, extricating his boot, he gingerly
climbed the rest of the way up and surveyed the attic. At the
top of the steps he took out his handkerchief and wiped the
dust off a small, circular window that was placed in such a way
as to throw light on the attic. It was badly situated, Sydney
could not help but notice; given his druthers, he would put
in a skylight and a strategically placed mirror. There was no
reason on earth why he couldn't hire a carpenter and a glazier
and do precisely that. He could kit the whole place out in log-
ically arranged windows and sensible lighting arrangements.

Letting the house quite literally rot had never been his
intention. In the immediate aftermath of grief he hadn't

had the wherewithal to do anything with it, and then he had been busy doing the work of two men. But allowing an entire house to sink into the earth was nothing if not a waste, and Sydney hadn't been raised to waste so much as a crust of bread, let alone an entire house. He could sell the place, if that didn't feel like a grossly presumptuous thing for him to do, considering his manner of inheriting it. He could let it, he supposed, and take the money and . . . add it to all the other money he couldn't bring himself to touch, the rest of that sum that had passed from Penny to Andrew to him. He could hand the whole thing over to Lex, who had at least a greater emotional claim to the place than Sydney did. Maybe that was what Lex had summoned him for—a plan to take the house off Sydney's hands. If Lex ever arrived, he would be sure to ask.

The next evening as Sydney returned to Pelham Hall after having supper at the inn, he passed a chaise and four heading in the opposite direction. He could think of only one reason for this, so he doubled his pace. When he reached the front door he all but threw it open.

There, seated on an overturned barrel in what had once been the manor's great hall, sat the Duke of Hereford. For one instant Sydney felt nothing but the purest relief that his friend was alive and well. But soon enough that passed and he recalled how long he had been waiting.

"Fifty miles, Lex. I traveled fifty miles to wait in a pile of rubble for over a week. I didn't know if you were alive or dead or hoaxing me."

"You make it sound as if you walked the distance in your

bare feet." Lex took a puff from a cigarillo, letting the ashes fall to the bare flagstone floor. "You probably took the stage-coach, because we both know you're too stingy to pay for a post chaise."

"Lex." Sydney tried again, summoning whatever scraps of patience he had left. "I need to return to my post. Not every-one can be as indolent as you."

Lex made a moue of distaste. "Surely they finished with that canal by now."

"One, it was a railway. Two, when it was finished, I started work on another railway. That is how employment works. One keeps working and earning one's living."

"So tedious." Lex crossed his legs and bounced one foot over the other. There was neither fire nor lamplight, and the windows were covered in ivy, so Lex's face was obscured by shadows. Still, Sydney could see streaks of silver in Lex's formerly dark hair. Sydney hadn't been the only one to lose a sibling that night: Sydney had lost Andrew, but Lex had lost his only sister. And since Sydney had last seen him, Lex's father and his only surviving brother had died, making Lex the duke, but also an orphan.

Sydney paced the length of the room. "Tell me why you sent for me. I've imagined every distressing scenario, so please put me out of my misery."

"I'm trying to make this interesting for you," Lex said peevishly. "Don't make me hurry my tale."

"Tell me this isn't some misbegotten attempt to get me back into your bed," Sydney said, more to provoke Lex than out of any concern that this might be true.

"Don't flatter yourself," Lex said. "If I needed someone in my bed that badly, I could find a willing volunteer nearer than Liverpool."

"Manchester," Sydney said.

"As you say," Lex said with a shrug, plainly not caring much for a geography lesson. Or for accuracy. Or for Sydney's patience. "In any event, I had to bend the truth a bit to ensure that you came. And I couldn't exactly write down the facts of the matter, in case the letter got intercepted."

"Are we spies now? How thrilling."

"Oh, my dear boy, I wish it were as easy as that. What we are is parents. Leontine, darling," he called. "Come here."

A child of about five years walked into the room, fixing Sydney with a bright smile. She had golden hair and a ruffled dress and a profile he would know anywhere. It was too dark to see much of the child's face, but when she stepped into the solitary beam of sunlight that made its way through a crack in the dirty windowpane, Sydney had all the proof he needed.

"How?" he managed, his voice hoarse and his eyes swimming with unshed tears.

"This charming parcel was delivered to Hereford House with a note explaining that she's Andrew's natural child," Lex said, dry as dust.

"Her mother?" He could not think of where they had been—he looked at the child, trying to calculate her age— five or six years ago. London, for a few months, then Durham. "When is your birthday?" he asked the child, kneeling in front of her.

"She doesn't speak English. Or if she does, she's being dashed stubborn about it. Try French."

"*Comment vous appelez-vous?*" he asked, certain he had bungled his pronunciation. The child tilted her head uncomprehendingly. He had probably said something unforgivably insulting. Andrew had always done the talking when they had been overseas. He had done the talking everywhere they went, for that matter; he had been the one who knew how to make himself liked and understood. Looking at this child, Andrew's daughter, Sydney felt a fresh surge of grief.

"It's Leontine," Lex said.

"*Bonjour, Leontine. Bienvenue.*" That much he could remember. The child smiled at him when she heard her name. He looked around the room for something to occupy her. He had not had anything to do with small children since Andrew had been this age and he had only been two years older. Sydney was grateful that he had, at least, swept the room clear of anything sharp or dangerous, except for a couple of workmen's tools in the corner. But he had also removed anything that could reasonably be played with. He took his watch from his pocket, dimly aware that babies were apparently amused by the ticking sound. She was not a baby, but perhaps the principle would hold. She took the object eagerly.

"A French mother," he said aloud. That, unfortunately, did not narrow down the field. He remembered the months they had spent in Flanders working on a bridge. "Who brought her to you?"

"She was left on my doorstep like a jug of milk. The note

said her name was Leontine, her father was Andrew God-dard, and her mother and aunts died of typhus. I assume mothers and aunts are euphemisms for residents of the bawdy house where the child undoubtedly was conceived."

Knowing Andrew's proclivities, that was entirely likely. For all his talk of sex not being a sin if it was mutually respectful, he had found a vast quantity of women to mutually respect. "Why did they bring her to you? You don't just sail across bodies of water and deliver children to the nearest duke."

"How the devil do you expect me to know what goes through the minds of French brothel keepers? I expect they were looking for Andrew, found he was dead, and decided his brother-in-law would do just as well."

"Good God." Sydney could only imagine how distressing it must have been for Lex to be reminded of his loss and burdened with a child all at once.

"Quite," Lex said tightly.

"All right," Sydney said, trying to collect himself. "I'll bring her back to Manchester presently. I'll engage a nurse and housekeeper. And I'll need to hire a house." He could hardly bring the child back to his bachelor lodgings.

"She's not going anywhere," Lex snapped, and it was the first time his mask of cool indifference slipped that day.

"I beg your pardon?"

"She was sick all over my trousers, my carriage, and my valet a dozen times in the past week. That's what took us so long to get here. I didn't want the creature to expire. And to be perfectly clear, I'm quite done in as well. I'm staying here until I recover my senses, or until the damp brings the sweet release of death, whichever comes first. In any event, Sydney, you'll be pleased to know that Carter already made up a bed for me in what he assures me is a room with four solid walls and a ceiling. I didn't ask about the status of the floor but trust his judgment implicitly. He's gone to the village to find a girl to take after our, eh, niece. It's a pity the house is barely habitable, though."

"Nobody told you to attempt to inhabit it," Sydney said. "I would have come to you in London. We could have gone to any of your properties. We could have stayed at an inn."

"No, we couldn't," Lex said. "I needed you to meet the child in private, because I didn't know what you'd want to do about her."

The child in question was, at the moment, sitting contentedly on the dusty flagstone floor studying Sydney's watch and comparing its time with that of an elderly longcase clock. The latter refused to settle upon a proper number of minutes per hour no matter how diligently Sydney tinkered with its workings.

"What on earth did you imagine I'd want to do?" Sydney asked, peeved. "Hide her in a convent? She's quite plainly my brother's child."

"Is she?" Lex asked softly.

"What do you mean, is she? I know it's been a while but surely you remember what Andrew looked like."

"Of course I remember," Lex said. "But I can't see her, you idiot. Can't see much of anything."

Sydney took note of the cane that was propped up against

Lex's leg. And he realized Lex hadn't once turned his head towards Sydney during the entire time they had been speaking. "Not from the fire," he said. Sydney had been in Durham when the fire broke out, and so a week had passed before he learned that his brother and sister-in-law were dead and his friend insensible after having been hit by a falling beam during his attempt to rescue them.

"Yes, of course from the fire. And I'm not completely blind. I can see light and sometimes movement, but not enough to identify whether a French urchin is related to my brother-in-law. In any event, I've gotten quite used to it and I find pity excessively boring, so save it. Besides, even if I had known that she was Andrew's, I still didn't know if you'd want the world made aware of her existence. You know perfectly well that a good many people won't have anything to do with their baseborn relations. To be honest, I don't know what to think of you since Andrew died. You certainly don't want anything to do with me."

This was simply too much. "You never wrote back! I wrote you six letters, and your secretary responded to each and every one of them."

"Because I can no longer read, you imbecile. And having my secretary read aloud letters from a former lover is rather lowering, not to mention a wonderful way to find oneself in the stocks."

"But I didn't know you had lost your sight!" Sydney said, so exasperated he hardly registered that Leontine had found a small fire iron and was using it to pry open the casement of the broken clock.

"You would have if you had visited. And don't tell me you never go to London. I'm quite aware that you testified before Parliament about steam or some such thing."

"Lounging around a ducal palace is not my idea of a good time, Lex. That much hasn't changed in the past two years." That had, in fact, been one of the many reasons their brief liaison had never become anything more. Sydney had needed to do things, to build things, to *work*, and Lex had been unapologetically idle and profligate. Sydney wanted no part of that world.

"As arrogant as ever, I see," Lex sniffed.

"I, arrogant? This from you, of all people."

"You don't need to be a duke to be arrogant."

"It certainly seems to help," Sydney retorted.

"Arrogant *and* rude. What would your mother say?"

The thought of what his mother would say was enough to make his mouth twitch into the beginnings of a smile. "She'd urge you to forsake Mammon and cast your sights heavenward," he lied. What she would actually do was attempt to persuade Lex to sign some kind of petition about mill workers, then leave with a hefty subscription to one of her favorite charities.

"She'd think I was charming." Lex buffed his fingernails on his lapel.

That was probably true, blast it. But the thought of his mother reminded him that this child was not only Andrew's child and Sydney's own niece, but his parents' only grandchild. And Sydney was the only living relation she had this side of the Atlantic. Leontine was the very spit of Andrew, from her golden curls to her apparent unconcern for things like not taking crowbars to clock cases. Just looking at her made Sydney's heart twist in a peculiar way.

He took a deep breath. He would not be cross with Lex for having dragged him to this place, because now he could give Andrew's child a good life. Not only was this what Andrew would have wanted, what Andrew would have done if he had been alive, but it was Sydney's duty. This time at Pelham Hall was a necessary evil, a pause on his way to righting wrongs and doing what was needful. He could do that.

The fact that this would give him time for more morning rambles with Amelia did not figure whatsoever into his complacency, he decided.

When Amelia set out the next morning at her usual time, she rather hoped to find Sydney waiting for her. That was a stupid thought, because she hadn't asked him to walk with her again, and she couldn't very well expect him to read her mind.

But there he was, leaning against the gatepost. "If you don't want company on your walk, I'll head in the other direction," he said. "But I thought you might need protection against any vicars' wives. No hard feelings whatsoever if you'd rather be alone."

Amelia chose not to investigate the surge of happy nervousness that raced through her. "I packed an extra sandwich," she said, lifting her basket.

"I brought a sack of plums. We'll have a feast. In what

direction are we walking?" Nan arrived then and gave Sydney her customary greeting, which was a cautious sniff followed by a rather halfhearted growl.

With this, they established a pattern of walking out together every morning. He waited for her by the gatepost, and they each brought food to share. If Amelia were being honest with herself, she had seldom more enjoyed spending time with anyone. Even years ago, before company had started to feel like a burden, she didn't think she had liked anyone quite this much. She tried not to think too much about what this might portend.

"Your walks have gotten much longer," Georgiana observed after a few days. "Sometimes you aren't back until noon."

"The weather's too lovely to waste indoors," Amelia said.

"Amelia, I've known you over ten years and you've never said such a thing in that entire time. You spent all of last summer holed up in your writing room and didn't seem to regret one minute of wasted sunshine."

Amelia busied herself in unlacing her boots. "I've been walking with a land surveyor," she admitted, not sure why it felt like a confession. A week ago she would have told Georgiana everything, from how near she had come to kissing him to the way he looked without his coat on. But now whatever existed between her and Sydney felt fragile, as if she might ruin it if she tried to assign it a name.

"A land surveyor?" Georgiana asked. "Have you taken an interest in geography?"

"I've, rather, um, taken an interest in the surveyor."

Georgiana's eyes and mouth both rounded comically. "Well. You're being careful?"

Had Amelia been less skilled in masking her emotions, she would have flushed bright red. "There's no need."

"That's what you think," Georgiana said darkly. "Men."

"He seems to be a decent man."

"Decent men still have penises," Georgiana intoned. "And probably entirely misguided notions of what they ought to do with them." Georgiana herself was perfectly indifferent to the charms of men and women alike.

The next morning Sydney wasn't at the gate. Amelia waited, unsure of whether he was late or if he had chosen not to come. Or perhaps he had gone back to Manchester. It had been nearly two weeks since she had first seen him, which surely was enough time to do whatever it was he was doing. Come to think, wasn't it a bit peculiar that he never seemed to have any maps or charts with him? Surveyors tended to have an assortment of tools, as well, and he never carried anything more than a satchel with his midday meal.

But then she saw him rounding the bend, and she didn't make any effort to conceal the smile that broke across her face.

"Good morning, Amelia," he said, smiling in return.

They grinned at one another, standing too close, looking too long. If she tipped her head up and rose to her toes, they'd already be kissing, and she didn't quite know why they weren't. "I thought you might not come today."

"I was up late last night patching a leak in the roof."

"At the Swan? I hope the landlord doesn't regularly ask you to do that sort of thing."

"No, no," he reassured her, but a flicker of unease crossed his brow. "Nothing like that."

He had purplish circles under his eyes, speaking to his lack of sleep, and his hair was adorably rumpled on one side. "Sydney, did you only now roll out of bed? You have a crease from your pillow still on your cheek." Laughing, she reached up and touched the red line with her thumb, tracing it from the warmth of his cheek to where it disappeared into his beard. "Lazy lie-abed. It's several whole minutes past dawn."

He huffed out a laugh. His skin was warm. She hadn't put gloves on and she was glad of it, because she could feel his skin and the bristles of his beard. He grasped her wrist in one big hand. At first she thought he meant to stop her from touching him, but instead he held her wrist still, almost pressing his cheek into her touch. Then he took a second glance at her hand.

"What happened to you? Did you overturn an ink-well onto yourself?" He held her hand carefully, his thumb moving over the pattern of ink blots on her palm.

"I got extremely upset with Edmund Tudor and broke a pen. The results are what you see before you."

He blinked. "I see," he said in a tone that indicated he definitely did not see, but was determined not to act as if anything she said was bizarre or required explanation. She felt a surge of affection.

"I'm writing a book about the Wars of the Roses. Murder,

treachery, all those good things. But Edmund Tudor is the worst." She was braced for questions about titles and plots. Her books weren't a secret; they were written under her own name—at least the three that wouldn't get her brought up on obscenity charges. It was just that she preferred not to talk about it, because she did not know how to explain that writing a three-volume history in which Margaret Beaufort went on a murder spree was the closest thing to personal fulfillment she feared she was presently capable of. She did not know how to talk about it without announcing to the world that she was deeply, irretrievably odd.

"They were all pretty bad that century," he said. "I imagine you're spoiled for choice as to villains."

"I know!" she said, delighted. "That's why I'm writing about it. Do you have a bit of extra time this morning? There's a spot I'd like to show you."

"I have all day," he said, and she felt his cheek warm under her touch. What must it be like, to have your emotions rush to the surface like that? Amelia couldn't even imagine. It must be like living one's entire life behind a window. "Let's be off, then," he said, and offered her his arm for the first time yet.

Chapter Five

Sydney had been looking forward to seeing Amelia since parting with her the previous day. He woke with her on his mind, and seeing her in person was as much of a relief as he had hoped. This was dangerous, he knew. Being with her, touching her, felt the same as nearly falling through the attic stairs due to his own poor planning. He was proceeding without a shadow of forethought; it was exhilarating but also more than a little terrifying.

Her hand rested on the inside of his elbow, and their sides frequently brushed against one another as they walked. She occasionally tilted her head up to look at him while she talked, and he caught himself helplessly gazing down at her. It was a wonder they didn't tumble headfirst into a briar patch.

When they reached the place she had wanted to show him, she kept her hand on his arm even after they stopped walking. It was a prominence with a good view of the valley below, and a conveniently placed boulder from which to watch the clouds make shadows on the opposite hillsides.

But instead of looking across the valley, she looked up at him, which he knew because he was already looking at her, because his brains were completely addled by sheer proximity to her. Then, God help him, she licked her lips. When her tongue darted out of her mouth and moistened her lower lip, Sydney thought he might freeze to the spot.

"Sydney," she said, her bare hand resting on his arm. "Are you quite all right?"

"Look at that very interesting sight over there," he said, gesturing in the general direction of the hills on the opposite side of the valley.

"It's . . . sheep," she said. "You're familiar with sheep?"

"They seemed fine specimens," he managed to say.

She smiled a particularly wolfish smile, as if she knew exactly what she was doing to his powers of thought.

"I'm wondering," he said, after they had sat on the boulder and passed his flask of ale back and forth a couple of times, "whether you plan to continue looking or if you have any further plans for me." He told himself he said the words to put her off, to let her know she was not being discreet and shock her into behaving in a more prudent manner. But he knew that wasn't the truth. He was goading her, daring her to do more.

"Well," she said consideringly, "I daresay that depends on what you'd like."

His mouth went dry. "Oh?"

"I'm hardly an expert but I believe the general belief is that best practice is for there to be two participants. Possibly more, in theory, but I don't see anyone else nearby."

"Participants," he repeated, his voice hoarse. Of course he knew what she meant. All morning she had been looking at him as if he were a table laid out for a banquet. She wasn't making any secret of liking what she saw, and he knew that she was capable of making her face keep any secrets she wanted.

She waved her hand impatiently. "Use whatever words you like."

He made a strangled sound. "I take it back. There are to be zero participants. You can't carry on like this."

"Like what? And why not? I daresay I can carry on precisely as I please."

His cheeks flamed with heat. "I can't—you are an unmarried girl—"

"No." She wrinkled her noise in disgust. "Do better. I mean, if you'd rather not kiss me and so forth then I'd be pleased to learn more about steam engines."

"Pardon?" he asked faintly. He was unaccustomed to approaching sex without a healthy dose of anxiety. With a man, he worried about being caught; with a woman, he still worried about being caught but also about pregnancy. In short, he worried.

"Do come up with a better excuse. Even if the reason you won't . . . participate with me is that you don't want to sully my honor"—here she made a particularly unladylike gagging sound—"do come up with a more creative reason."

"More creative." This was perhaps the least sensible conversation he had ever participated in, and he was certain he should not be enjoying it.

"I suppose you could say you don't fancy me, but we both know you've been looking at me as much as I've been looking at you."

"Impossible. Nobody has ever looked at anyone as much as you've looked at me. I feel quite cheapened." And then, because he was an idiot, he glanced at her chest, then hastily glanced away. Oh, hell. In for a penny. He returned his gaze to her, starting at the top of her head, then down to her forehead, where one eyebrow was arched in wry amusement. Then he traveled down to her lips, pale pink and quirked up in the beginning of a wry smile. He could lean in and kiss her—but no, now he was only looking. With his gaze, he traced the column of her neck, then the long sleeves of her gown, and back up again. He took in every curve, watched the way her chest rose and fell with every breath, and for one moment he let himself imagine what it would be like to let himself really want her, what it would be like to stop checking his admiration and fully experience it.

When she spoke, her voice was low, a bit throaty. "You owe it to yourself to invent a better excuse for not touching me. A vow of chastity, perhaps. I assure you I would be most respectful of any vows you've taken. A rare condition that causes you to lose consciousness when you become aroused. An insurmountable fear of redheads with ample bosoms. I could list a dozen more."

The woman was pathologically averse to the truth. Surely Sydney should not be so charmed. "I can't," he rasped. "I . . ." He swallowed, and she watched his throat work. "I took a vow of chastity," he blurted out.

"What?"

"As you said earlier. I took a vow of chastity and that's why I can't touch you."

"As long as it has nothing to do with my virtue."

"A pox on your virtue. It's *my* virtue, by which I mean my vow of chastity, that I'm concerned with."

"What kind of vow?" she asked promptly. "Are you in a monastic order?"

"Damn it, Amelia."

She shook her head as if he had let her down. "You can't have thought one line would be good enough. Do better."

He buried his face in his hands. "I swore an oath to my liege lord that I wouldn't lay a hand on any woman until I had brought back a holy relic."

"I thought Quakers didn't swear oaths."

He looked up at her in outrage. "I'm making up a story!"

She nodded approvingly. "Well done. I expect you to tell me more about your liege lord and the nature of your knightly quest at some other time, but first let's discuss the specifics of your oath. Are women allowed to touch you or did you swear to prevent them from doing so? If so, that would be a very comprehensive vow. Quite unprecedented."

"Amelia, are you looking for a loophole in my fictional vow of chastity?"

"Obviously," she said. "So we've established that you are a noble knight, unable to touch any fair lady, but also unsworn to defend your own virtue against any feminine explorations. Is that so?"

He blinked at her, dazed. Her lips were slightly parted,

and he could lean in and kiss her. She was all but asking him to do so, or maybe asking for permission to kiss him herself. "That's right."

"Are there any restrictions as to how a lady might touch you?"

"A lady might take care that we're very nearly in public," he said with an effort at asperity.

"A gentleman might notice that we're on an isolated hilltop. The sheep will keep our secrets. May I touch you, though?"

"Be my guest," he managed.

"I'm going to start with your beard."

"No, you can't," he said. "You can only touch over my clothes, otherwise I'm technically touching you and I'd be in defiance of the—" He broke off, realizing what he was saying. "Amelia, you've addled my brains."

"I know," she said delightedly. "Well, I'll start with your arms, then." She stroked her hands down his arms, slowly, as if relishing the solid feel of them under her fingers. He shifted under her touch, muscles bunching and rippling. He was suddenly very glad he had dispensed with his coat today.

"You're showing off for me," she said.

"That isn't against my vow."

She snorted in amusement. Excellent. She stopped just short of his cuff, then slid her hands back up the length of his arms and onto his shoulders. "Goodness, you're very large." She slid her hands down his chest, over the linen of his shirt and the wool of his waistcoat, over the muscles there. He groaned and let out a shaky breath.

He liked her. He liked her nonsense stories even though he was certain he ought to disapprove. He liked that she didn't make a secret of wanting him and didn't seem to think that their wanting one another meant they needed to do anything dramatic about it. He couldn't remember the last time he had enjoyed being in the same space as someone, and it must have been longer still since anyone returned the sentiment.

"Oh. Look at that," he said, gesturing at the sky. "It's noon."

"So it is," she agreed.

He liked her. He wanted her. She liked and wanted him. It was as easy as that, and was seldom so simple. He cleared his throat, but still when he spoke his words came out hoarse and thick. "Did you know that I get a dispensation from my vow each day at noon? Very brief. Only two or three minutes."

"Better hurry."

He took her chin in his hand, feeling how soft and smooth her skin was under his calloused fingers. "A kiss?"

"Clock's ticking," she said, and it was little more than a breath. She held herself perfectly still, waiting for him to make the decision.

He leaned in, let his lips brush over hers. He had forgotten how sensitive mouths could be, and was taken by surprise by the sparks of sensation awakened in him. He moved to the side and kissed the corner of her mouth. Her hand came to his jaw at the same time he deepened the kiss, testing the seam between her lips. She made a satisfied little sound that went straight to his groin. Then she pulled back, and for the merest instant he saw her discomposed, he saw what she looked like when she was honest. Eyes unfocused and hungry, lips pink and parted. Then she gathered herself up.

"My mother always said to leave people wanting more. Usually she was referring to when to leave a tea party, but I suppose it applies."

That brought him up short. Was that how she was raised? If so, it explained a lot. Sydney's mother was wont to say things like "waste not want not" and "don't buy cotton unless you know it was grown by free labor," and Amelia's mother was telling her when to leave tea parties.

"I couldn't possibly want you more," he admitted. "Even if you had kissed me for another half hour."

"Perhaps we could test that principle. Tomorrow, even." She bit her lip and looked up at him with laughing gray eyes.

"I leave tomorrow for Manchester."

"Oh! I see." She looked so openly disappointed that he nearly kissed her again.

"For a fortnight." He had to meet with the railway backers and then hire a house that would be suitable for Leontine. "Then I'll be back for a little while." He'd only be back long enough to collect his niece and take her to Manchester, but he didn't want to say so. "I'll look forward to seeing you," he said. And then, because that wasn't enough, he brushed his lips across her forehead. "I'll miss you."

"I'll miss you too," she whispered, and looked startled to have said it out loud. "Write me," she said. "You know where I live. And I'll write you back."

Even as he said yes, watching the smile spread over her face, he knew it was a bad idea. And he knew he would enjoy it anyway.

Sydney was more than a little surprised to find Leontine sitting on the gravel drive in front of Pelham Hall. Before her was spread a motley array of treasures: a bottle cap, several springs, a lump of sealing wax, some string. What was not present was the nursemaid who was supposed to be minding her.

"Where is your nurse?" he asked, before remembering that the child could not understand English. Or maybe she could, because she gazed in the direction of the house and gave a very Gallic shrug. If she were the sort of child who lived to escape supervision, as her father most definitely had been, she would need a trained governess, not a village girl who had been pressed into service. Perhaps she also needed a dog. Something that could follow her around and keep her safe, like Amelia's dog did for her.

"What are you building there?" he asked, crouching down beside her. She made a circular gesture with her hand and a buzzing sound. "A whirligig," he said, comprehending. She laughed and attempted to repeat the word, which made Sydney laugh as well. "I agree, it's a silly word. But your father and I used to make all manner of these. Here, let's look at what you're doing."

For the next half hour he watched her work, only contributing some conveniently sized sticks and congratulatory sounds. When they had a finished object, they brought it inside.

They found Lex sitting once again in the great hall, alone. He spent a great deal of time alone in the ruins of a house that had once been a happy place, and Sydney didn't quite know what to think about it. After he had admired the buzzing sound the whirligig made, and the maid had finally come along to bring Leontine to her tea, Lex tapped his cane on the floor. "Off to catch the stagecoach back to Manchester?" he asked, an odd edge to his question.

"You know I am. I need to arrange for a house and a maid, to say nothing of a governess for Leontine." He had run through the numbers last night. He'd need to use the money Andrew left him—rightfully Penny's, and only Sydney's due to the fact that the couple had wed so hastily there had been no time for settlements or wills. Sydney hadn't wanted to touch that money, it having all the taint of ill-gotten gains. But for Andrew's child, it felt almost right. "I need to do my duty."

"Of course," Lex said. "Your duty. How you make caring for people sound like such a chore, I'd like to know. Like emptying chamber pots."

Sydney strove for patience. "All I meant is that I'm all Leontine has in this world, and I'll do right by her."

"No, you aren't. She has you, me, and Pelham Hall."

"Pardon?"

"Really, Sydney, do keep up. If she's Andrew's child, this place ought to be hers."

That brought Sydney up short. The prospect of passing

Pelham Hall and all the memories and guilt that were tied up with it off to someone else felt like a millstone lifting from his neck. "Surely an illegitimate daughter has no claim on his property."

"Not legally, of course, but since when do you give a fig about that? Surely, if she's Andrew's daughter she has a claim to his property according to some principle you hold."

"Yes, principles, that's what they're called, Lex."

"Are you smiling?" Lex asked. "It sounds like you're smiling. Haven't heard that since I got here."

"But how do we go about proving she is who we think she is? How do I give it to her? Do I need to set up a trust?"

"You're being very tedious today. Were you always this tedious? I dare say you were, and I let your physique distract me. Nobody needs to prove who she is. Just give her the house. You clearly don't want it. Let the solicitors sort out the details and the child can stay here." He yawned. "Meanwhile I require dinner. You really ought to hire a cook. I'm very disturbed by the lack of hospitality I've received here."

"*Dégueulasse,*" Leontine said agreeably from the doorway. She had evidently escaped her nurse again. "*C'est une vraie porcherie, ça.*"

"Utterly *dégueulasse, ma petite,*" Lex agreed. "We must get your uncle to do something about it."

Sydney knew it was useless to argue with Lex when he was in a mood like this. Or really, ever. Amelia, for all her missing shawls and her levity, her insistence upon fictional vows of chastity and her too-sweet cakes, was a sensible person, and he had a sudden urge to turn to her for confirmation that Lex was being impossible. He could go to Crossbrook Cottage now, he supposed, but that seemed like a violation of their rules of engagement. They had only ever seen one another alone and outside and altering this made him uncomfortable in a way he couldn't identify.

Instead he climbed the stairs to the attic. Perhaps he'd find a doll or a couple of books that Leontine could amuse herself with while he was away, so that she needn't spend all her waking hours attempting to flee her nurse.

Along one side of the attic were a series of rooms tucked under the slope of the roof, nestled into the eaves. He suspected these had once been servants' quarters or lumber rooms. When he tried to open a door, he found it stuck, either the result of wood swollen by water damage or a hinge rusted in place. Pressing his shoulder to it, he jammed it open. Inside was an assortment of old furniture: a clothes press, a bedstead, a couple of chairs in need of mending. There was the baby's cradle Andrew had built himself—no, he would not look at that. He worked his way along the series of doors, shouldering each one open and examining the contents within. None of the windows up here were broken, and the contents of the rooms were safe and whole. He felt like he was snooping in another person's house.

And then he came across a too-familiar shape. Even covered in dust and cobwebs he would have known Andrew's trunk anywhere—it had accompanied them from Liverpool to Flanders to Durham to London and back again. And when Andrew had decided to stay in Derbyshire to marry Penny, his trunk had stayed with him. Sydney thought it had been destroyed in the fire along with everything else Andrew had owned. He was on his knees before he could think twice, throwing the lid open, staring down into its depths.

There was Andrew's hairbrush, his shaving kit, a few pairs of moth-eaten waistcoats that Sydney could still imagine his brother wearing. No, he couldn't quite cope with any of that, couldn't quite accept that this hairbrush existed when its owner did not. He shoved them aside, feeling for what he couldn't see in the faint light that made its way through the single small, dirty window. His fingers brushed against a smooth leather surface, and he knew he had it. He lifted the book out and looked at the cover. It was too dim to read but he knew the volume by heart, even after all those years: *Moral Tales for Young People* by Hannah Goddard. It was Andrew's copy of their mother's book. Andrew hadn't thought it even slightly embarrassing to carry around a book of children's stories written by his own mother, and hadn't cared who knew about it. He hadn't cared what anyone thought about anything, come to that. He had effortlessly managed to make everyone love him, and Sydney might have resented it if he hadn't loved Andrew as well.

When he opened the book, the pages fell open to the story of little Sally Cartwright who decides to learn the science behind exploding puddings and winds up boycotting sugar. That had been Andrew's favorite—the story of a child who isn't punished for her curiosity, but rewarded with both puddings and righteousness.

For a moment he was overwhelmed by how much he missed his brother, how much he wished Andrew had lived to know that he had a daughter. They could have dismantled every clock in the house together. Andrew had been rash and sometimes irresponsible, but he had never been stingy with his affections. He had been the sort of man who seemed to have a bottomless well of kindness and love, while Sydney only had duty. His caring for people did sometimes feel about as joyful as emptying a chamber pot, and he resented Lex for having got that right. Lex, a man who had certainly never emptied such a thing in his life.

He ran his fingers over the worn cover of his mother's book. He wished she were here, to ask for advice, to help raise Leontine, but also as living proof that Sydney was capable of affection, of loving and being loved. All he ever had from her were increasingly rare letters from America. All his connections seemed to deteriorate into unanswered letters—first Lex, now his mother, and he had always suspected that if he hadn't spent every day working alongside Andrew, his brother would have forgotten he existed. That would happen with Amelia as well. Perhaps he wasn't the sort of person one developed deeper feelings for. That was, he supposed, fine. He could still do what was right.

CHAPTER SIX

5 August, 1824
Dear Amelia,

I meant to ask you about your father. I suppose that's just the sort of opening guaranteed to have you toss the entire letter into the fire, which is no more than what I deserve, but the fact is that I did mean to ask you about your father, and now it's too late to come up with a more graceful way to ask. You probably think I ought to start the letter afresh on a new sheet of paper, but this single sheet was all I could persuade the innkeeper at the King's Arms in Peak Dale to part with. Why, you may well ask, am I at Peak Dale instead of Manchester? A sink hole opened in the middle of the road, caused the stagecoach to tip, and its passengers to undergo an adventure. If for some reason you've read this far (why, Amelia?) please note never to ask me about the condition of the roads from Bakewell to Manchester (for now I will confine *myself to noting that a certain turnpike trust ought to have hired me when presented with a chance).*

So, your father. When you mentioned that you would have died in his place, do you mean that you felt like it was your fault for having lived when he died? That your family would have been better off if he had survived? That, I'm afraid, is the sort of deranged notion that passes for thought in my mind these days. (But truly, my brother was a better man than I, and the world would have been a better place had he lived. He had a family—)

Please note that over the course of writing the last paragraph, I've muttered so many imprecations under my breath at my own presumptuousness that the respectable matron at the next table has pointedly found a new seat. You may well sympathize.

But you spoke of the matter with such perfect frankness and even humor that I think I'm not grossly overstepping, but I trust you'll put me in my place if I'm wrong.

Glancing out the window, I can see that it's pouring rain, which means you're going to be done out of your walk. Are you trapped inside as you read this? Do you get restless when you can't get out?

Sincerely yours,
Sydney [illegible]

P.S. If you take leave of your senses and wish to write me back, my address is 12 Booth Street, Manchester.

7 August, 1824

Dear Sydney,

*I thoroughly sympathize with the respectable matron
at the King's Arms in Peak Dale, if only because your
apologies are excessive and wear upon my patience. I will
proceed to cheerfully talk your ear off about the earnest
longing for the grave that ensued upon my father's death, but
first let me point out that most human beings would have
begun such a letter as yours not with a gentle request about
the nature of grief, but with the news that they had recently
had a narrow escape from their own death. May I assume
that you were uninjured, as that single sheet of paper is not
blotted with your own blood?*

*I suspect that for those of us who are accustomed to find
ourselves lacking in some capacity, especially by comparison
with those around us, our minds find self-recrimination a
very comfortable and familiar place. So when confronted
with a new and terrible sensation, such as grief, our idiot
brains retreat to the homely comfort of self-loathing. That,
at least, is how I think my own poor mind manages. It is, of
course, balderdash, and I know that now, but try telling that
to my brain.*

*It has been raining for two days straight. I've been
pacing the length of my sitting room for about an hour,
earning pitying glances from long-suffering Georgiana and
glares from the cat.*

I cannot read your signature, so will take my chances

and address this letter to Sydney Gibberish and hope for the best.

Sincerely yours,
Amelia Allenby

9 August, 1824

Dear Amelia,

 It occurred to me in the middle of the night (in my own bed in Manchester now, thank heavens) that women do not tend to write to men. Or perhaps the rule is that unmarried women do not write to men. There is quite literally nobody I could ask about this except my landlady, who is already very cross with me for planning to move out on short notice. In any event, our previous interactions have given me reason to suppose that you may not take such strictures very much to heart.

 The second paragraph of your letter rings uncomfortably true. A pox on you for being so correct. The truth is that my brother was everything I am not—generous, open-hearted, humorous. He was also impulsive, reckless, and absentminded, and I would feel disloyal for committing those thoughts to paper, but for how I am the inverse of those as well, but still manage to make it come out a flaw: I'm afraid I'm a bit of a bore.

Yours,
Sydney

11 August, 1824

Dear Sydney,

Are you calling me a lightskirt? I neither confirm nor deny these allegations.

As for your second paragraph, I do wonder if my letters have been intercepted by some boring, humorless, churlish man because the Sydney Gibberish of my acquaintance is none of those things. If you were angling for a compliment, consider it delivered.

Returning to your first paragraph, I will have you know you're hardly the first man I've corresponded with. Interpret that as you see fit.

13 August, 1824

Dear Amelia,

I am unfit for society in every capacity. I didn't mean to suggest that—oh bother. I'm making you pay the postage on this single sheet and I am awash in regret.

                                                        S

15 August, 1824

Dearest Sydney,

Honestly, you're always awash in regret, so don't try to make me feel special about it. If you wish, you can

make it all up to me with another kiss upon your return.
I expect your entire face is crimson now and I only wish
I could see it.

Now I'm making you pay the postage on this brief
missive, but I turned it into two paragraphs so I don't feel
bad about it.

A

Chapter Seven

On the stagecoach from Manchester, Sydney found his hand repeatedly drifting towards the coat pocket where he kept Amelia's letters. It shouldn't have come as a surprise that she was a good correspondent: she earned a living by writing, but so had Sydney's mother, who was one of humanity's worst letter writers. Case in point: the letter waiting at Sydney's lodgings, which read, in its entirety: "Out of prison for now, your father's gout is acting up." Amelia's letters, though, made him feel like she was beside him. In her words he could hear her voice and imagine her laugh. It wasn't the same as being near her, but it was close.

But without her presence, he found himself questioning more often what exactly they were doing together. When she was near, it was easy to go along with whatever hedonistic whim was impelling them both. They had never talked about the future, had never even alluded to the possibility that anything serious lay between them. But it also wasn't a carefree tumble. Not that Sydney had ever managed a carefree tumble—or a carefree anything—in his entire life. He suspected that this was more serious for him than it was for her, because in his experience everything was always more serious for him than it was for everyone else around him. He wanted to pin it down, know exactly what it was and precisely where in his mind to slot this experience, and decided that maybe he would have to be content with calling it friendship.

Sydney was half asleep on his feet when he arrived at Pelham Hall. The coach had left Manchester just past midnight and arrived in Bakewell a little before dawn, and he had only managed the briefest and least satisfying of naps during the journey. Surely his fatigue added to the dreamlike state of confusion with which he approached Pelham Hall. It hardly seemed real that after days and days of talking with the merchants who sponsored the railway and the other engineers who offered opinions of how to make the thing actually work, he was back here, looking at a house that stood almost precisely as it had a few hundred years ago.

He walked slowly up the drive to Pelham Hall, taking in its motley assortment of gables and window bays. He was surprised to find that the past weeks had softened the edges of his hatred for this place. It now housed his niece and his—well, he supposed Lex was still a friend—and it was close to Amelia. And he regretted that in a few weeks it would once again be empty, abandoned.

Except, as he got closer, he saw it was not precisely the same as it had stood two weeks ago, let alone a few hundred years before that. Before leaving, he entrusted Lex's man-servant with a draft on his bank and instructions to hire whatever servants were required to make the house safe and comfortable for Leontine and Lex. He arrived to find no fewer than two dozen workers on the premises. He counted three glaziers, a couple of masons, and more carpenters than he cared to think about.

Carter met him on the gravel drive. "His Grace and I had a difference of opinion on what work needed to be carried out," Lex's manservant said. "I'm afraid he insisted on paying for it himself."

Sydney passed a hand over his jaw and tried to remind himself that Lex was doing this for Leontine. And also that spending money was something Lex did the way other people breathed. "How long does he plan to stay?" Sydney asked. "I was under the impression that we were only staying until he and the child were well enough to travel."

Carter tactfully cleared his throat. "His Grace has paid the servants' wages for the next month."

A month! Good God. Lex was welcome to stay for twenty months but Sydney could not and would not.

"How many servants has he engaged?" Sydney asked. "And where, pray tell, are they sleeping?"

"Five, in addition to the nursery maids and several gardeners and laborers outdoors. As for their lodgings, there are quite a few rooms in the attics that only needed sweeping and airing. They were in a most unexceptional condition considering the state of the rest of the house. His Grace paid for the furnishings and linens."

"Anything else I ought to know about?"

Carter cleared his throat again. "I'm afraid I poached a

cook from one of the great houses near Bakewell. And I may have given her the impression that she would be working in a duke's establishment. So she was understandably dismayed to discover . . ."

"That she was cooking over an open flame in a pit of a kitchen. Yes, quite." He thanked Carter and headed into the house, where he discovered Lex and Leontine in the great hall, which, thanks to the light streaming through the now-spotless windows and an accumulation of mismatched furniture, somehow seemed even more dilapidated than it had two weeks earlier.

"Uncle!" Leontine cried. She sat on the floor at Lex's feet, a book open on her lap.

"We've been working on vocabulary," Lex said. "It seems we read English, but we do not speak it, so she's been reading aloud to me from this book of improving tales you left behind."

Sydney took a closer look at the book Leontine held and saw that it was his mother's book of fables. "I'm certain you found it an edifying experience," he said, trying and failing to keep a straight face. "Do you feel that your morals have been improved?"

"I'm mired in wickedness in ways I never contemplated. I've already been lectured in two languages about sugar, cotton, worldliness, and—in a true turn of events—bargaining."

Now Sydney was smiling openly. "My mother believes haggling is immoral because everyone should be charged the same price for the same good or service."

"*Écoeurant!*" Leontine supplied. "*Infâme.*"

"Indeed, my pet," said Lex. "I cannot wait for you to lecture your uncle on these topics as resoundingly as you have lectured me."

Sydney realized that the Lex he saw before him appeared years younger than the man he had parted with two weeks earlier. Not only were some of the signs of weariness gone from his face, but also he was smiling. Sydney had forgotten how dazzlingly handsome Lex could be. It was good to see him looking healthy and well.

Carter arrived with a tray of tea and biscuits. "Don't eat the biscuits," Lex warned. "They're paperweights."

Sydney picked one up anyway and tested it in between his teeth. Indeed, it was effectively made of bedrock, solid enough to support an impressively vast suspension bridge. He ought to introduce the substance to the men who still argued for building a bridge across the bottomless bog.

"Do I want to know why we have a tray of inedible biscuits?" he asked.

"The cook and I are working out our differences. Leontine," he said, raising his voice to get the child's attention. "Go to Mr. Carter and tell him you need a proper tea. Sweets. Bonbons."

At the last word, Leontine shot to her feet and left the room, stopping halfway to the door to drop into a hasty curtsey. When they were alone again, Lex said, "I'm glad your—our—niece exists and I'm glad to be able to spend time with her. Never thought six days of vomit would endear me to a brat, but there you have it. I confess that I had my doubts about whether you'd come back, but I'm glad you did. I half feared you'd send some formidable matron to whisk Leontine away."

"Of course I came back," Sydney said, now feeling churlish for wanting to take Leontine and leave at the earliest opportunity. "Why wouldn't I have come, Lex?"

"I rather thought you were—well, to say I thought you were cross with me doesn't quite cover it. These details do get lost to memory, but you may recall that your brother died because I let him keep gunpowder in the hayloft."

Sydney was stunned. It had never once occurred to him that Lex would blame himself for the fire. "I was too busy blaming myself," he admitted.

"You were in Durham, I believe, and can wash your hands of all responsibility. You couldn't have done a damned thing about it. Penny wanted a pyrotechnics display for her birthday, and Andrew was going to give it to her. You know how they were."

Of course he knew how they were—rash, careless, happy people. Andrew had always needed someone on hand to keep him out of trouble. That was *why* Sydney blamed himself. "If I had been here, you'd better believe that powder would have been kept someplace safe." Sydney stopped himself, remembering what Amelia had written him. Grief made the mind revert to comfortable—if demonstrably useless—patterns. "Look," he said, "you're not responsible for everything that happens around you."

"I damned well ought to be. What's the use of me if not

that?" He gestured at himself and his surroundings as if encompassing all of it—the title, the wealth, the generations that had come before him.

"I can think of a number of other uses."

"Oh, I bet you could," Lex said, one eyebrow hitched up.

"You know that's not what I meant." Sydney sighed. "In any event, it's the height of arrogance and pride for you to blame yourself for an explosion, when there was a trained engineer on the premises."

"Is there a man with a gun forcing you to say such reasonable things? I confess I'm shocked and a bit disconcerted," Lex said. "I really thought I could count on you to make me feel properly ashamed." He shook his head, as if trying to dislodge the thought. "In any event, what I was trying to say is that I'll turn three-and-forty this winter. I got rid of any residual angst over my amorous proclivities more than two decades ago, but I do regret not having had the opportunity to have children. I always thought there would be nieces and nephews. I was the oldest, and there were always children about. And now . . ." He shrugged. "It's very pleasant to be around a child, especially at Pelham Hall. We were all shipped off here every summer, you know, and we reverted to a state of nature while my parents indulged us. The house was part of my mother's marriage settlement, and when she married she left it to Penny. I have to imagine that Penny would have left it to a daughter."

Sydney's heart clenched. "I wish she had been able to." If there had been any justice in the world, Andrew and Penny would still be alive, Pelham Hall would still be standing, and—he tried very hard not to think about that cradle in the attic.

Lex tilted his head. "What I was trying to say was that even though Leontine is no blood relation of mine nor of Penny's, I find it doesn't matter." He spoke these words with something very near an actual smile.

"I'm not going to just take her away, all right?" Sydney said, because that was clearly what Lex was asking for. "I thought I'd have nieces and nephews too."

"I was surprised to find that you hadn't started a family of your own."

Sydney laughed. "Are you in league with my mother?" he asked. "I seldom live in one town for more than a year. I work ten-hour days for months, then sit idly at home as I wait for another project to start up, which hardly seems the sort of domestic life most people would want for themselves." That much was true, but he also doubted his ability to find a partner who wished to spend time with him. He was nearly thirty and hadn't even come close. The idea of having domestic happiness himself seemed faintly ludicrous. If he were another man, a very different man altogether, he might have thought that whatever he had with Amelia might lead in the direction of homes and hearths; he might even have given it a name. That was for warmer, kinder people; Sydney had steam and steel. He told himself that was enough.

"I'm asking for one little detail," Amelia pleaded. "A tiny little detail."

"You're a ghoul," Keating remonstrated, crouching on the ground to remove a stone from his horse's hoof.

"You're hoarding gossip," Amelia retorted. "You go up to Pelham Hall every day, for your own fell and mysterious purposes, which I've nobly refrained from asking you about, and still you won't tell me a single thing that's happening there. Janet says Pelham Hall has a ghost in its attic."

"There's a ghost in your attic," Keating said, tapping his head.

"Janet says the family is cursed. Apparently all the sons of the ducal line are doomed to die before their twenty-fifth birthday," Amelia persisted.

Keating snorted. "The duke is past forty, so I'd say the curse isn't worth much."

"So you *have* seen him," Amelia said. She was frantically trying to assemble information about this duke before she and Georgiana had to meet him. It was dawning on her that however strictly they had confined their letters to historical matters, an unmarried woman's correspondence with a man might open that woman up to rampant speculation. And for that man to have the social standing to dispose of a woman's good name with a flick of his quill across some very costly paper, made the matter considerably worse. She wished she knew more about the character of the man who held Georgiana's reputation in his hands. She could not remember ever having heard much gossip about him during her years in London, which could mean that he traveled in circles so exalted that even Alistair's connections couldn't gain Amelia's family entrée, or could mean that he was a retiring sort of person.

"All I can tell you is that there's a dozen workmen up there." Keating got to his feet and dusted his hands on his trousers. "Look, I know you don't want to hear this, but if anybody here makes trouble for you, you don't have to stay."

"I can't. I already ran away from London—"

"I know, love. But sometimes running is all you can do. We'll pack up the house and find another place to live." He looked down at her with a sympathy so far removed from his usual dry and short-tempered manner that she felt her eyes prickle.

"Right. You're right." She rubbed a tear with the back of her hand and strove to recover her composure.

"Look, there's somebody waiting for you." Keating gestured towards the lane.

Amelia actually let herself gasp out loud when she saw Sydney leaning against the fence post.

"You're back!" she cried, going to meet him. "Did you get everything done you needed to in Manchester? You look terrible." He had circles under his eyes. On the bright side, his scruff had grown into a proper beard. "I mean, relatively speaking. You started out looking perfectly well. Better than well." She paused to catch her breath. "I think I've made my feelings clear on that score."

He smiled, whether at her graceless rambling or the compliment, she did not know. When, she wondered, had she stopped trying to manage her reactions around him? She was very conscious of employing no artifice, no screen. Her honesty seemed to be enough for him.

"I spent six days arguing with businessmen about the

impracticality of laying rails over a bottomless bog and then another six days repeatedly explaining why the path must be level." He held out his arm for her, and she took it, relishing the solid warmth of him beside her. "That would be bad enough even if I hadn't already had precisely those same conversations with precisely those individuals a month ago. Compounding matters, I don't think I've slept more than a few hours straight since July. Last night a family of hedgehogs appeared from behind the wainscoting. And I've had nothing more nourishing today than a soapy tea cake."

"The conditions at the Swan are worse than I realized," she said, aghast. His arm went stiff under her touch and she looked at his face, which was sterner than usual. Every now and then she ran up against a brick wall when talking to him. Probably she ought to ask what it was that distressed him, but she decided he'd have already volunteered the information if he wanted to. The ease of their rapport was partly due to the fact that they didn't ask one another difficult, prying questions. They took one another as they were, without demanding explanations or excuses. "Well, at least you'll have some proper food today. I brought cucumber sandwiches and cold chicken."

"You're an angel," he said softly. "I did miss this. Thank you for your letters." His voice was gruff, his gaze intent on her, and she realized that he was . . . fond of her. Well, she already knew he enjoyed being with her and liked the looks of her. This other thing, this softness in his eyes, this *angel* business, that was only to be expected, she supposed. She had to acknowledge that she probably had a corresponding set of emotions. But it all felt somehow regrettable, a reminder that they couldn't go on like this forever, and however it concluded would be unpleasant in one way or another. She resolutely shoved all that aside; she was an expert at getting rid of inconvenient feelings.

"Did you hear that there's a duke living at Pelham Hall?" she asked, striving to make light conversation.

"I don't want to talk about dukes." His voice was low, almost a growl. "Bollocks on every last one of them."

"Are you a radical? What a relief. One doesn't like to ask, but what if I had kissed a Tory?"

He huffed out a laugh. "Yes, but that's not why I don't want to talk about dukes." He slipped his arm loose from her grip and instead took hold of her hand, giving it a squeeze. "I missed you, Amelia."

"Oh," she managed, hope and desire and nerves all mingling together to cloud her thoughts. "Dare I hope that what you have in mind is more kissing? Is that how you sweet talk all the girls? Bollocks on dukes, let's kiss? Unconventional but extremely effective, if so, because I'm—"

She broke off because he turned to face her, his hand coming up to cup her cheek. His eyes were lit up with laughter and she was glad his earlier seriousness had passed. "I do like you, Amelia. I haven't laughed like this in years. Maybe ever. Thank you for that." Before she could point out that he hardly laughed at all, he stepped nearer, and she could smell his soap, the smell of him, and her words disappeared from her tongue. "For two weeks, all I've been able to think about is how you kissed me."

"How I kissed you," she said. "That's rich. I do recall you kissing me back."

"I certainly did, and I'll do it again." He bent his head to kiss her and she almost moaned into his mouth at the contact. His beard was rough but his lips were gentle and soft. She opened her mouth a bit, hoping for more, and felt his hands clamp down on her hips. He was holding himself back, and she didn't want any part of that, so she put a hand to the back of his head and held him close. She licked into his mouth, tasting and exploring and wondering at how something so basic and unmysterious could act like a key in a lock.

"We're in the middle of a path," he said, murmuring the words into the edge of her mouth, as if he didn't want to pull away far enough to speak the words properly.

"That way," she said, indicating a point over her shoulder. "There's a spot a little bit further up the hill." She had found it when Nan chased a hare through the bramble.

Neither of them made any move to leave the path, though. He still looked down at her with an intensity that made her want to shrink away, or diffuse the tension with a silly remark. But instead she let him look at her, and she tried to return the look with one as open and honest. She couldn't do it, though. She felt bare and unprotected. Instead, she pulled him close and their lips met, no hesitation or gentleness this time. His chest was solid and warm against hers, his hands strong and sure on her waist. He kissed her as if this—this moment, this place, Amelia— were all he wanted, all he cared about. And she kissed him back with the same need.

This was the most honest she had ever been, the least artifice she had ever deployed, and she didn't know if it was because she was thinking with her body or because she was beyond thought altogether. Or maybe it was that Sydney let her be honest, let her be truly herself. Maybe he liked her the way she was, and that let her be truthful to him and to herself.

And that, more than anything, made her want this. She wanted a chance to see what happened if she kept being honest.

CHAPTER EIGHT

Amelia took his hand and led him through a stand of trees to what had once probably been a stable or barn but was now four stone walls in various stages of disintegration, each overgrown with ivy. Because of *course* Amelia thought this was an excellent place to—Sydney's thoughts skittered wildly around—to do whatever she wanted with him, frankly.

She leaned back against one of the walls and looked up at him with a smile that was halfway to a laugh, as if they were in on the same joke.

"Amelia," he breathed.

She was smiling fully now, wickedly, as if she knew exactly what she wanted and intended to have it, and Sydney found that he was very, very supportive of that, even though apparently what she wanted was to seduce him behind the ruins of some kind of barn in broad daylight. He had barely enough reason left in his brain to reflect that this was not the most prudent idea he had ever had. It was secluded, and they'd hear anyone coming, but Sydney was not sure he'd object even if they were in a shop window.

There was no coyness in her demeanor, no hesitation either. She raised an eyebrow, and as if a puppet on a string, he put a palm flat on the stone wall behind her head. The wall seemed solid, at least. That was good. He had just enough time to be satisfied with his forethought when she took hold of his collar and tugged him forward.

He brought his mouth close enough that he could feel her breath on his lips. It was she who closed the gap, brushing her lips over his. He pressed in closer, then ran a hand down her side, feeling where she was trapped between his body and the wall. He deepened the kiss and she opened for him, tilting her head back as far as the wall would allow.

He kissed her some more, one hand on the hard stone wall and the other on the softness of her waist, then kissed down her neck until he reached the edge of her gown. "What am I going to do with you?" he asked into the smooth skin of her throat, mortified to discover that it came out more a desperate question than a teasing threat.

Her fingers threaded through his hair, holding him close to her, and the tug at his scalp caused all his thoughts to careen wildly off the rails. That was—not something he knew he wanted. She did it again and he heard himself make a pleading noise into the skin behind her ear. A few strands of her hair had come down from her knot, and he pushed them off her neck to clear the way for more kisses. She tilted her chin up to give him better access. Now that he had his hands on her, and her hands on him, he felt like he couldn't get enough. He had been imagining this for longer than he cared to admit, even to himself. "What do you like?" he asked, deliriously proud of stringing those four words together.

She let out a breathy little laugh. "I don't think there's anything you could do that I wouldn't like."

He skimmed a hand along her bodice, her breast soft and heavy in his hand. "This all right?" he murmured.

"Not even close," she said, and reeled him in by the lapel for another kiss. She tasted of strawberries and sunshine, sweet and bright and lovely. He wanted to lay her down and strip her, taste every inch of her, learn every part of her. But she was panting against his mouth and he was hard in his trousers. He cupped her breast in his palm, running his thumbnail over the peak of one nipple. She groaned and— oh, God help him, she wrapped a leg around his waist. He got a hand under her hips and lifted, holding her against him so she could feel his hardness. She worked her hand under his shirt, feeling his back, his sides, as if she were trying to touch as much of him as possible. This felt precious and impossible, too good and bright and soft to be happening to him. Her fingernails dug into his skin, sharp and insistent.

"Amelia," he said, his still untouched cock twitching in his trousers. "You'll kill me." He kissed her again, as if they were in a sensible place for this to be happening, as if this were a sensible decision in the first place. But the softness of her hips under his hands, the sharpness of her teeth against his lower lip—these were arguments that superseded any-thing like reason.

"Please," she said. "I need more." She looked frantically at him, gray eyes blown wide.

If Amelia needed more, he was going to give her more, whether they were on a hilltop or a rooftop or the middle of the bottomless bog itself. He found the hem of her dress and slid his hand up her calf. "Can I touch you?"

"Yes," she said. And then, of all the damned things in the world to do at that moment, she laughed. "Sydney," she said, "it's not even noon. Whatever will your liege lord say?"

"He's dead," he said bluntly. "Tragic. What a loss." His hand cupped the back of her knee, lifted it.

"Are you being droll? Whoever would have—"

He kissed her and could feel her smile against his own. He caressed up her thigh until he found the wet heat of her, then traced his thumb along her opening. She made a desperate noise and pressed against his hand. "Tell me how you like it," he said.

"Inside," she said in a choked-sounding voice. He slid two fingers into her and she buried her face in his neck, kissing the sensitive place where his throat met his beard.

He moved his thumb to stroke her clitoris and she bit his neck. "Sweetheart, so good," he babbled as he continued to stroke her, his thoughts completely unraveled by the feel of her around his fingers, the contrast between the softness of her body and the sharpness of her teeth, her nails.

"Do that again," she said, pushing against his hand, "and don't stop."

He tried to memorize every sound she made as her need ratcheted up, which touches made her breath catch and her grip tighten. Then she was biting hard on his collarbone, clenching around his fingers, and then, finally, limp in his arms. He gentled his touch, reluctant to pull away.

"That was," she said after panting against his chest for a minute, her face buried in his coat, "a good start." Then she moved her hands to the fall of his trousers and unfastened them. He was as hard as a pikestaff and trying his best not to think about it. "May I?" she asked.

"You may do any damned thing you wish," he managed. "Enact any of your fantasies. Do your worst." And that was the last sensible sentence he said, because by then she had her hand wrapped around his erection, tentatively stroking it as if it might break. "Harder," he muttered. She increased the pressure marginally, and he was too desperate for friction to care for manners, so he wrapped his own hand around hers and showed her. "Yes," he groaned.

"Is that good?" she asked.

"Amelia, sweetheart—" He wanted to tell her that if she kept going, she'd see how good it was in about ten seconds, but the words wouldn't form. All he managed was a hoarse "Keep your skirts clear, I should think." She let go, the infernal woman. "Why," he begged. "Why?"

"I want you inside me," she said in a tone that carried no hesitation.

For an instant all the objections presented themselves in a swirl of judgment: they were outdoors, it was the middle of the day, she could fall pregnant, she could lose her reputation, it could be a ghastly and disappointing experience. But Amelia knew those things, and she was asking for this, and they both wanted it. And he was falling in love with her. He knew he shouldn't think about that. There were good reasons not to let his mind go to that place, and he'd remember whatever they were later.

He hoisted her up again, and she obligingly cleared her skirts away, leaving no obstacle between them. He nudged her opening with the head of his cock and she made a noise of desperation. He plunged in. She went still in his arms and he worried he had been too rough, too sudden. It had been a while—maybe he was out of practice. He held her close, not daring to move until she was ready. "So good," he said, kissing her softly. She whimpered into his mouth. "You feel so good." He shifted his hips and thrust tentatively into her, watching her for any sign of discomfort. But she made a sound of surprised pleasure, and then adjusted her legs around his waist, and the next thing he knew he was holding her entirely off the ground, driving into her as she whispered his name.

One of her hands was on his jaw, holding him still for a kiss, and the other drifted between them, pushing aside skirts and petticoats and touching where they joined. He pulled back with the idea of trying to watch her. He wanted to see what she was doing but an ocean of cotton and linen got in the way. He could see enough to know that she was stroking herself, and just knowing that she was doing so was enough to bring him perilously near the brink of his own climax. She shuddered again, squeezing and clenching him inside her, and with a muttered curse he eased her to the ground and gingerly pulled out of her. He took himself in hand and brought himself off in a few tugs.

"God help me," he said, catching his breath, one hand planted on the wall near Amelia's head. "Look at you." She was the picture of decadence. Red, kiss-swollen lips, hair tumbled around her shoulders, hand still under her dress, skirts still rucked up around her hips. "You look mighty pleased with yourself," he said, wiping his hand off on his handkerchief.

"I am," she said. "I'm pleased with you too," she added with an air of charitable concession.

He laughed and kissed her again, and couldn't remember if he had ever been so happy in anyone's arms.

"That wasn't bad, was it?" Amelia asked after she had made some efforts to rearrange her clothes into a semblance of presentability. They were sitting against the stone wall in a patch of sun. She was wondering if they could stay out here long enough to do that again, preferably with Sydney considerably more disrobed. Between her legs there was a dull ache, but she wanted more of that fullness, more of Sydney's hands on her, his body pressing against hers.

"Not bad?" Sydney asked. He still looked dazed, which was highly satisfactory from Amelia's point of view. "How lowering." But his fingers were twined with Amelia's and his voice held a hint of a laugh.

"I mean not bad for a novice. I don't think I was too terribly disappointing," she said with full confidence she had not been in the least disappointing.

His hand went still against hers. "You hadn't—you

were—Amelia, what are you trying to tell me? When in your letter you wrote that you had previous correspondents, I thought that was a code for—" He rubbed his face over his beard. "I am an idiot. Had you not done that before?"

"No," she said, dreading the follow-up.

His jaw set and his eyebrows slanted into dark slashes. "Are you telling me you were a virgin?"

She knew she shouldn't have said anything. But here she was, sated and happy and warm and she stupidly felt like she could be honest with this man. "Don't be like that," she said. "Don't mystify my hymen."

"Don't mystify—what—" he sputtered. "I'm not mystifying anything. But you've now put me in the position of having deflowered you up against a stone wall."

"I beg your pardon," Amelia said, getting to her feet, "I have not been deflowered, as you so vulgarly put it. My hymen—my entire vagina as well as the rest of my body, thank you very much—are mine to do with as I please, with the consent of my lovers—"

"You haven't had any lovers, that's the point!" Sydney scrambled to his feet beside her, tucking in his shirt.

"No it is not," she snapped. "My previous experience of this one specific act has nothing to do with you. I have no duty to tell you. It's none of your business. Besides, if I had told you, you would have gotten sentimental." Oh no, she shouldn't have said that last part. Far better to pretend that sentiment didn't enter into this, that it didn't even exist as a possibility between them.

He reached out to brush some dust off her sleeve. "And

what's so wrong with sentiment? I would have taken care, Amelia."

She glanced away. "I felt very much as if you did care for me," she said.

"I would have made an effort not to hurt you." He stepped nearer, and took her hand.

"You didn't, though. You didn't hurt me. I enjoyed myself, which I think was abundantly clear, was it not?"

"Yes, but—"

"And I think you did as well?"

He took her other hand and drew her against his chest. "Obviously."

"Then next time we can have the tearful deflowering you feel I cheated you out of this time," she offered, feeling diplomatic.

He stared down at her for long enough that she thought he really was upset with her. Then he laughed. "Amelia," he said when he collected himself. "As long as there is a next time, we can do whatever you please."

"Well, then," she said, trying not to sound smug, trying not to acknowledge the warm feeling of softness and fondness that bubbled up inside her whenever she caught his eye. "I suppose that settles it."

Chapter Nine

"Sydney, I have a matter to discuss with you," Lex called out when Sydney returned to Pelham Hall. He was lounging on a sofa that had definitely not been there yesterday. Every time Sydney walked into a room, he found that its contents had doubled in both quantity and quality. Leontine sat on a new rug in a patch of sunshine, apparently reassembling the clock that she had taken apart some weeks earlier. "Is something dripping? I hear water. If there's a leak in this roof I might actually cry."

"No, it's me. I went for a swim before coming in." He hoped Lex couldn't tell that he was blushing. After parting with Amelia, Sydney had been overheated in both mind and body, so had cast off his boots and coat and jumped into what had once been the trout pond but was now a clear lake. He felt much more sober and serious now, far less like a man who was perilously close to falling in love with a woman for whom this was all a lark. They had never once discussed the future, never even come close to stating what they were to one another, and now Sydney was devastatingly aware that all the idiotic feelings he had let himself acquire were very possibly unreturned.

"You took a—have you run mad? Even in the middle of August, that pond is one step removed from ice."

"It was perfectly comfortable," Sydney lied. He had sought out the sudden chill, hoping it would shock his mind into behaving reasonably.

"Get on dry clothes and when you come back you can help make sure that the house is ready for company," Lex said, as if offering a reward.

"Company," Sydney repeated, not sure why he was even surprised that Lex took it upon himself to issue invitations to a house that wasn't even his.

"Carter obliged me by writing out the invitations. All you'll need to do tomorrow is wear serviceable clothing and greet your guests."

When Sydney was dry, he returned to the hall.

"The time has come," Lex said, "for me to divulge to you my scheme. My ulterior motive in coming to Pelham Hall."

"Oh no," Sydney groaned.

"Oh yes. I've been corresponding with an amateur—*decidedly* amateur—historian who lives near Heatherby. I wish to make her acquaintance and persuade her of the error of her ways. I'd be grateful if you'd oblige me by reading aloud her latest missive so I can devote my attention to disproving its every thesis."

As far as schemes went, this was not as bad as Sydney

had expected. "Who usually reads and writes your letters?" he asked.

"My secretary," Lex said. "But he stayed in London because, frankly, he's used to better accommodations. No offense meant."

"None taken," Sydney said dryly. Well, reading aloud a letter hardly seemed an onerous task. He cleared his throat and got to work.

An hour later he regretted it. He had a headache, a scowling duke, and a child who had stopped playing with the clock in favor of casting intrigued glances at Lex every time he swore. He also had acquired more dubious knowledge about English history than he had ever wanted. Sydney was no student of history, but he was fairly certain that both Lex and his correspondent had the most fanciful notions of what constituted a fact. He would need to ask Amelia the next time he saw her.

He also had the niggling sense that Lex's correspondent was mocking him. Lex had always been prone to wild eccentricity, and Sydney didn't like the way this Miss Russell seemed to be laughing at Lex. He felt certain that this woman wouldn't have been quite as bold had she known she was corresponding with a duke.

"Read it again," Lex demanded when Sydney finished reading the letter.

"Absolutely not." There was a good deal Sydney would do for his friend, but spending an entire afternoon reading and rereading that piece of moonshine wasn't on the list.

Sydney exchanged a glance with the duke's valet, who had appeared in the doorway, carrying a tray of sandwiches. He gestured for Carter to put the tray on the footstool beside Lex.

"Are we certain these are edible?" Lex asked, sniffing the plate. "Yesterday's sandwiches consisted of candlewax and tomatoes. The day before her biscuits contained laundry soap. The cook and I continue to have our little disagreements."

"Is your disagreement over what constitutes food?" Sydney asked.

"She wants a new range, but I can't purchase her one, because that would be giving in to her demands. But I also can't sack her, because Carter shamelessly lured her away from the Earl of Stafford and one can't steal a servant and then send her packing. I'm afraid we're at an impasse."

Sydney would remember to walk into the village and purchase something edible for supper. Meanwhile, with the spirit of a man throwing himself into the breach, he took a bite of the sandwich. "Tastes like food," he declared.

"They must have been made by one of the kitchen maids," Lex declared. "At least one is a double agent." He nibbled at the edges of the sandwich in distaste. "Anyway, how is your lady love? Or is it a gentleman?"

"She—what, no, Lex, stop it."

"I knew it!" Lex crowed.

"There's nothing to know." Sydney's face was hot. Of course it was.

"I knew it was time for you to settle down. Your mother and I will be so proud of you."

"You think you're hilarious," Sydney said, rolling his eyes. He started to smile, but then sternly reminded himself that he could not indulge this sort of fanciful imagining, not without speaking seriously to Amelia. His thoughts insisted on drifting to a hazy future with her. He caught himself wondering whether she would like the house he had engaged in Manchester, considering whether he ought to hire painters or wait for Amelia to choose colors and furnishings that might please her. He was being wildly presumptuous and he knew it. Sydney had gone about this—love affair, or whatever it was—with a recklessness that was entirely new to him. Falling in love with a near stranger and simply hoping for the best was the sort of thing Andrew would have done. It was, in fact, exactly what Andrew *had* done when he met Penny, and the fact that Sydney only now was realizing that he was in a comparable situation was proof that he was not thinking clearly.

He took a deep breath and rose to his feet. He would need to talk to Amelia, that was all. Tomorrow, on their walk, he'd explain the regrettable state of his heart and ask if she felt the same. That was—well, it was terrifying. But fear was better than uncertainty, and he felt immeasurably better now that he had a plan.

Amelia held the invitation as if it were about to explode.

"You truly don't need to go," Georgiana said for perhaps the fifth time.

"It's addressed to both of us," Amelia said. That had been

a shock, but it shouldn't have been. Everyone in the village knew that Miss Russell and Miss Allenby lived at Crossbrook Cottage. It was hardly unexpected for a newcomer to familiarize himself with his nearest neighbors; a duke would be conversant enough with the rules of etiquette to understand that an invitation must be extended to all ladies living under a roof.

"Yes, my dear, but you don't need to go. You may decline the invitation. I'm hardly of an age that I require a chaperone."

"I'm not worried about you needing a chaperone," Amelia said. "I'm worried about the fact that we don't know this man or what his intentions are. As far as he knows, you're an unmarried woman who has been carrying on a shockingly improper correspondence with him. And even if he doesn't intend to harm you, he might wish to harm your reputation. We both know that I'm good at heading those sorts of things off at the pass."

Georgiana gazed at her levelly. "How long was I your governess? You think that after so many years under the same roof as Portia Allenby I don't know a thing or two about putting overbearing aristocrats in their place?"

"I've had more practice," Amelia said, and it came out more bitterly than she had intended.

Georgiana took hold of her hands, and Amelia realized she had been worrying at an imaginary mark underneath one of her cuffs.

"You don't have to do this," Georgiana repeated. "I can't stop you, but I can tell you that I'm very worried."

"If I don't do this now," Amelia said, "then it means I'm a prisoner here. I need to try."

"You could start by having tea with the vicar, not calling on a duke," Georgiana argued.

It was useless trying to explain that in Amelia's mind the difference was miniscule. Yes, the thought of entering a duke's drawing room was enough to make her skin crawl, but so was calling at the vicarage. Either way, she'd have to rebuild the defenses that she was just beginning to live without. She thought of how honest, how open, she had felt with Sydney that very morning, and how closed up and false she would have to make herself in order to go through with her plan to visit Pelham Hall.

If she let herself pay attention to her body, she could feel where he had been inside her, where his hands had gripped her hips. She shouldn't think about that. That woman had been defenseless, which was not something Amelia could afford to be. Not ever.

"In any event," Amelia said, trying to sound light and easy, "I'll be glad to see the inside of Pelham Hall. I'll put it in my next book as a place where somebody awful meets a grisly end."

"Amelia—" Georgiana protested.

"Don't worry, silly. We both know I can handle an unpleasant afternoon. I made it through an unpleasant *five years.*"

The next day she skipped her walk, choosing instead to work herself up to the task of putting on her metaphorical armor. She looked out the window and saw, at the end of the lane, Sydney leaning against the gatepost. She nearly threw open the window and called to him, asked him inside, told him everything that had happened and everything she feared. Instead she drew the curtain and put on her primmest gray gown.

Sydney surveyed the great hall. It had been furnished in a haphazard, make-do sort of way, odds and ends from the attics interspersed with items ordered from farther afield. But there were neither leaks nor broken glass, and so it would have to do. Given that Lex was blind and Sydney did not care for the opinion of a deranged historian or whoever she was, it was fit enough for company.

The duke, however, was decidedly unfit for company. He refused to be shaved, and was currently installed in the center of the drawing room on a throne-like velvet monstrosity that somebody had brought down from the attics. Whether there were mice living in the upholstery seemed very much an open question. He had tripped and hurt his ankle, so he had both legs propped up on a footstool that was shaped like a gargoyle holding a tea tray. Instead of a normal coat, he wore a banyan of embroidered scarlet silk. He looked utterly louche, like the monarch of a particularly disreputable kingdom. While Sydney would have liked to blame this on the man's inability to see his own reflection, he knew perfectly well the Duke of Hereford had always been like this.

"At least take off the spectacles," Sydney suggested when he heard carriage wheels on the drive. Lex had somehow acquired a pair of tinted spectacles that he insisted on wearing to disguise the fact that his eyes were clouded with milky white cataracts and that his gaze wandered. "They look incredibly peculiar."

"Samuel Pepys had a pair like these when syphilis caused his eyes to fail," Lex announced.

Sydney pressed his lips together so he wouldn't laugh. "You say that as if it's an endorsement."

"Of course it is. I fully intend to ensure that Miss Russell tells all her correspondents that the pox has ravaged my mind and my body." He gestured at his leg.

"You don't have the pox. You tripped over a hedgehog."

"Hush. That's the door." Lex actually rubbed his palms together in anticipation, and Sydney briefly pitied this poor woman who didn't know what she had gotten herself into.

However, the two women who entered the hall were at first glance so commonplace as to be utterly incongruous in company as outlandish as Lex's. The woman who was announced as Miss Russell was demurely clad in a muslin gown; she was very pretty, in a wide-eyed sort of way, and it was hard to imagine that she had developed a passion for Richard III. The other woman, clearly Miss Russell's chaperone, was of an indeterminate age and spinsterish mien, dressed in a frock of gray silk and a bonnet that shielded her face, the entire ensemble so demure Sydney's own mother wouldn't have objected to it. As Sydney stood beside Lex, flicking dust off his lapel, Carter announced her as—

Sydney thought he might fall over. He gripped the back of Lex's chair. Carter announced the elder of the women as Miss Allenby, and it took his mind a moment to catch up with the

words. At first he thought there had to be some confusion—
perhaps there were two nearly identical women in the neighborhood. Amelia had mentioned having sisters, had she not?
But this was indeed his Amelia, standing in his hall, wearing
a silk gown and a proper bonnet and bowing her head to him
as if they had never met. As if they had not been together in
the woods the previous morning. As if none of that had ever
happened.

"How do you do?" she asked in a tone so cool and civil it
stung more than any repudiation could ever have.

He remained speechless, his mouth dry, his heart racing.
They would think him rude, and so be it, because he had
nothing to say. The women sat, but Sydney walked over to
the window, and then turned back again to look at Amelia,
as if his eyes might have been mistaken. Somehow she made
herself small, shrinking into the corner of the sofa while still
holding herself perfectly erect. From her reticule she removed an embroidery hoop and began stabbing at it with a
needle, which she evidently meant as a sign that she did not
expect to be included in the conversation.

She had seen him and recognized him; she must have,
when she bowed her head in his general direction. The idea
that he held her in his arms the day before and now she was
pretending they had never met was totally incomprehensible
to him. When he tried to catch her eye, she did not so much
as flick a glance towards him.

Was this what it was like to have one's heart broken? It
didn't matter; Sydney would contend with his heart later,
or better yet, never. Instead he paid attention to the two

women, trying hard not to acknowledge the pounding of his heart or the sense that he was about to be sick. As Miss Russell talked with Lex about Richard the bloody Third, Amelia occasionally leaned over to contribute some murmured remark he could barely hear. As he watched, his eyes narrowed. Amelia was steering the conversation towards more general historical knowledge and away from the particulars of Lex's obsession. And that would only make sense if Miss Russell were not an expert in that area. Amelia, however, wrote books set in this exact period. With mounting dread, he recalled the letters Miss Russell had written Lex, and the letters Amelia had written him. Both displayed an excessive quantity of loops and adornment that surely he ought to have recognized as the sign of weak character and flighty disposition. There were blots and scratches and other indications of carelessness. He had been a fool not to have seen the similarity straightaway.

He recalled the arch, facetious tone of those letters she wrote Lex. He was gravely disappointed that Amelia would devote a months' long correspondence to mocking a stranger, and use her friend's name to do it. That was both careless and cruel. He hadn't thought Amelia either careless or cruel, but he also couldn't have anticipated a future in which she pretended he didn't exist.

He had badly misjudged both her character and the nature of their friendship, if it could even be called that. Whatever he had thought they had been to one another, the truth was that he was so inconsequential to her as to not even merit a greeting.

As soon as the women left, he would tell Lex everything. Lex wouldn't want to be made a fool of. He probably wouldn't even want to stay in the neighborhood. That thought calmed him down a bit. All he had to do was endure the rest of this visit, take Leontine to Manchester, and get on with his life. He sat heavily on a bench where he could see Amelia Allenby.

Tea arrived. Amelia put down her yarn and poured out tea for everyone, which was normal enough, and Sydney tried not to read deceit and treachery into her every movement. Each of the ladies took a biscuit. These were likely the same dish of biscuits that had appeared for tea the past several days in a row. As with most of the cook's creations, they were meant for warfare, not human consumption.

He watched Amelia bring one of the biscuits to her mouth, utterly unaware that it was of a consistency somewhere between hard tack and slate shingles, with the sense of witnessing an acrobat perform an especially ill-advised feat. She placed the biscuit between a set of perfectly straight little white teeth. Then, without batting an eyelash, she delicately removed the biscuit from between her lips and replaced it on her plate. She performed this without a flicker of discomfiture. Indeed, she did it as if that was what she had meant to do all along. Then, with equal finesse, she removed the biscuit from the other woman's plate and put it on her own. She did this all with utter serenity, as if rescuing her friend from inedible biscuits was a normal and expected part of any morning visit.

This, he realized, was her world: drawing rooms and manners and conversations sprinkled with "Your Grace."

The rest of it—sunshine and laughter and smiles that felt like gut punches—were meaningless diversions. She belonged here. Sydney didn't, nor did he want to. He had never known the real Amelia, and as he watched her he decided that he didn't want to.

Chapter Ten

Only years of hard training in the art of self-mastery allowed Amelia to retain control over herself when she walked into Pelham Hall and saw Sydney standing behind the duke's chair.

She was aware, several layers beneath the veil of icy composure she had summoned for this visit, that she wanted to go to him. She could smile as readily as she had when she saw him waiting for her at the gatepost. She could say his name, and explain truthfully that she hadn't expected to see him here. She could trust that he'd have some reasonable explanation for his own presence.

But at that moment, she could not set aside her chilly manners, because they were all that stood between her and near panic. If she dropped her armor for even an instant, she might make out traces of some other Amelia, a woman who had felt safe and bold in Sydney's arms, a woman who wondered why he was standing over there and refusing to come to her. If he came to her, she could be that Amelia for him. But he didn't. He only glowered. She shaped herself into a nondescript spinster of unimpeachable manners. The woman who might feel things about Sydney didn't matter; she wasn't even present. Sydney, for that matter, wasn't present. He was Mr. Goddard now. The woman who had been with Sydney was not present in this dim gray gown. And the man who had laughed and cupped her cheek was not the same man who glared at her from across the room. She had already known the intensity of his gaze, had known that when he looked at her, he was giving her his full attention and consideration. Now she knew how it felt when he looked at her without fondness, without humor, without anything but enmity.

Amelia brought her teacup to her lips and took a sip, not even tasting it. She absently touched a sore spot on her wrist where it had scraped against the stone wall yesterday. She decided that it didn't hurt. Later on she would need to pull that scab off with her fingernails, and that would hurt, and it would be such a relief, but for now she was as insensate as a dressmaker's dummy.

She stabbed her needle again and again into the fabric. She had meant to embroider a blanket for one of her nieces— Gilbert and Louisa were producing children faster than Amelia could produce blankets. A happy thought, and one that took her far away from Pelham Hall and angry glares: she tried to hold onto it. But her stitches were crooked and her thread kept knotting and she was just going to have to pull the whole thing apart and start over when she got home.

She buried all that—everything she felt in body and soul, everything that didn't have to do with what Georgiana was saying to the duke.

"On the contrary, Your Grace," Georgiana was saying. She had a gleam in her eye that made Amelia realize that her friend was actually enjoying this. "Despite our many differences, we see quite eye to eye on Richard III's innocence."

"Even a stopped clock is right twice a day," the duke said lightly. "I expect this is where you insist that the princes were killed by their sister as part of her bid for the throne."

"Oh, I'm quite bored with that theory and have an exciting new one that I expect you can't wait to hear about."

"I have the direst sense of foreboding that I'm about to be fed the most magnificent pack of lies," the duke said, crossing one leg over the other, an expectant look on his face. Amelia realized that he was enjoying this as well.

"I would never dare to bore you with a lie that was less than magnificent," Georgiana said sweetly. The duke transformed a stunned laugh into a coughing fit. Georgiana leaned in close. "It was their mother," she whispered theatrically.

"Well," the duke said, "Elizabeth of Woodville has been suspected of a good many things, but if you're going to accuse her of filicide I do feel that you ought to come up with at least some token of evidence."

"One might argue," Amelia murmured, "that the lady retreated to Bermondsey Abbey in repentance of some sin." This was utter silliness but it was the best she come up with. "Is the hearth in this room original to the house? And is that linenfold paneling I saw by the door?" She could navigate this sort of conversation in her sleep, and she could certainly do it while being glared at from across the room. She had, in fact, done it while being glared at from across the room.

She couldn't have anticipated receiving such a look from Sydney, and she didn't know why she was getting one now, but that was something she could settle in the future. Right now she could be polite, she could be invisible, and she could be silently furious. If Sydney had mentioned that he was at Pelham Hall to visit the duke this could have been avoided. Several times Amelia had mentioned Pelham Hall and Sydney had neglected to state that he had a connection with the place. That was suspicious and false. He had said he was a land surveyor. Had that been a lie? How much of what he had told her had been false?

After half an hour of being a milk-bland spinster while being stared at as if she were a felon, Amelia was starting to reach the end of her tether. She rose to her feet.

"My dear," she murmured to Georgiana in the same low baritone her mother always used when she wanted her voice to carry but seem like it was only intended for the person she stood nearest. "I'm afraid we must be going. We have many other calls to make."

Georgiana dutifully stood and they both said all the prescribed phrases that ladies had drilled into their skulls before they were allowed out of the schoolroom. But before they reached the hallway, the duke rapped his cane. "You'll come back." He did not make it into a question or even an invitation. This was a command. "And next time you'll bring your research so I can tell you exactly where you went astray and you can choose yet another queen to slander."

"Yes, Your Grace," Georgiana said, sinking into a curtsey, bless her. They hadn't planned it, but the man was in a throne and dressed like some kind of sultan. He hadn't even bothered to rise to his feet when she and Georgiana had entered the room. Clearly a curtsey would not go amiss.

They proceeded silently to the drive. Amelia said nothing until they were safely in the carriage, the door shut behind them.

"The duke's friend is the land surveyor," Amelia said despairingly.

"Oh!" Georgiana said. And then, with dawning comprehension, "Oh, dear. Not a particularly friendly meeting, was it? Why on earth did you not go to him?"

"Why did he not come to me?" Amelia retorted, trying hard not to think about how it would have felt to have had him by her side in that hellish room.

Georgiana pressed her lips together. "He did not strike me a man who is comfortable in company. Common accent, rough clothes, and those whiskers. I can't imagine how he came to be on intimate terms with a duke."

"How comfortable do you have to be to cross a room and say good-day?"

"You tell me," Georgiana said, eyebrow arched meaningfully.

Absently, one hand found the scab on the opposite wrist, and tore it off. She was aware of the brightness of the pain, the warmth of the blood. She shoved a handkerchief into her glove before her gown could be ruined. She wanted to go home and examine her arms for other things that could be torn off, other places that needed to be scratched. Good God, she was actually losing her mind, now. Here, in Derbyshire, over a hundred miles from London, she was finally becoming unhinged.

"Amelia?" Georgiana asked when the carriage stopped in front of the cottage. "Go upstairs and lie down. Janet will bring you tea."

Amelia went to her bedroom but it didn't do any good. She tried to shut her eyes with the idea that sleep would at least be a respite from her mind throwing a tantrum; instead, without distraction, her thoughts scattered with disjointed images of her visit with the duke, her life in London, Sydney's anger. She tried to imagine anything good—letters from home, Nan's fur, strawberries—but none of it would stick.

She could leave, as Keating had said. She could leave, and Georgiana could either come with her or return to London. That would solve the immediate problem of never seeing Sydney or his horrible friend ever again. But it wouldn't solve the problem of Amelia not wanting to be alone for the rest of her life. Letters and visits weren't enough. She wanted to be around people she loved, and who she loved in return. She wanted that to happen more than once every few months. Being around Sydney had reminded her of how much she needed that, and she felt even more unwilling than ever to spend the rest of her life shipwrecked on an island by her own absurd mind.

As Sydney watched the carriage disappear down the drive, his confusion at Amelia's behavior solidified into a hard ball of anger lodged in the vicinity of his heart.

"Write Miss Russell and Miss Allenby a letter thanking them for coming today and requesting the pleasure of their company for dinner next Thursday," Lex said as soon as they were alone—well, alone apart from Leontine, who sat before the empty hearth, dismantling a music box she must have found in the attics.

"But—"

"Yes, I know it's your house, that's why I'm asking you to write the invitations, please and thank you. Find me a respectable clergyman to invite, preferably one with a wife. That makes six. You'll need to do something about the dining room. Do you suppose the cook will be satisfied if we get her a few new pans? I wonder if she'll make jugged hare."

"But—"

"Dismissed! Send in Carter. I require a haircut."

"Stop talking about haircuts and listen to me! I cannot invite those women. Amelia Allenby is the woman I've been—" He hesitated, and felt his face flush to the tips of his ears. "Walking with."

"Ha! I knew there was someone. Nobody likes rustic rambles that much. I don't see why you can't invite her, however. In fact, even more reason why you ought to do so."

"Because she pretended not to recognize me."

"I didn't hear you correcting her impression."

"Well, no—"

"So you pretended not to recognize one another. It was a mutual deception."

Sydney bristled. "I pretended nothing of the sort!

After I noticed that she didn't want to acknowledge our acquaintance—"

"So dreadfully euphemistic," Lex murmured.

"—I decided not to embarrass her by announcing the truth."

"In other words you pretended not to recognize one another," Lex repeated patiently.

"You're being deliberately obtuse."

"Probably." Lex smoothed his lapels. "So. Dinner next Thursday."

Sydney squeezed his eyes shut. "Fine," he conceded, knowing Lex would get his way whether he liked it or not. "Buy the cook a new range, and I'll invite them," he grit out.

"She will have the finest range in the North," Lex agreed.

Sydney sat at the desk and wrote the invitations. The letter to the vicar was easy enough, but when writing Amelia's he gripped the pen so tightly that the paper tore and he had to start again. When he had written her the last time—reckless, foolhardy letters, he now thought them—he couldn't have imagined it would lead to this. Perhaps he should have, though. People born to wealth and status were accustomed to getting what they wanted, and everybody else got used to deferring. That sort of easy command made people careless, entitled, wont to play ducks and drakes with other people's lives. Lex was just as bad. Even Lady Penelope, with the very best intentions, had taken Andrew's entire life and blown it off course.

Amelia had written those silly letters to a stranger. She

had treated him as if he were invisible despite surely knowing at least some part of how he felt. Perhaps those two things were only connected by the thinnest of threads, or perhaps they weren't connected at all. He knew his mind wasn't reasoning particularly well, and that only made him more annoyed.

Delusional fool that he was, he had been daydreaming of marrying her and taking her with him to Manchester. For a moment he let himself mourn that half-imagined future, let himself grieve the loss of a person who hadn't existed in the first place. He ruthlessly squashed any lingering affection he might have felt.

He tucked the invitations into his pocket. He would hand deliver the letter for the vicar and leave the women's to be called for at the inn, because under no circumstances was he visiting Crossbrook Cottage today or ever. He walked the entire distance down the hill towards the village in undiminished irritation, when a figure barreled out of a lane and directly into his chest. She was going fast enough that she nearly propelled both of them into the hedge.

"Steady now," Sydney said, meaning that very literally, as he tried to arrange the woman into a more reliably vertical position. She had red hair, no bonnet, and—damn it—it was Amelia. Of course it was Amelia; every time he stepped foot outside he saw her and nobody else. They were cursed to be forever seeing one another.

"Amelia," he said flatly.

"Why didn't you tell me you were staying at Pelham Hall?" she asked. Her fists were clenched at her sides.

"Why didn't *I* tell *you*?" he repeated, stunned. "Why didn't you tell me you had been corresponding with my friend? Imagine my surprise when I learned that the woman I had . . ." He swallowed. "A woman I had considered a friend was in fact embroiled in a scheme to mock and disparage my friend."

"I beg your pardon. Yes, I wrote those letters, but I didn't know I was writing to your friend, perhaps because he and I both used false names and you did not tell me you had any connection with Pelham Hall. I realize this has all the makings of a French farce, but those letters contain no disparagement, no mockery." She took a full step back and glared at him. "Is that what you think? I thought you knew me better. What a fool I was to think that you were any different from the rest of them." And then, drawing herself up, "What are you doing here? Did you follow me home to dress me down in person?"

He nearly replied that he was on the way to the village with invitations; he even went so far as to reach for the invitation, but arrested the movement, instead brushing some dust off his sleeve. Her tone was so high and mighty; she was every last inch the aristocrat. He must have been out of his mind to think he could have so much as a friendship with her; he must have been out of his mind to even want to. "I thought you were kind. I knew you were flighty and unserious but I thought at least you were kind. I see that I was very much mistaken."

"Flighty and unserious," she repeated, the color rising on her cheeks. "I thought I had received every possible insult.

I really did. Flighty and unserious!" She gave a bitter little laugh.

He took a steadying breath. "You are the way you are and I daresay you can't change it. What I'm trying to say is that I realize now that whatever passed between us is a matter of little consequence to you. And however disappointed I am—"

And then—it happened so fast he hardly had time to realize what had transpired, just saw the tears in her eyes and felt the sting in his cheek. She had slapped him. He brought his hand to his face, stunned.

"Leave, why don't you?" she snapped. "Why are you still here? You've said what you meant to say. Surely that's enough." Her voice held a note of rising panic that reminded him of that first time they had spoken, in almost this precise spot.

Now, his cheek smarting and his heart racing, he felt so far from that moment, so far from the man he had been, so far from the hopes he had later harbored. So far, too, from the man he wanted to be. He didn't know exactly where he had gone wrong; she, after all, was the one who had revealed herself to be not at all the person he had thought her to be, but if she was looking at him like that, hurt and outraged, her cheeks flushed with anger, he knew he wasn't blameless. Some part of him wanted to go to her and make things right, but it was too late for that. He turned and walked away, feeling all the while that he had been given a chance to hold an object of immense value, and had chosen instead to cast it on the floor.

bother? Georgiana could see the evidence for herself, in the tears on Amelia's face and the color in her cheeks. "No. I'm far from fine. I can't imagine ever being fine again. I'm afraid I'm going to spend the rest of my life alone in this cottage or in an institution for women with delicate nerves."

"Oh, Amelia. I'm so sorry. First of all, you won't be alone so long as I can draw breath, you absolute idiot. Second—no, be quiet, why in heaven's name would you think working as a governess a preferable state to sharing a home with my dearest friend—*second*, nobody will put you in an institution, and I'll murder them for trying. Third, tell me what transpired between you and Mr. Goddard? You were so fond of him."

Amelia told her friend everything, from chance meetings and dog bites to that day in the ruins. Georgiana only offered fresh handkerchiefs and sugary tea.

"He said I was flighty and unserious and that he believed that what happened between us was of no consequence to me." Amelia's eyes pricked again with tears. "As if I've ever had the luxury of letting anything be inconsequential. As if I don't weigh the consequences of every step I take and every word I say, even when I don't want to. My God, if I could only stop doing that, then maybe I could leave." She blew her nose. "And then he had the nerve to say I was unkind. He accused us of writing those letters with the design of mocking the duke."

"What?" Georgiana squawked. "That's outrageous. We intended no such thing. He had written a badly researched diatribe and we had a bit of fun poking holes in his argument. He then seemed to amuse himself thoroughly in

CHAPTER ELEVEN

Amelia's cheeks were hot with outrage, and that was the final straw. She had spent years perfecting her ability to wipe her face clear of any emotion and Sydney had stripped her of that. She was furious with him, she was furious with the entire world, but most of all she was furious with herself. She didn't know how she had reached a point in her life where she assaulted a duke's friend in broad daylight. Even her ultimate disgrace in London hadn't quite risen to the level of public battery. Every last bit of armor she had constructed over the years was now ragged and useless, and she felt vulnerable and exposed.

"I slapped Mr. Goddard in the lane," she said when she returned indoors. Attempting a walk had clearly been a misguided notion. "No, don't ask, just use your imagination and you'll get exactly where you need to be."

"Are you all right?" Georgiana's eyes were wide.

She opened her mouth to reassure her friend that she would be fine, that she was the same as ever. But why even poking the holes in *our* badly researched arguments. His letters attacked our position as strenuously as we attacked his. Perhaps Mr. Goddard does not understand that people can amuse themselves by hurling polite insults at one another and accusing one another of sloppy research and utter illogic."

Amelia felt heartened. "I don't think Mr. Goddard understands that people can amuse themselves, full stop. I have no doubt that the duke amused himself greatly in our correspondence. That's why he invited us—you, rather—to see him. If he thought we were insulting him, he wouldn't have wished to see us."

"And he seemed quite pleased to meet us. I'm afraid that this is a case of Mr. Goddard misunderstanding what amuses his friend."

"That's his problem," Amelia retorted. "If his first inclination is to blame me rather than open his mouth and ask his friend, then he's a terrible friend to both me and the duke."

"Quite," Georgiana agreed. "You'll be well rid of him."

Amelia knew her friend was correct, that it was better to see Sydney's true character sooner rather than later, but she was stunned to have been so wrong. She had thought she could let down her guard with him, even just a little. She had liked him so much—more than merely liked, if she were honest with herself. But she had also thought he knew her and liked her too—such a small and paltry thing, to believe oneself *liked*, but it hadn't felt paltry coming from Sydney. She had felt valued, cherished even, which made his scorn and mistrust that much more painful.

It turned out that if you breathed slowly through your nose and out through your mouth, you could resist the urge to throw a potted fern at the nearest duke.

Temporarily.

"I say, Syd," Lex said in tones of sincere fascination. "You can't just go around getting yourself slapped by young ladies."

"I don't want to talk about it," Sydney growled. He had been an idiot to mention it in the first place.

"I, however, very much want to talk about it. Enlighten me. Did you give her a slip on the shoulder? Make her an indecent proposal?" Lex asked, riveted. "I didn't think mousy spinsters were in your line."

"She isn't a mousy spinster," Sydney protested. "She has red hair and she can't be five-and-twenty. Nothing mousy or spinsterish about her." Now Lex was smiling much too broadly. "She covered her hair when she visited you," Sydney clarified. "It was all part of her deception."

"Bonnets do cover the hair," Lex said slowly. "That's what they do. That's how hats work. Besides, you can't go around getting assaulted by every redheaded girl you meet, for heaven's sake. Don't know how they do things in Manchester but it's just not done in decent society."

"I'm so glad to amuse you," Sydney said through clenched teeth.

"Quite excessive of you," Lex went on, ignoring him. He was enjoying this far too much. "One may be assaulted by at most a third of the redheaded girls one meets. Anything more speaks of a character flaw."

"I did not set out to get myself assaulted by anyone of any gender or hair color."

"Is she pretty?" Lex asked.

"That is not the point," Sydney answered.

Lex hummed with interest. "It's going to be terribly awkward at dinner. Frankly, I can't wait."

Sydney looked heavenward. "You can't really mean for me to host that dinner now?"

"Please tell me where else in the nation I'm likely to find a wife who is not only conversant in the finer points of English history, but finds arguing about it amusing enough to write me meticulously researched twice-monthly letters?"

"They were making sport of you! And what on earth are you talking about? Wife?"

Lex waved a dismissive hand. "We were making sport of one another. I daresay my letters to them were even more objectionable than those they wrote me. My secretary did warn me I was only spurring her on, but that was the point of the game."

"You call it a game," Sydney protested. "This is rich people nonsense. Normal people don't act like that." He fiercely suppressed the possibility that Lex was correct, that Amelia had meant no harm—because if she hadn't then he had gravely insulted her for no reason.

"Andrew did," Lex pointed out.

Sydney bristled at the comparison. "He was an outlier."

"You're being exceptionally stupid about this. Do you want to know what I think?"

"Not especially, thank you."

"I think you fell in love with this girl. And for whatever reason, she ignored you or thought you were ignoring her, and now you have it in your head that she's some kind of harpy or jezebel."

"She's neither of those things!"

"Precisely," said Lex, unreasonably smug. "You behaved like an ass, she slapped you, and any reasonable man would have already arrived at her house with flowers and an abject apology. The only reason you haven't, is that you're pretty sure she'd throw both the flowers and the apology back in your face." His tone gentled, and that more than anything braced Sydney for what was to come. "Things do end, Syd, but that isn't any reason not to start them in the first place."

"You're talking nonsense," Sydney said.

"You really are a curmudgeon." Lex's voice returned to its usual acerbity, thank God. "Have you not smiled once since your brother died? I did worry about you. Ought to have made you visit me sooner. Poor Syd. I bet your eyebrows are doing that thing they do."

"They're doing nothing at all," he snapped. Was Lex intent on discussing all Sydney's least favorite topics? He didn't want to think of the past two years since Andrew's death. He had worked, and that was satisfying in its way. He hadn't been particularly happy, but he had chalked that up to missing his brother. And he had missed Andrew, of course he had, but he saw now that he had been missing something else—joy, maybe. Something sweet and sharp that he felt when he saw Leontine tinkering with a clock, or when Lex ribbed him, or when—every minute he spent with Amelia, but he wouldn't let himself think about that. Whatever it was, he didn't need it, didn't want it. It was something for other people. He cleared his throat and turned his attention to what Lex had been saying a minute earlier. "Why are you looking for a wife?" He knew that Lex was never attracted to women, but also that marriages had been formed without a basis of attraction. Perhaps now that Lex's brothers had all died, he thought he needed an heir.

"Previously, I had always supposed that any woman I'd be fond enough of to endow with all my worldly goods and also endure at the breakfast table wouldn't deserve a husband indifferent to her charms. But I've found a woman of good family and learning who enjoys arguing with me and may even be willing to exchange marital happiness for an obscene settlement. I intend to woo Miss Russell."

"Of course," Sydney said, burying his face in his hands. "Of course you don't want to marry someone you like, and who likes you. How stupid of me to think otherwise. But there's a flaw in your plan." There were a dozen flaws, but Sydney would content himself with the one. "Georgiana didn't write those letters. Amelia did. I've, ah, had occasion to see the lady's writing."

"You're a master of euphemism, Sydney. I assume you mean you were exchanging billets-doux with the young lady. How roguish of you. Shocking. Besides, I daresay they did it together," Lex said, unconcerned. "It's precisely the sort of mischief young ladies would get up to. Sometimes I forget you don't have sisters. I daresay, if participating in a jest about Plantagenet history is the sort of thing Miss Russell does for amusement, then we'll get along splendidly. As for Miss Allenby, a woman of her predilections can be forgiven for enjoying a bit of a lark with regard to her area of expertise, such as it is."

"Miss Allenby's predilections?" he repeated.

"She is Amelia Allenby." At Sydney's uncomprehending stare, he continued. "The authoress of several exceptionally silly historical novels. Imagine Sir Walter Scott, but if every woman in English history dabbled in witchcraft or murder. You really didn't know?"

"I knew she wrote but I haven't read—I don't read novels," he finished stiffly.

"Lucky you, I've sent Carter out to get me her books. You can begin reading them to me tonight. It's a pity I can't marry Amelia Allenby herself. But, alas, the lady's affections would appear to be engaged elsewhere," he said pointedly. "Besides, I'm not here to litigate my marital intentions. I want to contract a marriage on as fair a basis as a man in my circumstances can. I want children."

"You realize not all marriages result in children, don't you?" Sydney managed when he had recovered his senses.

"Are you saying my lady wife will not effortlessly pluck a baby from the cabbage patch?" He flung a biscuit in the general direction of Sydney's head. "Give me some credit, Sydney. I want to give myself a fighting chance to have a family. Surely you can understand that."

Lex could not have come up with a word more suited to play upon Sydney's sympathies. Family was precisely what had been lost in the fire—Andrew and Penny, their expected child. Both Lex and Sydney had lost their families that day. Maybe this was a way to make it right. Maybe he would remember this summer as the time he had met Leontine and helped Lex find happiness, rather than the time he had finally understood that he was not to have that sort of happiness for himself.

Chapter Twelve

By the next day, Amelia had progressed from confusion and sorrow to incandescent rage. When she heard a knock on the cottage door she was prepared to answer it for the mere satisfaction of slamming it shut again. When she flung open the door, her cheeks were already hot with anger, and only got hotter when she saw Mr. Goddard standing before her. He was composed of fifty percent shoulders and fifty percent stern disapproval and she didn't want any of it.

"No," Amelia said, already moving to shut the door. "There's nothing left for you to say. Take yourself off. Certainly not."

"I came to apologize for misjudging your motives in writing to my friend," Mr. Goddard said. "I can do that by shouting at you through a closed door or at a normal volume like a civilized person. The choice is yours."

"I don't want your apology, whether it be shouted, whispered, or delivered in semaphore. You can take your apology and"—no, she was not going to be vulgar, this man did not deserve the satisfaction—"put it in your pipe and smoke it."

"I see," Mr. Goddard said through clenched teeth, then let out a breath.

"No you don't. What I'm saying is that your apology does me no good. It doesn't undo what you said. If you think yesterday was the first time anyone has thought the worst of me, you're as innocent as a baby. You're probably only here to make yourself feel better, and I don't care in the least how you feel. I can't think of anything I care about less." As she delivered this speech, she watched a flush rise in Mr. Goddard's cheeks. He passed his hand over his beard in a gesture of frustration so familiar she was outraged: how dare he resemble that man she had cared about. This unfeeling, unthinking, insensitive brute was a stranger.

"I have an invitation from the duke," he said, very much in the tone of a man striving for patience. "It's for dinner Thursday night." From his coat pocket, he produced a folded rectangle of ivory paper and held it out to her.

"I don't want that either," she said, shaking her head in wonder that *this* was the man she had thought she might be falling in love with. "Give the duke our regrets, if you please."

He opened his mouth to speak and snapped it shut again, as if thinking better of what he planned to say. As she watched, his chest rose and fell for the count of four breaths. It was a pity that she knew how his shoulders and chest felt against her palms, how up close he was somehow even broader and larger than he seemed halfway across a room. He passed one of his absurdly large hands across the scruff of his beard.

"Did you tell the duke that you suspected us of making sport of him?" she asked. She still had a hand on the door, ready to shut it in his face.

"Of course I did," he said, plainly affronted. "I'm not in the habit of keeping secrets from friends."

Well, that certainly put her in her place. She supposed she had never been his friend, then. Some of her thoughts must have shown on her face, because he winced. "I didn't deliberately—"

"I'm not interested," she said crisply. "I am surprised that you invite us despite your poor estimate of our characters."

"The duke invited you because he enjoys discussing history. He doesn't get much of an opportunity for it. I advised him not to invite you, considering what passed between us, but he disagreed, and I'm doing him the favor of delivering his invitations."

"You keep making it worse. It's really incredible." She half wanted him to keep going; maybe after a few more idiotic sentences she'd forget why she ever liked him in the first place.

He took a deep breath, as if gathering up his courage to make a distasteful admission. "He is effectively stranded in my house. He's blind and he recently injured his leg. Conversing with your friend is one of the few things that has brought him interest in a long while. Perhaps you could put aside your objections to me, however justifiable, and do a kindness to your neighbor."

For the first time since he knocked on her door, Amelia really paid attention to what Mr. Goddard was saying. He clearly swallowed a great deal of pride in apologizing. But that didn't move her—she had spent her entire life being aware that people had to swallow their pride to acknowledge her, and she didn't want any part of it. What she noticed was that he was doing it for a friend. And someone who made sacrifices for a friend was not entirely bad. He had to be at least one percent not-horrible, and she didn't like having to admit it. She much preferred to think that he was a villain, and that she had been naïve and stupid to think otherwise.

She coolly extended her hand for the invitation. Whatever her feelings for Mr. Goddard, she would not let anyone say she would ignore a neighbor in need. "Dare I hope you'll have the courtesy to refuse to attend this dinner?"

He grimaced. "I'm afraid I have no choice but to attend, because it's my house."

"Your house," she repeated. "Pelham Hall belongs to you? I spoke of Pelham Hall many times to you and you never alluded to the fact that you own it. And if you own Pelham Hall, you must own this cottage. You knew I live here." She thought back to the letters they had exchanged. "I believe you deliberately rendered your signature illegible. If I had known you were named Goddard I might have connected you with the Mr. Goddard who owns Pelham Hall." He looked momentarily guilty and she knew she had been right. "I trusted you," she said. She had trusted him with her feelings and with her body, and based on his blush she knew he understood her meaning. "Not only have you proven my trust unfounded, but you have met my trust with nothing but distrust." She felt her chest tighten but recovered her composure. "It's time for you to leave my house," she said coolly.

He solemnly nodded at her and left without saying another word, as if glad to remove himself from her presence.
She shut the door before she could watch him retreat down
the lane. Her heart racing, she ran her hands up and down
her forearms and tried not to remember the expression of
stricken shame that crossed Mr. Goddard's face when she
had accused him of dishonesty. At that moment she had
watched him realize that he had done wrong, and the look
on his face had been that of a man who had known himself to
have made the gravest error, a man who had, through his own
folly, lost something he had once held dear.

"What the devil is that smell?" asked Lex as Carter but-
toned him into his evening coat. "Don't tell me the hedgehogs
got back in."

"It's a dog," Sydney explained. Leontine had escaped the
nursemaid's clutches several times over the past few days,
causing great consternation in the household. Sydney had
determined that something had to be done. Remembering
how Nan followed Amelia about the countryside, keeping
her safe and alerting her to danger, he thought a dog would
be just the thing. He had gone to the nearest farm and acquired a pup from a rat terrier's litter, an animal apparently
unsuited to farm life but otherwise healthy. He soon found
out why exactly the dog was useless to the farmer: this was
a dog without ambition. He had not thought it possible
for an animal to sleep twenty-three hours a day, only rousing
herself to trot alongside him with her tongue lolling and

one ear flopping in a way that did nothing to increase Sydney's estimation of her intelligence. He could not seem to impress upon the creature that her sole function in life was to protect Leontine. Something had to be wrong with it. Well, at least she would be easy to transport back to Manchester.

"Has the dog taken a moral stance against bathing?" Lex asked. "Because otherwise it needs to be put under the pump. Carter," he said, as the valet arranged his cravat, "will you wash the dog?"

The servant cleared his throat, which Lex evidently took as a signal to begin negotiations. "Three bob?"

"Make it four, Your Grace, and we have a deal."

"Excellent. What's its name?" Lex asked Sydney.

"She doesn't have a name. And even if she did, she sleeps too much to answer to anything."

"Francine," Lex declared, promptly. "Had an aunt Francine who smelled just like that and slept all day too."

Carter wrapped Francine in a blanket and took her off for her ablutions.

"You see what's happened since I purchased that range for the cook? All the staff believe they can negotiate with me." Lex sounded cheerful, however.

"You're in a fine mood," Sydney observed.

"I really am. I forgot that I knew how to do that."

"Do what?"

"Be happy. I'm not sure if it's hearing Leontine's English come along, or if it's being back here, or if it's a chance to scold people for being wrong about Richard III."

"You told me you enjoyed that woman's company," Sydney protested. He had compunctions about inviting people to dinner if Lex planned to torture them.

"I just told you that I did."

"No, you told me that you enjoyed scolding other people for being wrong."

"Precisely. Good God, Sydney, it's as if you don't know me at all."

"Are you going to be rude to them?" Sydney asked. He struggled for a way to explain that Amelia Allenby found social intercourse difficult in some way he did not quite understand. He cleared his throat and adopted a stern tone. "I'd hate to think I'm complicit at a bear baiting."

Lex visibly bristled. "My, how you've changed your tune. A few days ago you wanted me to bar the door to these women. I don't need you to tell me how to act. I may be abrupt and difficult, but I don't make sport of people."

"I know that," Sydney said, chastened.

"And since we're giving one another advice, I'll suggest that you not hold a bit of carefree levity against Miss Allenby. Evidently you've spent the past two years deliberately forgetting that we aren't all saints. Andrew was no saint, neither am I, and neither are you. So get off your high horse, Sydney. We're all fallen, and all we have is one another. So kindly bugger off. Carter!"

Sydney's cheeks heated with shame, because he knew his friend was right. He had misjudged Amelia. Feeling the full weight of his wrongdoing, Sydney went to the dining room to make sure everything was in order for dinner.

Amelia was stepping into her dinner dress when Georgiana burst into her bedroom wearing a dressing gown and wielding a pair of sewing shears.

"I knew it!" she cried. "I knew you'd mean to wear that gray watered silk."

"It suits me!" Amelia protested, holding the dress behind her back, away from the scissors.

"Ha!" Georgiana exclaimed. "It's so boring I could weep."

Amelia cast a concerned glance at the scissors her friend continued to brandish. "Did you mean to cut me out of it? Or to threaten me with violence?"

"What? No, I need to trim your ribbons to the proper length. Where's that emerald green dinner gown your mother sent last month?" But even as she spoke, she dug through Amelia's clothes press.

Amelia sighed. She had not wanted to accept the duke's dinner invitation. She could compile a list as long as her arm of things she would rather do: weed the garden, finish the mending, walk directly into the woods and never return. But what Sydney had said about the duke being stranded, bored, and alone had needled her. She, too, was stranded, bored, and alone, and she didn't wish that on anyone. To soothe herself, she had begun reading advertisements for houses to let in even more isolated places.

Georgiana thrust the emerald silk gown at Amelia. "You cannot expect me to wear this," Amelia said, regarding her friend.

"Of course you won't wear it," Georgiana scoffed. "I only

wanted you to look at yourself. Here. Hold it up in front of you, and look at yourself." She spun Amelia to face the mirror.

Amelia instinctively opened her mouth to protest. Even in London, she had preferred her various white muslin frocks, a sedate nut-brown pelisse, and an evening gown of dove gray. All were perfectly ordinary, unobjectionable, a sort of social camouflage. Amelia had been delighted to discover that she could, with the proper attire, blend in with the other young ladies. Her nondescript frocks made her feel unremarkable, as if all her efforts not to stick out like a sore thumb had finally been successful.

However, during her years in London, her mother and sisters insisted that with every safe, boring dress she ordered, she also purchase something special. Something that will make you look as special on the outside as you are on the inside, was what her mother always said. Amelia found that a nightmarish prospect, and therefore had never worn any of these special dresses out of the house.

Amelia did as she was asked and regarded her reflection. Her first impulse was to hastily look away. Red hair and a green dress were . . . striking. Amelia did not enjoy being striking. There would be no fading into the background in this gown.

"Do you see?" Georgiana asked. "You look impressive. You're very good at making yourself invisible when you want to, which is all well and good. But this is who you are when I look at you. You look beautiful, but that isn't the point. You also look powerful. The woman in this looking glass could be terrifying if she wanted to. Nobody else would stand a chance."

Poor Georgiana, she really was deluded if she thought Amelia was powerful. Amelia could hardly walk out of her house without hysterics. A week ago she had been strong enough to go to Pelham Hall and think she could emerge unscathed; not only that, but she thought she'd be so undamaged by the experience that she might be able to return to living a normal life. Now she didn't even have that hope. The best she could hope for was a return to numbness.

She folded the gown and returned it to the clothes press.

Chapter Thirteen

Pelham Hall was the sort of house that was pretty rather than grand. The part of the structure that survived the fire looked to Amelia to have been built in the sixteenth century as a small manor house. Certainly it had been built before the fashion for overgrown baroque rectangles like Chatsworth, or the nearby Stanton House. It was quaint, with its tiny windows and its profusion of ivy. If she had been visiting under any other circumstances, she would have been eager to explore. As it was, she felt almost rigid with anxiety. She hardly felt the stones beneath her feet as she climbed the steps into the house.

Usually, when Amelia entered a room in which she did not know everyone present, she made directly for an elderly lady or a clergyman. She wound balls of wool, asked about grandchildren, and untangled embroidery floss until it was time to go home. That was all she wanted to do this evening. She would happily sit by the vicar's wife. She would even submit to a lecture about her need for a chaperone.

But the first person she saw upon entering Pelham Hall was Mr. Goddard, looking like a very large storm cloud. Much to her relief, her anxiety evaporated, replaced by searing hot anger.

She knew what it was to be stared at, suspected, and judged. Those stares had pierced her skin and reached as deep as her bones, until they formed part of who she was. She had always reacted by trying to deserve approval or at least escape censure and it never ever worked: there was always more judgment. This, however, was the worst yet. It was judgment from someone she thought had really known her.

She suppressed the urge to retreat to a dark corner of the room, unwilling to let him think he had won. Instead, she pretended not to notice him. She made a show of rummaging through her reticule for something, then smoothing the gray silk of her skirts.

Mr. Goddard appeared by her side. "Might I speak to you for a moment?" he asked, his voice little more than a rumble.

She steeled herself against anything like emotion. "I suppose," she said, regarding him with bored expectation.

"Privately?" he asked.

She was about to oblige him, just for the sake of getting this over with, when she realized she didn't have to. She could stay precisely where she was. Just because she was uncomfortable and out of her element didn't mean she had to drift around at other people's will. She owed nothing to this man, and his judgment did not matter in the least bit; it was a drop in the ocean.

"No," she said.

"I beg your pardon."

She straightened her spine and snapped her reticule shut. "No, you may not speak with me privately. Regardless of our previous acquaintance, there's nothing you need to say to me that can't be said publicly."

To his credit, Mr. Goddard nodded, although his jaw was tight and his eyebrows especially antagonistic. "I'd like for you and your friend to visit once a week during the remainder of the duke's stay in Derbyshire and talk to him about"—he made an expression that Amelia took to be a smile and which she resolutely did not respond to—"Richard III."

"I don't even want to be here tonight," she said in a tone that indicated precisely how irrelevant his words were to her. She pointedly glanced around the room, as if willing something more interesting into existence. "I can't imagine why you think I'd want to repeat the experience."

"I suppose I deserve that."

Amelia flicked some lint off her sleeve and pointedly said nothing.

"You need not come, if you choose not to," he went on.

"How kind of you to clarify that this is an invitation, not a summons from a magistrate." Now he was blushing. She determinedly did not care. She looked him straight in the eye and tried not to remember a time when those dark eyes had been warm and kind. "If you think I'm turning over my friend to a strange man in an isolated house you're very much mistaken."

"That's not what—I didn't mean anything untoward. Surely you know . . ." His cheekbones darkened above his

beard. Amelia believed him. He didn't have the imagination
to orchestrate illicit liaisons, nor the cunning to do anything
sly. He had all the subtlety of a puppy, all the capacity for
guile of a newborn baby. How revolting. What kind of life
did a person need to lead in order to be so transparent? Some
people were raised without the constant need for secrecy and
subterfuge and it showed.

Amelia was not having any of it. She had been putting on
a performance since she was old enough to walk. Some of her
earliest memories were her mother taking her around ("be
silent Amelia, and don't speak until you're spoken to, then
we'll get you a Bath bun on the way home") with the express
purpose of making her father's friends sit in the same room
as his mistress and illegitimate daughter. That was when
she had learned to be invisible, but it was also when she had
learned the inverse: the power of making people look at you.

By God, she was making Sydney Goddard look at her
tonight.

She knew exactly how a lady was supposed to behave to
put people at their ease, or, alternatively, to do the opposite.
Her mother had taught her how to use her manners to
ingratiate herself and win favor. Well, if this man thought
she was careless and rude, she'd give him careless and rude.
Some people were born with the knack of making themselves likable, but Amelia had learned those skills the way
she had acquired languages. All she had to do in order to
be profoundly unlikable and difficult to be around was to
drop her veneer of manners entirely—all she had to do was
to be the worst version of herself. So that's what she did

now—she said exactly what she would say if she hadn't had any upbringing whatsoever, but dressed up her rudeness in a cloak of satin suitable for a duke's drawing room.

She imbued her voice with an acid politeness, replicating the exact tone with which grand ladies put her in her place. "I know nothing of the sort. I might have once thought that we knew one another, but I was wrong, was I not?" It was an insult masked as a question and he knew it. He blinked at her then slowly looked away.

"I was wrong about a good many things. I didn't think you were the sort of man to deceive a friend about something as relevant as your name, and if I were not in a charitable frame of mind I might point out that a good deal of misunderstanding would have been avoided if you had been honest on that point."

"It was indeed a lie of omission, and I'm ashamed of myself for it. But I—"

"I don't care for your excuses, Mr. Goddard," she said, idly folding her gloves, as if she couldn't be bothered to give him her full attention.

"It's not an excuse," he said, his voice so insistent that she looked up at him. "I came into ownership of this house through means I prefer not to think of, and I found it a relief not to be reminded of those circumstances during our time together." He spoke those last words quietly, almost intimately, and she had to fight back a blush.

"I see," she said, even though she did not see at all.

"I did not treat you as a friend. I assumed the worst. And I am sorry for that. I try to do better by my friends."

That was a better apology than she had yet gotten from him, and it was the closest he had yet come to resembling the man she knew from her walks.

"That's what I should have said earlier," he continued. "When I thought you were refusing to acknowledge me, it cut me to the quick. I thought I was being insulted by someone I—someone I esteemed. I should have spoken to you, but instead of doing that, I hurt you, and I regret it." He set his jaw, as if waiting for her rebuke. She remembered kissing that jaw, she remembered the scratch of his beard against her mouth, the feel of his lips against her own. She tried to push those memories away. "The fault is entirely mine."

He bowed and left her. Only after he had turned away did she allow her cheeks to heat.

Sydney hardly even tasted the unprecedentedly edible meal the cook had sent up as a condition of her truce with Lex. He was quite beyond making conversation with his dinner companions. He sat in between the vicar's wife and Georgiana Russell, both of whom seemed determined not to let him get a word in edgewise, so there was no need for his contributions anyway. He was able to sit silently and regard Amelia Allenby across the table. He could barely detect a trace of the woman he had known on their walks—she was composed, silent except for the occasional platitude or commonplace, and bland. Throughout the meal, it was as if she had donned an impenetrable mask, through which he couldn't see her.

When she walked into Pelham Hall for the first time the

previous week, she had been equally distant, equally cold. That was what had tipped him off that she was putting on some kind of show; he knew the real Amelia Allenby, and she was light and fun and slightly silly. He had assumed these were the airs and graces of a woman who didn't wish to be bothered in acknowledging their connection. But what if this was just how she was in company? She had told him outright that she had difficulty around people—what if that coldness were the result? She had become angry when she saw him that first time on what she regarded as her path. She asked him to shield her from the vicar's wife, who was present at this very dinner party.

What if what he was seeing was plain self-defense? What if she developed this impassive mask as a sort of camouflage, so she would blend in with her surroundings the way a moth resembled tree bark?

What if, when she had walked into Pelham Hall that first time, he had greeted her as a friend, a person he cared for, a person he respected and admired? He tried to imagine telling his mother—he was conscious that perhaps at his age he ought to have a moral arbiter other than his mother, but there were few people whose opinion he regarded more than he did hers—what had happened. He had made a friend, and then at the first sign of trouble, abandoned her. His face heated with shame.

This, come to think, was exactly what he had done with Lex. He knew Lex was injured in the fire, but when Lex failed to respond personally to his letters, Sydney assumed Lex wanted nothing further to do with him.

His food—which, as the cook had promised, was not only edible but delicious—turned to ashes in his mouth.

With such a small party and no proper hostess, there was no sense in having the women withdraw first, so they all proceeded from the dining room to the hall together. He hung back so he could walk next to Amelia.

"Are you all right?" he asked, pitching his voice low enough that he would not be overheard. "Can I be of any assistance?"

"I beg your pardon?" Amelia's voice was icy.

"I don't want to presume, but—" He realized he had not planned what to say, and doubted whether there even was a delicate way to ask a person whether they were about to be overcome by a fit of nerves, if that was even what was happening. "You once said you wished to be a recluse, and I . . ." He cleared his throat. "I remember how distressed you were the first time we met, and all of that leads me to suppose—well, I suppose this is not easy for you." He wasn't sure what *this* constituted. Dinner parties? Dukes? And he had no standing to ask. All he could do was offer his aid.

"Do I seem troubled?" she asked, her chin tipped up.

"Not at all," he said honestly. "You're the picture of elegance and composure. If I hadn't known you otherwise, I'd think this was your natural state. But now I do know otherwise, and I ought to have figured it out before. I'm desperately sorry that I hurt you, Amelia. That isn't why I pulled you aside, though. I thought you might want an excuse to leave early. Would you like to have a sudden sickness?" he offered.

That got him a faint smile, and he smiled in return until

he realized he was smiling daftly upon her in a dark corner of the dining room, which surely she did not want. He mustered up some self-control.

"No thank you," she said. "I'm well accustomed to enduring these gatherings."

He watched her progress coolly out of the dining room, conscious that this conversation had been the best part of his day.

CHAPTER FOURTEEN

"I really could get used to meals that consist of actual food," Lex said as he ate the shirred eggs and kippers the cook sent up for breakfast.

Sydney noticed that the eggs and the kippers were in silver dishes that hadn't been on the table yesterday morning. Come to think, he wasn't entirely certain where all the serving dishes from last night's dinner had come from either. He was trying not to dwell on how much Lex was spending on this house, its restoration, and its servants. First, Sydney in general considered paying laborers, craftsmen, and tradesmen to be a fine use of money. Second, Sydney was all too glad to think of this house as Leontine's rather than his own and if Lex wanted to spend money on the child's property, then that was fine. Still, he couldn't let this continue on without saying something.

"What's going to happen to all this"—he sought for a polite way to say *ostentation*, but couldn't come up with anything—"all these items you've purchased when we all leave?" he asked.

Lex's answer consisted of a triangle of toast, launched in Sydney's direction.

"All I meant was that she's not your niece and you're not under any duty to provide for her," Sydney said, catching the toast in midair and laying it on his plate.

"You and your duty," Lex said, his mouth full, "can both kiss my arse. I'm perfectly aware I have no duty to look after her, but we both know that if Andrew and Penny were alive, they would raise the child as a daughter. I have no other nieces or nephews, I like the brat, and she likes me. I realize that I have no legal claim to her so if you mean to take me to court for guardianship—"

"I intend nothing of the sort," Sydney said. "But I do need to get back to work. We can't stay here indefinitely."

"Maybe *you* can't," Lex said. "The rest of us can. Hedgehogs and French urchins and dukes don't have jobs waiting for them in Birmingham."

"Manchester," Sydney corrected. "My point is that if you intend to requisition this house to raise our niece, we ought to at least discuss it."

"Requisition, indeed. You make it sound desperately boring. I've stolen your house out from under your feet, which is a very dashing thing to do and you ought to give me credit."

Sydney laughed despite himself. "Good God, you're welcome to it. You know how I feel about this place."

Lex put down his fork. "No, Sydney, I do not."

"I inherited it because my brother died."

"People do tend to inherit things after the death of a loved one. I'm intimately familiar with the process," Lex said dryly.

"And Andrew only owned the place because of antiquated property laws. It ought to have remained in your sister's possession after the marriage, for her to dispose of as she wished."

"Everything I own is mine due to antiquated property laws and the death of loved ones. I'm not seeing your objection to Pelham Hall. This is more of your guilt, isn't it?"

"You make it sound irrelevant."

"It's not irrelevant, but irrational. It was never your fault that your brother accidentally blew up the stables and killed himself in the process."

"I know that," Sydney snapped. "I don't blame myself for his death. I blame myself for being alive."

The room fell silent. "Very grim," Lex finally said. "Typical of you, frankly."

"I'm well aware," Sydney said dryly. It was true, though, even though it was a truth he hadn't let himself realize until Amelia had mentioned feeling much the same thing after her father's death. "What I mean is that he was a better man than I."

"I beg your pardon," Lex said in tones of outrage. "If we were sentencing people to death based on merit I would have been on the chopping block decades ago. How revolutionary. Disgusting of you. Also, it's very absurd of you to think Andrew was better than you. He was more fun. Infinitely more sympathetic. Better looking, too."

"You have such a soothing way," Sydney said.

"My point is that you have your own qualities. You're dependable. I have total confidence that whatever bridge or canals you're building—"

"Railways, damn it."

"I have total confidence they won't plunge people to a watery death or flood a town of innocent peasants or what have you. That may not be a quality one values overmuch at the dinner table or a house party but it's very boring of you to make me explain how building things that don't kill people is an admirable quality. Please never make me pay you compliments again. Can we go back to talking about Leontine?"

"I did miss you, Lex."

"You disgust me. Now, I'm here to solve your problems. You have a house you don't want and a penniless ward. You give the house to the ward and raise the ward in the house."

"Except for how *my work is in Manchester*," Sydney said.

"Do they not have work in Derbyshire? Do they not build things here?"

"I cannot walk away from my career."

"So don't. Let me raise Leontine. Well, me and my army of servants. You've said yourself that you work long days. Here, she'd at least have me."

Sydney pinched the bridge of his nose, realizing that there was going to be no arguing with Lex at the moment, and also suspecting that there was more than a germ of truth in what Lex had said. "Please tell me that you don't expect this Russell woman to raise Leontine."

"God no. She's one of the Somerset Russells," Lex said.

"A cadet branch of the family, and very poor, but with a pedigree that would satisfy anyone. She and I talked about it last night. Her father was a few years ahead of me at Eton. Incidentally, as for the Allenby girl, she's one of the Marquess of Pembroke's daughters," Lex said. "All you have to do is look at her and you'll see the resemblance. Red hair, freckles, general tendency to *en bon point*."

"Now, how can you know that?" Sydney asked, exasperated. "You can't tell me you got that from her voice."

"Don't need to see. I have my sources. Besides, it turns out you don't need to see to know what people look like. I wish you'd worn something a bit less demoralizing, for example. A pair of trousers from five years ago and a coat of unspeakable origin. Quite depressing. Did you shave?"

"No," Sydney said. He rubbed a thumb over his chin.

"Ugh. Next time you're to appear at my table, try to make an effort," Lex said genially.

"*Your* table," Sydney began, then broke off. "Wait. A marquess's daughter uses a title, doesn't she?"

"Not when she's born on the wrong side of the blanket, as our Miss Allenby was. Her mother was a woman of some notoriety about twenty-five years ago. She appeared from nowhere, then not only wound up in Pembroke's bed, but got the old rascal to buy her a house in Mayfair. She must have been especially quick on her feet to get her brood accepted as something more than Pembroke's other by-blows. I don't think anybody's ever tried counting how many children he had. In any event, Miss Allenby vanished from society about a year ago after leaving a ball right in the middle of a dance.

She simply picked up her skirts and left her dancing partner standing stupidly in the middle of the floor, according to my informants. It caused a slight ruckus, as the man she was dancing with was the Russian ambassador."

He had known abstractly that Amelia was a part of this world of balls and ambassadors. He had known as much from the first time she opened her mouth. But more distressing was that he could see it—he could see her freezing in the middle of a ballroom and deciding that she was done with it. And, what was worse, he could imagine how returning to a similar situation—a duke, a drawing room—might engender the same response. It was no wonder she hadn't managed to treat him cordially. He could have spared them both a good deal of turmoil if he had simply gone to her instead of assuming the worst. But at the time it had seemed impossible that she could want him, let alone need him.

When he rose from the table, he nearly tripped over Leontine's pup. "You again," he said accusingly as he scooped her up. "You don't belong here." She swiped her tongue over his cheek. "You're supposed to be with *Leontine*," he said, as if that could mean anything to this wriggling ball of fur. In fact, he was unsure why he was bothering to talk to her in the first place. "You are not a Francine," he told her. She thumped her tail. By the time he stepped outdoors, the animal was already asleep.

That dinner party had not been the most unpleasant Amelia had endured. There was the usual skin-crawling horror of sitting in a drawing room, combined with the fervent wish to be safe at home. But the crumbling, fairy-story charm of Pelham Hall was nothing like a London drawing room, and the Duke of Hereford was as far removed as London society as one could get while still being a duke. Amelia was familiar with, if not precisely comfortable with, the vicar and Mrs. Trevelyan. Everyone seemed content to ignore her, and she spent the hour after dinner with a gangly terrier puppy asleep in her lap. She strongly suspected that Sydney had said something to the duke to make him focus his attention on Georgiana, and meanwhile Sydney seemed intent on occupying Mr. and Mrs. Trevelyan.

She was trying not to consider what role her conversation with Sydney played in her assessment of the evening. She was trying not to think about Sydney at all, because that look of abject regret on his face had been so much like something she might have expected from *her* Sydney, not the cruel stranger she had met the previous week.

When, the next day, Georgiana announced that she meant to call at Pelham Hall, Amelia automatically reached for her boots and shawl.

"You don't need to come along," Georgiana said. "I only mean to bring Hereford some of our strawberries and let him amuse me with his bad opinions."

Amelia narrowed her eyes. "You two were as thick as thieves last night." She glanced at the basket of strawberries that was looped over Georgiana's arm. "Georgiana Russell, are you throwing your cap at the duke?" She meant it as a joke, and was stunned to see Georgiana blush.

"Not in the way you mean," Georgiana said. "You know I have no interest in men, not in that way. But I like him. So you needn't accompany me unless you have a longing to see Pelham Hall in the daylight."

Amelia *had* wanted a chance to properly see the grounds of Pelham Hall, but that was before things went so wrong with Sydney. "I could walk around the garden," she said, surprised to find that the idea didn't distress her. "It would just be a walk."

"And if you hate it, you can turn on your heel and return home," Georgiana said.

As they approached Pelham Hall, they were greeted by a small child wearing nothing but a shift, running helter-skelter down the lane, followed by a woman in a pinafore and cap.

"Stop, you wretched child. *Arrêt!*" the woman said. "Oh, heaven help me, please don't run into the brook, you imp!"

The child ran into the brook. Before Amelia could quite make sense of what she had seen, Georgiana stepped out of her boots and waded into the water. The water was low, so the child was merrily splashing rather than actively drowning, but Georgiana had her out in half a minute.

"What could you have been thinking?" Georgiana asked in a tone Amelia knew quite well from when her younger sisters had gotten into mischief. "Do you think your mama wants to ruin her boots chasing after you?"

"*Maman est morte,*" the child said. "*Mes tantes sont mortes. Mon oncle monsieur le duc n'est pas morte mais il est fou.*"

"*C'est toi qui es folle,*" Georgiana said, slipping into brisk French. "*Et c'est toi qui doit te sécher et t'excuser auprès de*"— she glanced at the woman in the cap—"*de ta bonne.*"

Heavy footsteps pounded down the lane, and Amelia whipped around to see Mr. Goddard running towards them.

"Is she—"

"She's quite all right," Amelia reassured him. "No, really, there's no need to run after her. She doesn't need two adults ruining their clothes."

Georgiana led the child out of the water. She clapped her hands together and gestured for the child to go to the maid. "*Vas-y!*" she said.

The child flashed a sullen glance at Georgiana but proceeded to the maid. "*Je suis désolée, Marie,*" she said dutifully. Then she caught sight of Mr. Goddard and all but flung herself into his arms, babbling in broken English. He responded in halting French.

There was an obvious family resemblance between Mr. Goddard and the little girl. She was fair where he was dark, but the likeness was there nonetheless. Was she a niece? His own daughter? Whatever the case, he was fond of the child, and she returned the sentiment. It was yet another unwanted reminder that Mr. Goddard was capable of warmth, that he was more than stern disapproval and furrowed dark eyebrows. In fact, if she disregarded that one terrible day at Pelham Hall and their subsequent encounter in the lane, Sydney had been unfailingly kind to her from the beginning. She rather wished she had not come to that realization, because now she felt the pull of whatever they had been to one another. If she were another person, she might be able to let herself be pulled, to let her heart go unguarded. But that was so laughably far from what she felt herself capable of that she felt alone, mere inches from him.

CHAPTER FIFTEEN

"Thank you," Sydney said to Georgiana Russell. "I can't begin to thank you. Leontine recently lost her mother and I'm afraid we've been spoiling her terribly."

"Children are all very naughty at that age," Georgiana said. "Miss Allenby's youngest sister used to climb out on the roof. She gave the entire household nightmares."

"Miss Russell was my governess," Amelia explained.

"And it would seem a very competent one," Sydney added.

"Certainly an experienced one," Georgiana said. "From when I was sixteen, until last year when Amelia carried me away." She smiled fondly at Amelia.

Sydney added that to the paltry store of actual facts he had collected about Amelia Allenby: she was the illegitimate daughter of a marquess and a woman with social aspirations, she seemed to support herself by writing, she had left London under a cloud, she tried to be a good friend. It seemed grossly unfair that he only got to know her after things were impossible between them. He knew he only had himself to blame for that.

"The duke is on the terrace," Sydney said. "Or, it's more or less a terrace, minus a few flagstones." He had cleared most of the rubble away with his own hands so Lex could safely walk outside.

"Excellent," Georgiana said brightly. She strode off ahead, leaving Sydney alone with Amelia.

Sydney couldn't have said whether he tilted his arm to Amelia, or whether she reached for him, or whether they moved at the same time, their bodies remembering a friendship that their minds had discarded. But either way, Amelia's hand rested lightly on his forearm as they continued to walk.

They reached the back of the house, where there had once been a maze or labyrinth. It was all overgrown and riddled with weeds, and would likely need to be torn out. Only after wondering whether the gardener Lex had hired could manage the task on his own, or whether he would need to hire helpers, did Sydney realize he was starting to envision a future at Pelham Hall. He immediately pushed the thought aside.

"If you look," he said, gesturing around the corner of a dilapidated trellis, "you can see where your friend and the duke are on the terrace. You had mentioned once that you wished to explore the ruins here. If you still wish to do so, I can assure you that they're all very safe, as far as ruins go. Leontine has clambered across the lot of them," he said dryly. "Otherwise, you're free to treat the gardens or the house as your own. I know it's not your ordinary time for a walk, but I thought that would be more agreeable for you than sitting."

They had reoriented themselves so instead of standing side by side, they faced one another. He was suddenly very conscious of how close they stood, and how her hand still rested on his forearm. Her skirts touched his trousers and he could feel the heat from her hand on his arm. He tried very hard not to think of the last time they had been this close, the last time he had felt the warmth of her body and the heat of the sun. But the harder he tried, the more insistently his mind provided flashes of memory: her parted lips, her roving hands, the sounds she made. He ought to leave her to her walk; that was the only answer. Surely one of them ought to step away.

Neither of them were stepping away.

Before he could quite work out how to extricate himself—or, more pressingly, why he wasn't extricating himself—the blasted dog flopped onto the ground between them.

"What on earth," Amelia asked.

He sighed. "That's Francine. All she does is find new and ingenious places to lounge. Devil take you, dog. Beg your pardon, Amelia. She ought to be with Leontine but she seems not to understand the first thing about responsibility. Be off with you, you shiftless reprobate."

They stood perfectly still, utterly silent, as if they were both uncomfortably conscious of the fact that he had in that moment spoken to her as if she were his friend, as if she were the same person who had walked with him, the same person who had kissed him and touched him and laughed with him. They stared at one another, eyes wide.

Amelia cleared her throat and looked away. "I believe she's snoring," she said in some amazement. "She spent yesterday evening asleep in my lap. Imagine being able to sleep so easily."

"That's all she does. It's her one talent. She finds the least likely spot in the room and lapses into unconsciousness. I've almost tripped over the beast a dozen times now. I'd like to know how you trained Nan to attack interlopers, because I've had no luck at all."

Amelia pulled her skirt aside and regarded the dog, who was in fact asleep on her boots. They were a perfectly ordinary pair of boots, the same ones she wore when rambling through the hills. And above them her calves were covered in a perfectly ordinary pair of white stockings. He could only see about an inch of stocking, but he remembered how they had felt under his fingertips as he slid his hand up her leg. After everything they had done together, surely he should not be completely incapacitated by an inch of stocking. He dragged his gaze up to her face, and saw she was regarding him curiously.

"She's exactly the color of the dirt," she said, evidently striving for a normal tone. "What a cunning disguise. Well, I suppose I'm here for the duration. That's the law. The custom of my people, rather. If an animal sleeps on you, you can't move."

With a pang, he realized she was making a joke, the sort of idle silliness he had once found so baffling but endearing. Vows of chastity, and now dog laws. She was peering carefully at his face, as if waiting for his verdict on her jest. So he tried to smile, to show her that he liked it, but what he achieved must have been more of a baring of teeth, because she nearly flinched. Damn it. He was bollixing this up. There was only one thing to do.

He dropped to his knees, shoved her skirt to the side, and lifted the dog off her boots. "Never say I won't rescue a fair maiden," he said, his voice perilously low. "That, Amelia Allenby, is the custom of my people." There. He had shown her that he was still capable of entering into her silliness, and also, judging by the direction of her gaze, that he had arm muscles she found attractive. He felt absurdly satisfied by the dazed intensity with which she regarded him.

Hefting the dog under one arm, he made a gesture as if to tip his hat, had he been wearing one, and left her in the middle of the garden.

Amelia almost wanted to call him back, ask him to join her on her explorations, ask him if they could put bygones behind them and go back to when they had made easy conversation. They had been friends, at least, and that had to count for something. A braver woman might have called him back, but Amelia didn't have any reserves of courage left. Instead she watched him go, his shirt straining across his broad shoulders.

Both last night and today he had tried to make her comfortable. Today he had gracefully found an excuse for her to be alone and had not even tried to burden her with his company. He had even pointed out that Georgiana would be in her sight at all times. That had been kind. The fact that Sydney did not think she was difficult or eccentric was not, she knew, a feather in his cap. It only meant he had achieved a minimum level of humanity. And yet, when so many people failed to do so, she could not help but feel grateful that he had casually observed her limitations and done his best to accommodate them.

She walked the circumference of the knot garden, wondering how long it had been since anyone had trimmed the hedges. She climbed up onto the remnants of a bird bath and tried to see what was at the center. Usually there was a statue or a fountain. But the greenery was too overgrown for her to see anything, so she left it behind and headed towards the ruined wing of the house. There were still blackened timbers visible among the rubble.

The child had referred to the duke as her uncle. The duke's sister had owned Pelham Hall, Sydney's brother had died, and now Sydney owned the house. Amelia didn't have a copy of *Debrett's* but she suspected that if she did, she would find that the Duke of Hereford's sister had married Sydney's brother. If the house hadn't been properly settled on Hereford's sister, then upon her marriage it would have passed on to her husband. Sydney, then, might have inherited the house after his brother's death.

He had said that he didn't care for the manner in which he had come into possession of the house, and now she could see why: he was saddled with a half-destroyed home that held nothing but guilt and bad memories.

There were details she couldn't quite figure out. Why, after leaving the house empty and deteriorating for two years, had Sydney chosen to come to Pelham Hall with his brother-in-law and begin restoring the place? And why had he brought the child? There were other oddities, too. Most of the servants had been hired locally. According to Janet, the duke had arrived with a valet and a groom. In Amelia's experience, rich men traveled with a small army of retainers. And Janet had also mentioned that the servants and laborers were hired and the furnishings were purchased after the duke arrived, rather than earlier, so as to make the house ready for his stay. That was very odd indeed.

As she let her path take her closer to the terrace, she could hear the duke laughing at something Georgiana had said.

"I tell you," Georgiana said in tones of high delight. "She carried a vial of cyanide—"

"They didn't even have cyanide in England in 1480—" the duke interrupted. Amelia nearly opened her mouth to protest that they certainly did, but Georgiana got there first.

"She had it anyway. Vats of the stuff. And she went about putting it in everybody's tea—"

"They didn't have tea either," the duke said.

"In their chocolate, then," she said blithely. The duke cackled. Amelia smiled broadly. Georgiana knew enough about history—she had been a governess for ten years, for heaven's sake—to know the Plantagenets hadn't been drinking chocolate either. "Here, have this. I took the stem out," Georgiana said, handing the duke a strawberry.

"It's probably poisoned."

"You say the nicest things."

Amelia climbed up the steps to the terrace, making her footsteps loud enough that the duke would hear.

"There you are, Amelia," Georgiana said. "Tell His Grace about your murder queens. He's very much enjoying your book."

"*The Wolf and the Huntress*," the duke said. "I'm about halfway through. I didn't know I even liked Isabella of France."

"Wait," she said, remembering that the duke could not see. "Who is reading it aloud to you, Your Grace?"

A smile spread across the duke's face. "Sydney, and I fully intend to make him stay up tonight until we finish it."

"I'm becoming quite the expert in arcane murder rituals," Sydney said, coming up behind the duke.

Amelia let herself smile, a polite, discreet curve of her lips. "And are you enjoying it?"

"I am." His voice was low. Intimate. Just for Amelia. "Especially when I can hear the author's voice in my own head."

Amelia tried her best to keep her guarded smile from spreading into something real and broad and dangerous, but in the end she decided not to bother.

When they arrived at Pelham Hall the next day, a mist had settled over the valley. It muffled the sound of the horses' feet and carriage wheels crunching over the newly graveled drive and gave the house the appearance of having been cut off from the outside world. Inside the hall, a fire had been lit.

"Damn those hedgehogs, my leg hurts enough without daring the universe to give me rheumatism," the duke said from where he sat on the sofa, "so I intend to spend the afternoon indoors getting lied to about the Plantagenets. Miss Allenby, if you prefer to take your chances in the garden and risk being rained upon, we'll have tea waiting for you by the terrace."

Amelia supposed this meant that either Sydney or Georgiana had explained her predicament to the duke, and she did not know whether to be grateful or annoyed. She couldn't even imagine what words they might have used to describe her requirements, because she could hardly do so herself. "That's very kind," she said.

"Nothing of the sort," he said, scowling. "Be off with you, so I can corrupt Miss Russell in peace." Amelia glanced at Georgiana, who made a shooing motion with her hand. "If you see Goddard, let him know that he too can feel free to get rained upon. The brat has a cold, so he's reading to her. A tract against popery or the moral righteousness of sad-looking coats, no doubt."

"I beg your pardon?" Amelia asked.

"*Mother Goddard's Moral Tales for Young People*," the duke said. "His mother wrote it. As it seems to be the only book to have survived the fire, Leontine has the entire thing by heart."

Amelia supposed that if Sydney had been raised by the

sort of woman who wrote improving tales for children, that might explain why he was so rigid and unsmiling, why it took so much work to coax a laugh out of him. Most children weren't so fortunate as to be raised by a parent as pragmatic as Amelia's mother, and she felt vaguely resentful of this Mother Goddard. Amelia had read her share of stories that were meant to instill virtues in recalcitrant children, and they all seemed to work on the principle that a child who was deeply ashamed of herself would behave better—and better usually meant in a manner more convenient to adults. It might very well be a sound idea: Amelia had been both ashamed and extremely well-behaved. But she also had lost years of her life to that shame.

She had been about to take the duke up on his offer to explore the gardens, but now she found that she wanted to take the book and throw it out the window before it could rob Leontine of her happiness.

"If I wanted to hear these improving tales, where would I find Mr. Goddard and Leontine?" she asked.

"Take my advice and don't let curiosity get the better of you," the duke advised.

"Don't mind him. He's being a giant baby because he doesn't like having to listen to stories about girls getting their monthlies," Georgiana said. "We all know that's why you're cross, so save it, Your Grace. Now, let's discuss murder and treachery."

Before Amelia could ask what on earth Georgiana was talking about, the duke spoke. "Top of the stairs, second door on your left," he said, then turned his attention back to Georgiana.

This was the first time she had ventured beyond the great hall and dining room of Pelham Hall. The rest of the house seemed much of a piece: old woodwork marred by centuries of nicks and dents but brightly polished nonetheless, mullioned windows still darkened by ivy, the lingering smell of sawdust and paint speaking to the recent spate of improvements and repairs. It had to be inescapably drafty in the winter and damp in the spring, and probably ought to be knocked down and replaced with something newer, a red-brick manor with evenly placed windows and a sensible arrangement of corridors and chimneys. But she also guessed that the duke was attached to this place and that he wasn't going to let it go easily, even if it didn't belong to him anymore. She wondered what Sydney planned to do about it.

At the top of the stairs, she heard Sydney's voice. She would have liked to linger outside the door and listen to what he was reading, but every floorboard in this house seemed to creak, so there was no hope her approach had gone unnoticed. Standing in the open doorway, she raised her hand in an awkward wave.

Sydney sat in a hard-backed chair beside the bed, a book open in his lap. Upon seeing Amelia, he shut the book and smiled. It was such an unguarded, instinctive reaction that Amelia was momentarily robbed of speech. Despite everything, when he saw her, he smiled.

"Don't stop on my account," she whispered.

"She's asleep," Sydney whispered back. Sure enough, Leontine—her nose red and her bed littered with handkerchiefs—slept, curled on her side. He gestured at the empty chair beside his own. "I don't want to leave her. I know it's only a summer cold, but I—"

"You don't need to explain." Amelia remembered her mother sitting up with her during childhood illnesses, and she also remembered the times her mother couldn't do so because her father required her or because she had an engagement she couldn't avoid. Amelia sat in the empty chair, and even though it was more than six inches away from Sydney's, he felt even nearer in the silence of this little room.

She reached over and took the book off his lap. "'*Moral Tales for Young People*,'" she read aloud. That did sound dire. "I had a book very much like this one, in which children who didn't wash their hands or kiss their mothers met with terrible fates."

"We had one like that too," Sydney said, his voice so low it was hardly more than a rumble. "Which is why my mother wrote her own version."

She opened the book. The flyleaf looked typical enough—there was a woodcut of a plainly dressed child sitting primly on a bench. The table of contents listed stories with such titles as "Little Susan Eats a Scone" and "Brother William Goes to Market."

Amelia drew in her breath. She was glad that she and Sydney were on a decent footing now, that they weren't enemies, even if they would never return to their previous closeness. And she knew she was going to jeopardize that by what she said, but she had to speak up. "Leontine has been through a lot in the past few months," she said, thinking of what the child had said to Georgiana outdoors. "Perhaps this isn't the time to read her stories about how she ought to deport herself." Amelia thought it was never the right time for that, but she was trying to appeal to Sydney's sense of decency.

To her surprise, Sydney smiled again. "This isn't a book about deportment. It'll have any child deporting themselves right out of polite society," he said. "And right into prison, if my mother's any example."

"What?"

"Go ahead, read it." When she only blinked at him, he pitched his voice even lower. "Trust me." Amelia shivered.

"I've never wanted to read a book more," said Amelia, trying to keep her tone light. "'Will send you right out of polite society' ought to be on the cover." She cleared her throat. "'Rosie's New Shoes,'" she began, reading aloud. "'Once there was a girl of ten years named Rosie. In her pocket she had sixpence which she was meant to use to get her shoes mended, but what she really wanted to do was buy the pretty purple vase she saw in a shop window. Rosie's mother warned her that she would have no more money until next month, but that if she chose to spend her money on the vase that was her choice.'"

She looked up, wrinkling her nose. "I've read this," said Amelia. "It's a terrible story. Rosie buys the vase and when she gets home she discovers it isn't purple at all but rather filled with dirty water. And her mother won't give her a bowl to put the dirty water in."

"I know that story," Sydney added. "The father was worse. He made Rosie stay at home because she looked slovenly with her worn-out shoes. But you haven't read this version of the story."

Amelia skimmed ahead, flipping forward to the next page. "'Rosie's mother, being a wise and kind woman, showed her a place where the dirty water could be safely disposed of. Then Rosie's father took Rosie and the empty vase back to the shopkeeper and demanded that he either take back the vase and return Rosie's sixpence, or refund part of the price as compensation for his dishonesty. The pretty vase was, of course, worldly nonsense, but everyone, especially children, likes a bit of nonsense in moderation, and Rosie's parents knew that. That night Rosie's mother apologized to Rosie for making a child of her tender years choose between shoes and a pretty thing, because there are many children who have neither shoes nor pretty things, and it made a mockery of their suffering to force Rosie to go shoeless as well.'"

The next story was entitled "The Calendar," and turned out not to be a story at all, but several informative pages about menstruation.

"She got in trouble for that bit," Sydney said. His cheeks were slightly pink. "My mother never met a fight she didn't want to hurl herself bodily into. I miss her."

"Oh. Is she—"

"She's alive and well. She's in America," he said. "I haven't seen her in three years."

"What is she doing in America?" Amelia asked.

"She's in and out of prison," he said fondly.

"What?" she exclaimed, taken aback. Leontine stirred at the sudden noise.

"She went over because there's been some division between American Friends and those of us in Britain. She couldn't resist leaping directly into the fray," he said, smiling. "And then she started hiding enslaved people when they tried to cross into free states. That's how she wound up imprisoned."

"That's very noble of her," Amelia said, meaning it, but also more than a little stunned that this stern, upright man had a mother who had been to jail.

"Oh, never tell her that. She'll tell you that helping people who are fleeing bondage is the bare minimum a person can do. She has my father there to bring her good food and clean clothes, so she's not in danger. She's not a peaceable woman, my mother. She wrote that book because she didn't think the world needed another generation of peaceable women, or complacent adults of any gender. I do wish she could see Leontine."

Amelia swallowed, not certain if she were going to disrupt the fragile peace between them. "Sydney, I know this is a personal question but—"

"You can ask me anything," he answered, his voice husky.

"Is Leontine your daughter?"

"No," he said, "she's my niece. My brother's child. I thought you knew."

"I didn't want to ask because I know too well that these questions are usually unwanted."

He nodded, thoughtful. "It wouldn't have bothered you to know I had a natural child?"

"It would bother me to know you had any child who you didn't take care of. You plainly care a good deal for her."

Leontine rolled over and murmured something unintelligible, and they fell silent until her breathing resumed the steadiness of sleep. Then Amelia began to rise to her feet, but was checked by Sydney's hand on her arm.

"Stay, Amelia. We're having a conversation indoors, for once." He swallowed, and she watched his throat work. "And I missed you."

She opened her mouth to tell him that she missed him too, that she was beginning to suspect that she'd spend months and years missing him after this summer had passed. But no words came out.

"You can read the rest of my mother's book, if you like," he went on. "I too have a book to read." He took a book from the bedside table, and she was mortified to see *The Wolf and the Huntress*. That startled a laugh out of her.

"If you think I can sit here calmly while you read my book—"

"Oh, I've already read your book. I'm rereading my favorite passages now."

"Nooo," she moaned. But she was smiling, and he smiled back.

"Will you stay, though?" He indicated the window, where rain had begun to patter against the glass. "It's no weather for a walk. Stay inside with me, warm and dry, and we can read."

He said it so pleadingly, almost wheedlingly, that she

would have laughed if there hadn't been a sleeping child a few feet away. "Fine," she said.

Amelia read the rest of the book to herself. There was the tale of two sisters, one of whom always told their parents the good and evil deeds she had done that day, and the other who always lied to avoid punishment. Amelia's own childhood book of improving tales had contained a similar story, the moral of which had been that dishonest children are reviled and honest ones beloved. But in this book, a wise grandmother scolds the parents for giving the naughty child an incentive to lie. "Why would she tell you the truth," the grandmother asks, "if the truth isn't good enough?"

She felt that she had been given the key to understanding Sydney. He was a person who had been raised to listen to his own conscience rather than prevailing notions of right and wrong. And more important than any sterile notion of good and evil was the duty of one person to another. She could see that in how he treated her and how he looked after Leontine and even the duke. He had once told her that he was aware he was large and did not want to impose on her; he seemed to carry that principle into all aspects of his life.

Amelia had been raised to blend in, to behave, to make herself unobjectionable and sometimes invisible. She knew her mother and maybe even her sisters would object to that characterization; her mother would say that she had given her daughters the tools to survive in a cruel world. And so she had: here Amelia was, surviving. And yet—it all felt so small and constrained. She once thought this constraint had to do with her limitations, that of course a person's world was small if it only consisted of a tiny corner of Derbyshire. But that wasn't it at all: the constraint came from within, from the voice that told her to hide away her true self, to squash feelings before they even fully formed. If she could stop doing that, she could have an entire universe without even stepping foot outside.

She closed the book and looked at the man beside her. One of his boots was propped up on the edge of the bed frame, and she could see Nan's tooth marks. As he read, he occasionally stroked his beard. A lock of his dark hair fell in his eyes. She reached out to push it back, and it was silky in between her fingers. He didn't turn his head, but she could tell that he wasn't looking at the book anymore. With the back of her hand, she stroked down his cheek, feeling the softness of his beard with her knuckles. He grasped her hand—not stopping her, just holding her hand in place— then kissed her palm.

Chapter Sixteen

Amelia stood obediently still while Janet and Georgiana fussed over her, occasionally taking a step this way or that so they could pin and tuck things into place. It really was an absurd gown. Around the hem were flounces that looked like barnacles, and the waist was defined with a wide ribbon that Amelia's mother claimed was the latest mode from Paris. The sleeves somehow looked inflated, like tiny hot air balloons.

Amelia was only trying the dress on. That was all. It was an experiment. She just wanted to see what it looked like when she chose not to be invisible.

But when she looked at her reflection, she had to concede that it didn't look bad. In fact, the overall effect was . . . good. Her mother had always insisted that if one had a good figure, one might as well have as much of it as possible, and Amelia felt almost statuesque in this gown. There was no denying the curve of her breasts or the roundness of her stomach in all these yards of green silk.

"You look very handsome, miss," Janet said.

That was the word. She had never aspired to prettiness. But at some point in the past few years she had lost all traces of girlishness, and now she looked handsome. Distinguished, even. Her mother had always counseled her to be confident, or, failing that, to act confident. Amelia couldn't do it, so she resorted to invisibility: quiet, polite, unobjectionable, utterly and flawlessly composed. But this gown was not the attire of a woman who wound wool and faded into the shadows.

There were times when she didn't want to fade into the shadows. Of course there were—she wasn't reserved around Georgiana or her family. She was as bold as she pleased around Sydney. And, if she were honest with herself, it was Sydney who she was thinking of when she took this dress out of the clothes press. Not the ton, not her mother, not the judgment of strangers and the fear that followed her. Only Sydney. She liked when he looked at her, when he gave her one of those dark and hungry glances as if he couldn't possibly look his fill.

Well, she wanted to give him something to look at.

"All right," she said to her reflection. "I'll wear it."

"I'm torn between wanting to hustle you out of the house before you change your mind, and asking whether you're certain you want to come in the first place," Georgiana said.

Tonight they were dining at Pelham Hall, and Amelia was surprised to find that the prospect didn't fill her with dread. Pelham Hall was becoming a place where she felt safe. She hadn't known she was capable of expanding her world, but now she had Crossbrook Cottage, her paths along the hills, and Pelham Hall. It was still a small universe, but it was, perhaps, large enough.

"It's not a real dinner party," she said. "It's four people eating a meal in a sad excuse for a house."

"It's the exact same assortment of people who were there that first day we went to Pelham Hall," Georgiana pointed out. "And that was hard for you."

"But this time it's among friends," Amelia said, and the words were out of her mouth before she could reflect on the fact that she had resumed thinking of Sydney as a friend.

"Hmm," Georgiana said, regarding Amelia thoughtfully.

When they arrived at Pelham Hall, they found the duke alone in the great hall, standing before the fire. "Miss Russell, play *vingt-et-un* with Miss Allenby while we wait for Sydney to come downstairs," he ordered by way of greeting.

"I beg your pardon, Hereford, but I'll do nothing of the sort," Georgiana said. "She'll do me out of all my money and make me look a proper fool." She settled in a chair by the fire and was promptly joined by Francine the dog.

The duke arched an eyebrow. "Am I to understand that you're some kind of card sharp, Miss Allenby?"

"That, and I cheat," she said cheerfully. She didn't really cheat, not in company, but with her sisters and Georgiana the usual rules of most card games had by common consent been cast aside in favor of anarchy and cunning. When Georgiana and Amelia played cards now, they did so with the same lack of principle they had years ago.

Footsteps sounded behind her, and she turned to see Sydney approaching. His hair was combed, it looked like he had trimmed his beard, and he was wearing a black coat. She knew that she had seen him dressed for dinner before, but that last and lonely time they had dined at Pelham Hall, she had done her best to avoid looking at him. She was so used to seeing him dressed in attire more suited to manual labor, with bits and pieces missing as the weather dictated, that the sight of him dressed in a starched collar and a plain but well-cut dinner coat took her breath away. Men with broad shoulders, she decided, should always wear well-tailored coats. Or perhaps they should never wear any coats at all. Really, either option was highly satisfactory.

"Everyone fell silent when Sydney came in," the duke observed. "Either that means he looks like more of a ragamuffin than usual or he took my advice and dressed presentably for once. If memory serves, he cleans up well. Does he not, Miss Allenby?"

Amelia resisted the urge to glare at the duke, for embarrassing her and for embarrassing Sydney. "He looks well in whatever he chooses to wear," she said coolly, in the tone her mother was accustomed to use when dressing down fraudulent wine merchants. Only after the words left her mouth did she realize that her response had only opened her to the duke's scrutiny. What he had doubtless intended as an offhand remark, some reference to a running joke between himself and his friend, she had taken personally, and thereby announced that she admired Sydney Goddard's looks.

"Is that so?" the duke said. "Sydney, Miss Allenby says you look good in anything you wear. We both know this to be patently false, despite your manifold physical charms, so I'm left to assume—"

"Enough, Lex," Sydney said with finality. "You aren't

allowed to toy with my friend. Besides, Amelia is well aware that I admire her no matter what she is wearing, so it's kind of her to return the compliment."

The duke seemed stunned into speechlessness by this. Speechlessness, but also enormous curiosity, and Amelia very much feared that the next words out of his mouth were going to be even worse.

Georgiana saved the moment by intervening. "You'll never guess what I heard about the Battle of Bosworth Field."

Amelia couldn't pay attention to whatever tales Georgiana had chosen to weave about kings long dead. None of it could matter, because Sydney had come to sit beside her on the sofa. She was very conscious of every inch that separated them.

"Lex is impossible," he said, too quietly for anyone but Amelia to hear.

"I have two younger sisters," Amelia said. "I'm familiar with people who express their affection through attempts to embarrass one to death."

"Perhaps the experience with your younger sisters has rendered your friend equal to dealing with Lex." They both regarded the duke and Georgiana. Whatever she said had the duke's shoulders shaking with laughter.

"I'm not certain about that," Amelia said slowly. "She brought him the last of our strawberries. That's as good as promising him her firstborn." Only after the words had left her mouth did she realize that she might have stumbled across the truth. Was Hereford . . . courting Georgiana? More intriguingly, was Georgiana letting him? When she darted a glance at Sydney, she saw that he was flushed to the tips of his ears. "Don't worry," she said. "I won't ask what has you blushing like that."

He let out a bashful laugh and scrubbed his hand across his beard, and she was almost overcome by the surge of fondness she felt for him. Every time she saw him, the threads of desire and affection that lay between them grew stronger and she felt herself being drawn in by them. Love, or whatever this was, crept past her defenses, and she found that she didn't want to stop it.

Sydney was alarmed to discover that Amelia wasn't wearing one of her simple cotton frocks, nor did she have on the plain gray silk. Instead she wore a gown of green, the color of summer grass, the same bright green as the hills they had climbed together. It was trimmed with a profusion of nonsense that Sydney could not begin to understand, let alone describe. He was no connoisseur of women's fashion, and firmly believed it to all be worldly nonsense, but he found that he was strongly appreciative of this particular piece of worldly nonsense.

She looked beautiful, but that was no surprise. For weeks he had known he liked the looks of her. What mattered was that she was wearing it, that she had chosen to wear it. He knew a person could choose to dress in a certain way for reasons that had nothing to do with how they appeared; he chose his clothing based on comfort and a desire to abide at least somewhat by the principles of plain dressing. Usually Amelia seemed to want to make a camouflage out of her clothes, but tonight she had dressed herself in a way that she must know would draw the eye. His eye, in particular, he hoped.

Then Lex had to go and make everything awkward by insinuating that Amelia fancied him. Of course, there had been more than mere fancying between them, but Lex didn't know the extent of it. Whatever existed, past or present, had been mutual, and at that moment it seemed important to let Lex know that. If he had the use of his eyes, he'd probably already know from the fact that Sydney couldn't stop looking at Amelia, regardless of what she wore. Sydney was done with secrets, with half-truths, with lies of omission. He was foolish fond of Amelia and he didn't care who knew it.

Mr. and Mrs. Trevelyan had at the last minute sent word that they were unable to attend, so it was only the four of them at the table. Sydney wouldn't have been able to make conversation with the vicar or his wife anyway. All he could do was watch Amelia and blush furiously every time she caught his eye.

In her hair, she wore three curled ostrich plumes and a banded ribbon of the same shade of green as her gown. Whenever she leaned in to speak to Georgiana, she tipped slightly over the table in a way that caused her ostrich plumes to dip slightly, and made Sydney glance hopefully at the bosom of her gown, despite his best intentions.

When she caught him looking at her, she didn't glance away in embarrassment. It was as if she accepted his regard as her due, and that thought gladdened him in a way he couldn't make sense of. She looked like a goddess, like a queen, and he wondered when he started considering either of those to be compliments. She was the kind of person people built monuments to, carved statues of, worshipped from afar and hesitated to approach, and he had held her in his arms.

After dinner, she dealt him into a game of *vingt-et-un*. Lex and Georgiana discussed historical lunacy, the dog dozed at his feet, and Sydney was glad there was nobody else playing cards with them because the only thing in the room he could pay attention to was Amelia Allenby.

Amelia deftly shuffled the deck and held it out for him to cut.

"I ought to warn you," Sydney said, "that I'm truly awful at all card games I've ever tried, and probably all those I haven't, so we can skip the game and I'll just empty my coin purse into yours."

"But I like playing cards. And I like winning." She glanced up at him with a predatory smile that went straight to his groin. "We can play for farthings, or perhaps a couple of your shirt studs and a few of my hairpins. Those would do admirably."

The idea of taking out one of his shirt studs a mere few feet away from her was enough to make Sydney flush with some strange combination of embarrassment and want. So he shoved up his coat sleeve and removed a cuff link. When he placed it in the center of the table, he glanced up at her and saw that her gaze was fixed on the exposed triangle of skin on his wrist. As he watched her, she licked her lips. Sydney sucked in a breath.

"And here I thought you were an honest man," she said with mock sadness. "I said you could wager a shirt stud." She cast a glance at his chest. "Not a cuff link. I get to pick your next wager."

"Is that so?"

For an answer, she leaned forward to take the cuff links and slowly, deliberately dropped them into the bodice of her gown. "What would you have me wager?"

"Perhaps the ante you've stolen from me," he managed, keeping his eyes resolutely on her face.

"No," she said, shaking her head and delicately patting her bodice. "That's now the bank."

"You're making these rules up."

"These are Italian rules. You wouldn't know them." She said this so calmly, only a flicker of an eyebrow to let him know she was jesting.

"I've utterly underestimated you," he said.

"I know," she responded promptly. "Men do that." She took the deck of cards and shuffled them. "It's just like Elizabeth of York. I don't call it underestimating to think too highly of a woman's character to think her above murder and cheating."

They played another hand, using farthings gathered from both their coin purses as the stakes. She won easily.

"If I didn't already regret having lived my life in such a way that I'm no longer allowed to touch you, the way you look right now would have done the job," he murmured. "Not only the gown," he clarified. "But the way you look when you're winning."

She was silent for a few seconds, and he thought he might have gone too far. Then she fanned out her cards in front of her, facedown. "Tell me more."

He let out a long breath, glad for a chance to properly apologize. "One of the stupider things I've done in my life was to assume the worst of you that first day you came to Pelham Hall. I can think of a dozen ways I could have put you at ease, and I utterly failed as a friend by not doing so. And then I compounded that by insulting you. Under the circumstances it's remarkable that you'll still talk to me at all. I can only assume that you do this so that Lex isn't left with nobody but me as company, which is very admirable of you."

She stared at him, her gray eyes wide. "I'll disregard the second half of that, because it's too stupid to deserve a reply. I meant tell me more about how you wish you could touch me."

He could do that. He could do that for hours. He scrubbed a hand along the back of his neck. "When we were together," he whispered, "I wish I had taken more time. I wish I had seen all of you, touched all of you, tasted all of you. And I didn't, because I'm an idiot, and that's something I'm going to be reminded of every time I see you."

"You're assuming you won't get another chance," she said, doing something with the cards and helping herself to some more of Sydney's farthings.

Sydney dropped his cards and she tutted over his lack of dexterity, but smiled at him over the top of the cards she had fanned out in her hand.

"**Y**ou were serious," she said. "You're truly bad at cards." For reasons she chose not to fully examine, his total lack of competence at something as basic as *vingt-et-un* endeared him to her. It was like finding a three-legged dog or a cat with one ear: one had to look after it. "You have no sense of strategy." The utter guilelessness of this man both charmed Amelia and made her want to wrap him in a blanket and keep him safe. "I dare say that's why you find it such a trial to talk with the railway backers," she said. "They're trying to negotiate with you, and you're telling them what your best cards are." She returned the various hairpins and cuff links that had served as stakes.

He frowned. "My brother used to handle that sort of thing. And now I make do the best I can, which I'm afraid isn't very good at all."

She knew the way guilt and grief could tangle together. There was nothing she could do about that. "Why railways?" she asked.

It took Sydney a moment to follow her meaning. "Why do I build railways? I want to make it easier for things and people to move around. Change is coming and we need to be ready for it. If we don't get the railways laid properly now, we'll be in a mad rush in a few years."

"Why?" she persisted.

"Look." He swept the cards aside and shook his remaining coins onto the table. "Here's Portsmouth. Here's Liverpool. Manchester." He dropped a farthing piece in the middle. "That's us." And now a crown. "There's France." He hesitated a moment, then took out a guinea. "Here's New York. Right now, in order to get a round of cheese from eastern France to here, it has to travel over bad roads, good roads, and canals before being loaded on a ship that sails to Liverpool. Then it has to travel overland to Manchester, and then from there to a cheesemonger in Bakewell."

"There are no French cheeses to be had in Bakewell," she pointed out. "Not for love or money."

"But there would be if the roads were good, the ships faster, and the railways ever got built."

"Seems a lot of bother just for cheese."

He rested his forearms on the table, his head inches from hers. "Imagine that instead of cheese, it's people that we're moving about." He gestured at their makeshift map. "Where are your mother and sisters? London?" He placed a penny on London. "And you've mentioned a brother, I believe?"

"Two brothers. Kent and Shropshire, respectively."

He placed coins accordingly. "Anyone else?"

"A pair of friends not far from Worksop," she said. He placed a coin a few miles to the east of where they were, near to Weybourne Priory, where Verity and Ash lived when they weren't in London.

They both regarded the map. She knew the minute he saw the pattern, because his eyebrows rose and he looked hard at her, his dark eyes seeing things he wasn't meant to. "You took a house in a place that was almost on the way to two of these places. Your brother"—he indicated Shropshire—"and friend"—he indicated Worksop—"are less than a day traveling post. And the roads from here to London are serviceable.

You deliberately situated yourself where you'd be far enough away to be private, but not so far as to be remote. You know the value of roads, Amelia. Your people have the money to come see you and the education to write you letters. Not everybody has that."

"And your railways would change that?"

"One day. That's why it matters. The better we get at moving things about, the more we bridge the gap between people. Think of it. People will travel from one end of the nation to the other without stopping at inns. Friends will think nothing of a distance of hundreds of miles. Everything you think you know will change."

She had meant to parlay his words into something intelligent he could say to investors or parliamentarians. But instead she was dazzled by this image of a future where she could just see people when she wanted and then promptly go home when she was done. "Why does it matter to you?" she asked. "To you in particular?"

"I've always been a tinkerer," he said. "My brother and I built our first engine when I was sixteen. We got work with an engineering firm and then, a few years ago, we started our own firm. That's how we came here. We were surveying the route for a potential tramway. One afternoon, as we were quarreling over whether the grade of an incline was too steep to work with, we came across Lex's sister. She had turned her ankle, Andrew very gallantly carried her home, and within two months they were married. They said it was love at first sight, which I thought was the silliest rubbish until—" He broke off and looked at her, startled. For an instant she thought he'd try to backtrack, try to pretend he hadn't suggested what she thought he had. But instead he let out a chagrined laugh. "Well, I suppose that wherever he is now, he's feeling properly smug."

"So," she said, her mind reeling, "you build railways because you enjoy creating things?"

He spun a coin. "I'm an engineer because I like solving problems and making things work. But I build railways—or, God help me, I'm trying to—because I, well, I suppose that if people could move about more easily then I'd be less alone." He swallowed. "Which I suppose is very silly because people would still have to actually want to see me."

She was not going to cry. She had too much practice masking her feelings to shed a spontaneous tear. But Sydney looked like he could do with some air. "Step outside with me?" she asked, rising to her feet.

"Are you all right?" Sydney asked as he followed her onto the terrace.

"Yes, but you aren't. How thick is your head not to understand that you have friends? Do you not see that the duke thinks the world of you?"

"That's not friendship. It's just lingering fondness for a former—" He broke off, eyes wide.

Amelia had the distinct impression that Sydney was not about to finish that sentence with *brother-in-law*. Well, not for nothing had she been schooled in the art of putting people at their ease. "The world is filled with former acquaintances and former lovers and all manner of people one used to know. I spent a season kissing a French poetess at every opportunity, and if today she summoned me across the country I certainly wouldn't go." There. She had put that out in the open, established equal footing, and done it in two concise sentences. This, she felt certain, was the best use she had ever found for her mother's teachings.

He had his back against the stone wall of the terrace. As she spoke, she walked towards him, until now they were almost standing chest-to-chest. She traced a finger down the length of his sleeve, appreciating the bulk of his arm, even beneath the wool of his coat. Just when she was wondering if she had misjudged the situation, he put a hand on her hip, letting out a sigh as if the contact came as a relief to him.

"I've wanted to touch you too," she said. "It's like my body forgot we were quarreling."

"Can we agree that it was only a quarrel, Amelia? Not a rupture?"

Her instinct was to reassure him that everything was fine, to deny to both him and herself that she felt anything at all. "I hope so," she answered instead. But what did it mean if they really did put the past two weeks behind them? Where did that leave them? Their time together had been almost anonymous, entirely free of cares and responsibilities, and she didn't think they could go back to that. Now they knew one another's weaknesses. They knew one another, full stop, and continuing would bring about something irrevocable. She closed her eyes and remembered that this was how she could expand her world from the inside.

"We're quite in the shadows," she said conversationally.

The corner of his mouth turned up in that lopsided smile

that she was starting to regard as her favorite expression in the world. "I'm beginning to think you just like kissing strange men out of doors," he murmured, then bent his head. He brushed his lips across hers, but even at that slight touch, she knew they had done something new and different, and there was no going back. What had come before, out on the hills and in the open, had been lovely and fine, but it hadn't been real. Or maybe it had been real, but it had been something they could deny, something they could walk away from. They nearly had, come to that. But this, this was new. Sydney saw her now, he saw the real her. She wasn't invisible to him, and that was terrifying.

She took a moment to relish the feel of his strong arms wrapped around her, solid and secure. Then she pressed up onto her toes and kissed him again, deeper and with intent. He groaned and hauled her even closer. This must be what it was like to dive into a lake from a great height, or to jump fences on a horse. Her heart was racing and every inch of her skin felt alive with exhilaration. One hand on his shoulder, she pressed her other palm into the stone wall behind him. Remembering the last time they had kissed, that time she with the wall at her back and Sydney at her chest, she pressed her hips into him and felt the hard length of him against her belly. His grip on her waist tightened. And then, slowly, he gentled his kiss and put a little distance between them. He eased her down from that precipice, stroking her back and whispering nonsense until the desire she felt for him wasn't an all-consuming thing. What was left was a tenderness, a warmth, that was somehow even more forceful. And when she looked up at him, she saw him gazing down at her with a dazed and adoring expression that she knew mirrored her own.

"We could have gone upstairs," Amelia said, leaning against the wall beside him. The only place they touched was where their hands clasped, but he could still feel the echoes of her hands, her lips. "There seem to be quite a few unoccupied bedrooms."

Sydney snorted. "They're filled with hedgehogs and spiders. Which you probably find very titillating, what with your mania for doing lewd things in the great outdoors." He could not believe he was jesting about this. It was a serious matter, the fact that he was on the verge of giving his heart away to this woman, but he couldn't stop smiling.

"You know, Sydney, I intend to collect on that deflowering you owe me. Don't think I've forgotten."

He made a noise that was definitely not a whimper, then cleared his throat. "No worries. I'm a man of my word."

"What will you do?" she asked. "That you didn't do already, I mean."

He was about to explain that he'd be sure not to hurt her, instead of throwing her against walls like some kind of brute, but then he turned his head and saw the glint in her eye and understood what she was really asking. She wanted to play one of her games of make-believe. He swallowed. "First, I'd kiss you. Very softly."

"No tongue?" she asked in a tone of academic curiosity.

"No tongue," he affirmed somberly. "Only delicate brushes of my lips over yours."

"Because I'd be utterly inexperienced and you wouldn't want to shock me."

"If you're going to take issue with how I'd pretend to deflower you, why don't you take the reins? If you're such an expert at deflowerings," he said in mock annoyance.

"Fine. You'd very tentatively touch my breasts." She mimicked the action herself, bringing pale hands to cover the green silk of her bodice. "But I'd like it and you'd be able to tell, so you'd begin to unfasten my dress."

"Would I? I work fast."

"In this scenario, I'm impatient, so you'd better." She was still caressing her breast, and he didn't even bother to pretend that he wasn't watching intently. She had on a corset and likely a couple layers of petticoats and a chemise, but he imagined that she was focusing her attention on her hardened nipples.

"Then what do I do?" His voice was hoarse.

"You slide my gown down my shoulders just enough to lick—"

"Stop," he groaned. "I can't take it." He was hard in his trousers and if he ever wanted to go back inside he needed to get some control over himself. "Look, I'd take your gown off and, well, I'd fold it and put it someplace safe because it looks expensive." God help him, had ever a man been less skilled at this. He tried again. "Then I'd get my mouth all over you. And I'd be ready to die from the need, but I wouldn't try to make love to you until you were ready. I'd go slow and make sure I didn't hurt you. I'd make sure you liked it. Because I care an awful lot about you and I can't pretend otherwise, Amelia." She looked up at him with an unreadable expression, probably because this was probably the least successful bedroom talk anyone had ever attempted.

"I wouldn't undo that first time together, not for anything," she said after staring at him for a moment. "Because it was lovely and you were lovely." She squeezed his hand. "And we were lovely together."

He swallowed. "What are we doing here, Amelia? I don't think this is a passing fancy for either of us."

"I don't think you've had a passing fancy even once in your life, Sydney Goddard. And no, it's not that for me either."

Sydney ought to be pleased to hear that, surely. Instead his heart raced, his stomach turned—he was terrified. He had an insane urge to tell her that she must be mistaken, to present her with all manner of compelling arguments that she was not particularly fond of him after all. He had barely enough sense not to do so. "What does this mean?" he asked. "In any other circumstance I'd have already asked you to marry me." Knowing her as he did, he couldn't even consider asking her to come with him to a city that could be as disastrous to her as London had been. "But, I ought to tell you, the only reason I've been able to spend this much time away from Manchester is that I haven't yet been appointed head engineer. Once construction starts, I'll be lucky if I can get away for more than a day at a time."

"I see," she said slowly. "I understand if you want to keep your distance when you return. In the interest of avoiding heartbreak."

He made a sound that was in between a cough and a laugh. "No, Amelia, that's not what I meant. I haven't the faintest interest in keeping my distance. As for heartbreak, I think we've already done that." He lifted her knuckles to his mouth and kissed them. "At least I have. What I mean is that if we try to mend this"—oh, God help him, he was about to launch into an extended engineering metaphor—"we need to make sure it's, um, structurally sound. Better than before. No gaps in knowledge or intent."

"Structurally sound," she repeated, her eyes laughing. "You want to make sure our hearts are structurally sound."

He tried to bury his face in his hands but she kissed the corner of his mouth. "You need to know I won't be here so often, in the future."

"Fair. And I need you to know that I don't think I can live in a city."

This was very much the opposite of structural soundness. He very much feared they were headed for another—emotional equivalent of a bridge collapse, he supposed. But standing here with her in the moonlight, he knew that nothing was going to stop him from seeing her. Nothing was going to stop him from falling further in love with her, and if he got his heart resoundingly broken at the end of it, he'd simply have to live with that.

CHAPTER SEVENTEEN

In the morning, Sydney packed his bag. He had little to cram into his satchel, because most of his belongings were, naturally, in Manchester. That was his home, and he would do well to remember it. He tried not to remember that he had somehow acquired two changes of clothes, a spare shaving kit, and a cake of soap, all of which sat in the wardrobe in his room at Pelham Hall, waiting for his return.

He heard footsteps and turned to see Lex in the doorway, holding his cane. "Carter said you're packing your bag."

"I have a meeting with the railway backers."

"You told me that wasn't until next week. Tell me you aren't running away from the Allenby woman."

"I'm doing no such—"

"I swear to God I can actually hear you blushing right now. You're a terrible liar." Lex tapped the ground with his cane until he found the bed, then shoved Sydney's clothing aside and sat. "You're smitten with her."

"I am," Sydney admitted.

"And she's smitten with you."

"I believe she is."

"You sound unsure."

Sydney swallowed. He thought of what she had said, and the way she looked at him and touched him. She was fond of him. That wasn't news, precisely. It was just difficult to believe. "I'm trying not to be."

"And so you're running away."

"I'm getting some space so I can think about this clearly." After the previous night's conversation, he needed to pause before rushing headlong into disaster. Maybe there was a way to mitigate damages, some way to take whatever they were feeling and shove it into a less dangerous shape. Maybe, with some distance, it could become a casual affair, a summertime romance, and they would only be slightly miserable at the end of it.

"As I said, running away. Of course you are. You'll need time to come up with a better reason to drive her away this time. I doubt you're up to the task, if I'm honest."

"What on earth are you talking about."

Lex arranged himself against Sydney's pillows, his booted feet crossed on top of Sydney's folded shirts. "When someone's fond of you, you immediately stage a tactical retreat."

Sydney opened his mouth to object but Lex carried on. "One," he said, holding up a single finger. "You were terribly standoffish with both me and Penny. My God, the lengths we had to go to for you to join in our frolics. We asked Andrew if you hated us but he insisted that this was how you were. Two." He held up another finger. "You ran off to Durham as soon as you and I became something more than occasional bedmates."

"That's not fair," Sydney said hoarsely. But he remembered that summer, remembered the realization that he was in over his head, and wanting to get as far away from Lex as possible. "I had work in Durham."

Lex ignored him. "Three. You jumped to the worst possible conclusion about Miss Allenby when she and Miss Russell visited. Surely you realize how irrational that was. You went so far as to insult the poor woman. I can only assume you were deliberately trying to alienate her."

"I don't need to try to alienate anyone," Sydney said. "It just happens. It's my nature."

"Four. You didn't come to me in London."

Now that was simply going too far. "You didn't ask me!"

"You were the only person who had suffered the same loss as I had. We were—we are—family. I needed you and I couldn't tell you because my secretary doesn't need to be privy to my every thought, and you didn't come."

Sydney clenched his fists in frustration. "Your letters were so chilly. And they were dictated, Lex. I thought you were trying to put me off."

"You knew me. You knew better than to think that I'd shrink from telling you to keep away if that was what I wanted. I think that you didn't want to see me because you were afraid."

"What was I afraid of, Lex?" Sydney asked, exasperated.

Lex tapped his long fingers on the coverlet. "Of being liked and wanted. Of being loved. And I don't mean in the carnal sense. You seem to have no difficulties understanding your appeal in that arena. You spent so many years in Andrew's shadow. No, that isn't right. *As* Andrew's shadow. You were so different from one another, that I think you decided that since he was so likable, you must therefore be unlikable."

"I'm really not particularly likable," Sydney pointed out.

Lex groped on the bed, found a hair comb, and flung it at Sydney. "You're surrounded by evidence to the contrary. Surrounded, you monumental lackwit. Nobody should let you build bridges if you're this stupid."

"They're railways! Not bridges!"

"Bugger the entire lot of them. This is why you're so devoted to duty, isn't it? You've reduced all your relationships to duty, and it's never once occurred to you that someone might want something else from you."

"This is balderdash."

"In any event," Lex said, swinging his feet to the floor and rising. "When you come to your senses I will *not* be gracious about it."

"You're never gracious about anything!" Sydney called to Lex's retreating form. The infuriating part was that Lex was right. When Sydney suspected someone was fond of him, his first thought was that there must have been some sort of emotional calculation error. Perhaps they hadn't carried the one, perhaps they hadn't noticed that he was gruff and abrupt and bad at friendship. But he also found it hard to believe that sharp-eyed, keen-witted Amelia saw him for anything other than who and what he was, and that she liked him anyway. And, yes, that made him uncomfortable in a way he couldn't quite understand. All the more reason, then, for him to step away from the confusion in his mind and heart and see if he could make some sense of it at a comfortable remove. He told himself very firmly that this was best for both of them.

When Amelia and Georgiana arrived at Pelham Hall, Sydney was waiting on the drive for them, a satchel in his hand. Amelia's heart sank.

"I'm headed to Manchester for at least a week," he said. His voice was pleasant. Detached. She hated it. "Are there any errands or services I can perform for you?"

"You've had me longing for French cheese all day," Amelia said, striving for the same level of detachment. "A round of Camembert would be delightful with the berries we've been gathering."

"Eight yards of nankeen," Georgiana said promptly.

Amelia blinked. "Are you going to recover all the furniture at the cottage?"

"Leontine needs new clothes. The dresses she arrived with are already too small and can't be let out any further. Some pretty ribbons for her hair would not go amiss. The mercer on the high street doesn't have anything suitable. And she needs books. Not copy books or primers—there will be time for that later—but stories to read in French and English. I would know where to get them in London but the stationer in Bakewell doesn't have what I need. I can make a list," Georgiana offered, when Amelia and Sydney both continued to stare at her.

"No, quite all right," Sydney said, removing a notebook and pencil from his pocket. "I'll take care of it."

"And while you're at it, you need a proper governess. Your niece is a lady, whatever her origins are. Especially given what her origins are, in fact. She mustn't be raised in a slipshod manner. It's all well and good to be camping here for the time being, but if you mean for Pelham Hall to be her home, you must hire a full staff and see that she has other children of a similar station to play with."

"When she goes to Manchester with me, she'll go to school," Sydney said.

"You might want to confirm those details with His Grace," Georgiana said. "Because he's laboring under the impression that Leontine will continue to live here with him. They're exceedingly fond of one another and given that they've both had recent losses, you certainly wouldn't want to separate them." With that, Georgiana bid Sydney farewell and went inside.

"What just happened?" Sydney asked, passing a hand over his face.

"I think Georgiana has decided to manage your life," Amelia said. "It's really not a bad thing. She's quite good at managing. It's been so long since I've seen her lift a finger that I forgot what it's like when she decides to take matters in hand. I didn't know she still had it in her." Amelia swallowed, not certain how to approach the topic diplomatically. "Also, she is entirely correct that your niece needs to be raised as a lady if you intend for her to be a lady. Georgiana helped my mother in that regard. She is an expert in tricking society to accept baseborn children."

Sydney's jaw tensed. "I'm not certain I like hearing you refer to yourself or Leontine as baseborn."

"It's a sight nicer than the alternatives," Amelia responded. "Illegitimate sounds like I'm a grifter. Bastard is unconscionable. By-blow is crass. Born out of wedlock is entirely silly, as it makes it sound like the child was born in an improperly fastened jewelry case. As for natural, what on earth does that make the rest of you? Unnatural?"

"Maybe it's not a concept we need to dignify with a word."

"Well, when everybody stops treating it like the gravest error a person can make is to be born to an unmarried parent, then we'll stop needing a word for it," she said crisply.

"I see," Sydney responded. "I defer to your greater wisdom in this area."

"However," she said slowly, not sure if she were intruding too much into an area that was not her concern, "you do need to settle this with the duke."

He frowned. "I'm aware that taking Leontine away will distress Lex, but I haven't a notion of what else to do. She's my niece. She doesn't talk much, but when she does it's clear that she was passed from pillar to post after her mother died. I'm her only blood relation in England, and it's my duty to look after her." He stopped, as if his thoughts had snagged on one of his own words. Then he swiftly shook his head. "She's my only family as well. And that matters, Amelia. You have scores of relations but she and I haven't."

"Blood isn't the only thing that makes a family," she observed. "I have blood relations who pretend I don't exist. Until I was eighteen, my eldest brother was one of them. My father's sisters won't even look at me. There are things that matter so much more than blood."

"Damn it. I know that. I'm sorry. I keep saying the wrong thing." He stood up straight and hefted his satchel higher on his shoulder. "I shouldn't have bothered you with all my domestic troubles. They're my own responsibility to sort out."

That was too much. She was not letting him part from her like this. "You aren't bothering me," she said. "I care what happens to you." Well, wasn't that about as tepid a declaration as a woman could produce from the bottom of her heart. "I care about you," she tried again, and no, that wasn't much better. It didn't help that Sydney was staring at her as if she were speaking in tongues.

"I care about you too," he said. "That, if you'll forgive me, is the problem."

"You have a funny understanding of what constitutes a problem."

He let out a choked laugh and kissed the corner of her mouth.

"Write to me," she said, and hastened up the stairs into the house.

Sydney found Leontine thoroughly caked in filth, and only vivid memories of her father having been similarly muddy stopped him from grabbing her out of the mud puddle and delivering her directly to the tender mercies of the bathtub.

"I'm going to be away for a fortnight," he said.

"Uncle and mademoiselle will take care of me," she said, not looking up from her twigs.

"What are you making?" he asked, thinking she'd tell him about fairy houses or mud pies.

"A road," she said. "For shipments of cheese." She indicated a leaf that was laden with acorns.

"Very sensible," he said solemnly. "Why must the cheese be delivered across the mud puddle?" he asked, crouching down to her level.

She cast him a pitying glance. "So the *lutins*—the . . ." She broke off, plainly searching for an English word. "The creatures who live in the woods? Little magic people?" Her tone was serious, as if she spoke of trestles and railway gauges.

"Fairies, or maybe brownies," Sydney supplied with equal gravity.

"So the brownies or fairies can get the cheese quickly. They do not care to wait for the cheese to go around the bog."

"Entirely practical," he said. "Your papa would have caused the bog to be dredged and a canal to be built."

"*Ça c'est stupide*," she said. "Then the boxes have to be hauled from cart to boat and back again. People will steal the cheese, then, and say it fell overboard."

"Precisely how much of my conversations with your uncle Lex have you overheard this summer?" Sydney asked.

"Enough," she said with a shrug.

He leaned closer, entirely aware that the hem of his coat was going to get muddy, but he wanted a closer view of what she was doing. "Are you building a bridge across the bog?"

"Not a bridge. A road, like I said." She gestured at the twigs that lay across the surface of the puddle. Then she placed the leaf—already laden with its acorn cargo—on top. "See, it does not sink. It floats."

Sydney stared at her. "You are very much like your papa, you know. He had the cleverest ideas. Did you know that a man once built a road like that across a bog, just like you're doing now? He was blind, like your uncle. Anyway, he made the road out of rush rafts, all tied together. It was strong enough to support horses and carriages, because the weight of anything that traveled across it tightened all the rafts together."

"*Naturellement*, like ocean ships can hold horses and great cannons," she said pityingly, as if she were now going to have to explain the most rudimentary principles of flotation.

"Chat Moss," Sydney said. "No need to go around it. No need to risk lives trying to lay pylons in the bottomless muck. The road floats right on top, and disturbs nothing at all." He got to his feet. "Leontine, my love, you are a genius."

He needed to get to Manchester, and he needed to do it right away. He repeated to himself: no need to bypass the bog, no need to plow through it, just float lightly over the top of it. It was elegant and practical and probably half the cost of circumventing the bog. He'd be awarded this contract and then he'd be near enough to Amelia to at least make things work in the short term—stolen days and rushed meetings.

Except that was just circumventing the problem, and it was as short-sighted and inefficient as circumventing the bog. A better solution wouldn't treat his friendship with Amelia as a problem, but as a part of the landscape.

After kissing Leontine's head, he rose to his feet.

"You have to take Fancy with you," she said, pointing at the terrier who had appeared at Lex's side. "Or she will be so sad."

"Fancy?" Oh, Francine. And sure enough the dog did look like she would pine away if he didn't bring her. She was doing something reprehensibly manipulative with her eyes, and her ears didn't even bear thinking about. "Fine," he said. There was no use fighting. He scooped the dog up and made his way to the inn.

Chapter Eighteen

---

1 September, 1824

Dearest Amelia,

    I shamelessly stole your most recent book from Lex's bookcase and left Moral Tales in its place. I stayed up unconscionably late reading it. I found myself wishing that Mary, Queen of Scots really had killed all those people. Unfortunately, this means I've now read all your books. When will the next be finished?

Yours,
Sydney

3 September, 1824

Dearest Sydney,

    The next book is still in its larval stages and we won't speak of it. However, in the spirit of full disclosure, I can

tell you that I have written another book, but I couldn't
put my name on it for reasons that would make themselves
abundantly clear as soon as you saw it.

    You may be interested to know that I have not had
a single blackberry in over a week because Georgiana
has brought them all to the duke and Leontine. First the
strawberries, and now this. It's nothing less than robbery.
This might seem unremarkable if you did not know how
jealously Georgiana guards her sweets.

Yours,

Amelia

5 September, 1824

Dearest Amelia,

    *Are you telling me what I think you're telling me? Give
me the title. I promise I'll destroy the letter immediately upon
receipt.*

Yours,

Sydney

7 September, 1824

S—

    A Princely Imposition.

—A

9 September, 1824

Dearest Amelia,

If you had told me two months ago that I would have had occasion to visit the sort of bookseller that carries obscene literature behind the counter, and would look forward to it, I would have assumed I had run mad. Booksellers of illicit material are very warm and welcoming, as it turns out. I only blushed the color of a tomato and stammered four times before I could utter the title aloud. The engravings are very educational and I've also learned a good deal about history.

Ever yours,
Sydney

11 September, 1824

Dear Sydney,

I'll regret to my dying day that I wasn't present to see you blush and stammer at the bookseller. I ought to tell you that I didn't write the entire book. I was responsible for the historical content while a friend wrote the more interpersonal segments.

Yours,
Amelia

13 September, 1824

Dearest Amelia,

I've gotten the post and am now the head engineer of the Liverpool and Manchester Railway, despite having sat through the interview with a dog asleep at my feet. Look forward to my building a scale model of how one goes about laying a road over a bottomless pit.

I spent the morning inspecting the new whitewashing at the house I hired the last time I was in town. The house is neat and clean, with flowered wallpaper in the dining parlor and a tidy nursery for Leontine at the top of the stairs. There are no mysterious noises in the dead of night, no creaking floorboards, no leaks, no damp, no hedgehogs. I should be quite pleased. I can't understand why I find the place entirely unlivable.

That's a lie. I know why I find it unlivable, and it's because I can't quite imagine you here. I'd ask you to tell me this is merely a failure of imagination on my part, but we both know it isn't.

Yours ever,

Sydney

13 September, 1824

Dearest Amelia,

Damn it, I went about that all wrong. What I'm asking is—oh, never mind, there's a reason this sort of thing is done in person, isn't there?

S

CHAPTER NINETEEN

As Sydney descended from the coach at the George and Dragon in Bakewell, he felt that he was in a strange in-between space, straddling two separate lives, two different versions of himself, and he didn't want to choose between them. He wanted to live in this liminal state, like dusk or dawn, neither here nor there, but temporary, transient, never quite real.

He tried to imagine Amelia as his wife. That was what he had been getting at in his last letter, unhinged and illiterate as it was. There really was only one thing to do with a person one loved, and that was marry them. Well, unless they didn't want to marry you, in which case you left them in peace. And this was all supposing one was legally able to marry the object of one's affections—he supposed the case would alter if he and Amelia had been of the same gender. But the fact was that they were both free to marry, and fond of one another, and Sydney was conventional enough to think this settled the matter. Except, he was starting to suspect that it didn't. Maybe they didn't need to let convention settle their fates for them.

He readjusted his satchel across his chest as he passed the stile and made his way along the lane towards Crossbrook Cottage. The only time he had ever proceeded beyond the gate was when he attempted to apologize to her, and he had been too angry and ashamed to get a good look at the place. It wasn't a proper cottage, he saw at once, but what had once been a farmhouse or a small manor house. It was made of the pale honey-colored limestone that was common in the area. Morning glories climbed up one wall, and the path to the door led through an artfully chaotic flower garden. Sydney smiled to himself as he realized that this was exactly what a pair of gently-reared London ladies would fancy as their country cottage. He peered around the back of the cottage and saw a small stable, a neatly trellised kitchen garden, a well with what looked like a new pump, and outbuildings that were decorously screened by a shrubbery. Yes, this was the precise level of rustication that he expected from Amelia Allenby and Georgiana Russell. He imagined Amelia choosing this house—near her friends, accessible by good roads, modern roof, newly glazed windows. He really wanted a closer look at that pump handle though. It had an unusual design. Was it cast iron? Wrought iron? He stepped closer. "Come, Fancy," he said, not even bothering to check over his shoulder for the dog he knew to be in his shadow. "Let's have a look."

"Stop there," said a gruff voice.

Sydney turned to face a man of somewhere between forty

and fifty, with close-cropped gray hair and the attire of a groom or stable hand. Amelia had referred to a Keating—an old family retainer or something of the sort.

"I'm here to call on the ladies of the house but I'm afraid I got carried away admiring the garden. Are you John Keating?"

"Depends on who's asking." He had his hand on the hip in a way that made Sydney strongly suspect that he had carried a sidearm or at least a knife of some kind. He ordinarily didn't much appreciate encountering rough-looking men who carried weapons but he found that he was glad Amelia had on hand a man who was willing to spill blood for her.

"I'm Sydney Goddard."

"The duke's friend," Keating said suspiciously. "You're supposed to be in Manchester."

"I only now returned." He gestured to his satchel. "And I have parcels for the women."

"Miss Allenby's indoors," Keating said, with a strongly implied *I'll be watching you.*

"Keating," came a high, clear voice. "I found this interloper being frightened out of his wits by Georgiana's cat." Nan trailed rather sheepishly behind her mistress. Beside Sydney, Fancy's ears pricked up. "She was hiding under the sofa."

"Not my dog, not my problem, miss," Keating said, very much with the air of a man who has had the same conversation many times.

"Keating," Amelia protested, laughing, "she has to be somebody's dog." She was dressed in one of her plain walking dresses and her bonnet was under her arm, her hair in a neat knot at the back of her head. He wanted to memorize the sight of her, learn her entirely by heart, so he could think of her the next time he was away.

"She's her own dog," Keating said, but the dog had already gone to hide behind his legs. "You've got company." He shrugged a shoulder in Sydney's direction.

Her face broke out in a smile before Sydney could explain that he was only stopping by and would leave if she didn't like it. He had seen a dozen varieties of her smile and knew them all by heart, and he knew this one to be genuine. He smiled back.

"We didn't expect you until tomorrow," she said. "And what have you done with your face!"

"I shaved before my meeting," he said, absently running a hand over the stubble that had already grown in on his jaw. "I finished my work early and—" And he couldn't stay away, that was the bare fact of the thing. "I have half a bolt of nankeen and three books," he said, taking off his satchel.

"Bring it indoors," she said. "Georgiana's at Pelham Hall and I'd love to give you tea instead of doing any work. I have scones! Janet made them with the good sugar. The fair sugar. Free sugar? The sort that's mentioned in your mother's book."

Sydney let out a totally unexpected burst of laughter, not only at the idea of Amelia reading his mother's book and taking its lessons to heart, but at the unvarnished thrill on Amelia's face at having found the right sugar. "I'll be sure to let her know in my next letter."

And it occurred to him that his mother would like

Amelia. They would disagree six times out of ten, but they would both enjoy doing so. They would respect one another. It also occurred to Sydney that this mattered to him more than he could have anticipated.

When they stepped into the cottage, the room Sydney saw before him was very much of a piece with the outside of the house. Mismatched chintz furniture, books scattered in a somewhat even layer across every surface, vases of flowers wedged in between the books, a fine dusting of cat hair throughout. Sunlight streamed in through a large window. Fancy promptly hopped onto the sofa and shut her eyes.

"Is this where you write?" he asked.

"No, that's upstairs. Do you want to see?"

"Of course I want to see. I need to know where the muses live when they whisper murderous nothings into your ear. Lead the way." He was dimly aware that this was inappropriate, but then he remembered that things between them had progressed quite beyond the stage where traditional concepts of propriety were even remotely applicable.

Her writing room was a small, low-ceilinged garret at the top of the house, into which an improbable quantity of furniture had been crammed. There were a desk and chair, two bookcases, and a sofa that he guessed was deemed too shabby for downstairs. There was an abundance of blankets and cushions throughout. The result of all this—he hesitated to call it clutter—was that he and Amelia were standing very close.

"It's a mess," she said. "Always is, no matter what I do."

"I'd expect nothing less." The words came out gruffly,

and she turned towards him in question. "I missed you," he said. "But I missed you even before I left. I missed our walks and"—he swallowed—"all that, and I suppose it stands to reason that I'd miss you even more not even being in the same county." She was looking at him with an expression that shifted from confused to pleased to something heated and hungry. "In any event—"

She shut him up with a kiss, rising onto her toes and meeting his mouth as if they had done this a dozen times, as if they had spent half a lifetime doing this. And when she licked into his mouth, that's how it felt—like she had always been there, like she would always be there, like they had been waiting and looking for one another without realizing it.

"I missed you too," she said, pulling away enough to speak the words. Her hands were in his hair, pulling him close, and he staggered under the force of it, accidentally pushing her against the wall. The memory of the last time they had been in this position, their hands all over one another, their breaths coming hot and fast, made his desire coalesce into something urgent and needful.

"Amelia," he said. He thought that maybe he ought to step back, stop pawing at her, but she didn't seem to want him to stop and God knew he didn't either. So he hauled her into his arms and deposited her onto her desk.

"Please tell me you're not going to sit me here and then go away," she said, laughter in her voice, the sunshine from the window behind her making her hair into a fiery crown.

"Sweetheart," he said, "I'll stay as long as you want me." He almost believed it was true.

It was extremely gratifying to be hauled about as if she were no more substantial than a cup of tea or a bunch of grapes. It was also gratifying that Sydney seemed utterly unconscious that he had knocked over a stack of books and sent a sheaf of papers floating to the floor. All he seemed to care about was touching as much of her as possible, and as that aligned nicely with her own interests, she did not protest.

Sitting on the edge of the desk did nothing to level out the difference in their heights; if anything, it exaggerated the difference, so that Sydney had to bend over her to properly kiss her, and it seemed only logical for her to wrap her legs around his waist for leverage. His mouth was soft on her own, a pleasant contrast with the coarseness of his stubbled jaw. One of his hands was at the small of her back, holding her in place, and the other cupped her breast, his thumbnail sliding across the fabric that covered her nipple. He bent his head and kissed that place, biting gently until she gasped.

"This gown has to go," he said, his voice rough. "God help me, get it off before I tear it off." The hand that fumbled at the buttons and tapes at the waist of her gown was shaking, and she put her own hand over it, holding it steady against her waist.

"The fastenings are at the back," she said, "but really I wouldn't mind if you tore it."

He set her on her feet, then with a firm hand on her hips, spun her around so her back was to him. "Another time," he said. "Another time I'll tear anything you please." And that

almost made her laugh because it was a thoroughgoing lie—
he'd never ruin her gown.

As he worked open the fastenings, he pressed a kiss over
each inch of exposed skin on the nape of her neck down to
the middle of her back. She expected him to whisk the gown
over her head, but instead he shoved it down a bit, then un-
laced her corset. She let out a shaky breath when she felt his
hands slide purposefully under her dress, then tug the corset
down, letting it fall in two pieces to the floor. Now his hands
were on her breasts, thumbing over her nipples, as he kissed
the side of her neck.

The hardness of his erection pressed against the small
of her back, and she pushed back against him. His arm
came around her middle, pressing her to him. And then,
with a groan that sounded like capitulation, he eased her
forward, so her hands were on the desk before her. The
hem of her skirt brushed against the back of her thighs as
he lifted her shift, the air suddenly cool against her skin.
She looked over her shoulder and watched him looking at
her, his eyes frantic and hungry, his body totally still, as if
paralyzed by want. She knew she was exposed, she knew
he liked what he saw. He unfastened his trousers and took
himself in hand.

"What are you going to do about that?" she asked, and
with a helpless laugh he passed his hand over his jaw.

"Amelia," he groaned, "you'll be the death of me." With a
steadying hand on her hip, he slid between her legs, hot and
close but not actually entering her. Instead, he got his hand
under her skirts and touched her clitoris. She held on to the

edges of the desk, wanting to push forward into his hand and back against his erection, but at the same time wanting to rub her breasts on the smooth surface of the desk. She was made of sensation, her nerves on fire. He was kissing the back of her neck as he touched between her legs, his erection hot and heavy, and she wanted it inside her.

"Please," she said, rocking back into him.

He laughed, a warm burst of air at the nape of her neck. Then he shifted his stance, widening her legs with his knees in a way that made her groan with anticipation. He slid into her, filling her, stretching her, and—this was what all the fuss was about. The first time had been good, but now there was no sting to undercut the pleasure, only the sensation of it being too much and just right all at once. She understood how people could make terrible choices, decisions that would alter the course of their lives, chasing after this feeling.

He entered her slowly, building up to a steady rhythm that she felt she knew by heart. As she edged closer to her climax, his breathing grew ragged, and it was the knowledge that he was barely holding on to control that pushed her over into her orgasm. Her fingernails dug into the varnish on the desk as the wave of pleasure crested over her. And then his hands were covering hers, his lips on hers as she turned her head, and he thrust a few final times into her before he withdrew.

Without the solid presence of him behind her, she sank to her knees, but he caught her and hauled her to the sofa. He sat sideways, and pulled her against his chest.

"Be careful," she said, "it's an old sofa."

"I noticed," he answered. "That's why we used the desk."

She didn't know why, but this foresight—he had bent her over the desk so as to spare her sofa a misfortune—made her laugh. "How chivalrous," she said. And maybe the orgasm had made her giddy, because another inane thought occurred to her. "Was that meant to be my tearful deflowering?" she asked.

"What?" He sounded gratifyingly dazed.

"Did this qualify?"

He gave a helpless little laugh into her throat. "You're mad and I adore you."

She thought her heart might burst from happiness. Maybe she was mad, maybe he did adore her, maybe those facts weren't connected by a *despite* or an *even though* but a simple *and*.

"Well, I suppose we'll just have to dedicate ourselves to doing it right next time," she said. His cheek was scratchy against her own and she wanted to nuzzle into it like a cat. "We could even do it in a bed. I hear that's considered de rigeur in some circles."

He laughed, a rumble she felt against her back, but then went still. "Look, I'm about to make history's worst marriage proposal, so I apologize in advance."

"I'll try to withhold judgment," she said, her mouth dry.

"I work fourteen-hour days for weeks on end and then sit idle for a month or longer. When the railway is completed, I'll likely go to an entirely different part of the country and repeat the process. I can't imagine that this life would appeal to anyone, and I'm mortified that I'm asking you to share it. I've already canceled my lease."

"You did?"

"I told you, it was unlivable. But what if we took a house in the country outside Manchester proper. I'd take the knockers off the door and, I don't know, put up quarantine signs or surround the house with skulls on pikes or do whatever it took to keep people away." He made a frustrated sound into her hair. "I told you this would be a bad proposal but I didn't really foresee decapitated heads coming into it."

"That was a nice touch," she said. "But here's the problem." She had been thinking about this in the days since she had received his last two letters. "I don't think I can move to a town, or even reasonably near a town. I would effectively be trapped inside the house."

"We could live even further afield," he said promptly.

God, he was trying, and somehow that made it all worse. "So, after I learned that a duke was moving into Pelham Hall—weeks before that debacle the first time I visited—I began to suspect that Crossbrook Cottage might not be isolated enough. Even the prospect of meeting with people who belong to that world is enough to make me want to bar the doors and draw the curtains. I have a nice collection of advertisements for houses to let in places like the Hebrides. I haven't entirely ruled that out, but for now Crossbrook Cottage feels safe again. Pelham Hall even feels safe. And I think that given time I might be able to expand that circle a little bit, but not so far as Manchester."

"I see," he said.

Without turning around, she knew his eyebrows were in

a deplorable state. She stroked his arm. "This is my home, Sydney. I've worked hard to get to the point where every day isn't a disaster, where I'm glad to know that there will be a tomorrow. And while I'd like my tomorrows to include you, they won't be in Manchester, or Liverpool, or Edinburgh, or any city at all. There are days when I feel like I can barely even manage this much." She shifted so she was facing him, then cupped his cheek in her hand. "I don't expect you to understand, just to believe me when I say that I know my limits. I'm done thinking it's my fault, or that I can make it go away by ignoring it. You've helped with that."

"I have?" He looked up, startled.

"You always accept my boundaries and treat them as normal. It's gotten me in the habit of paying myself the same courtesy."

"I was under the impression that Georgiana didn't push you to go beyond your capacity," he said carefully.

"She doesn't! But she'd do anything for me because that's her nature, whereas you—" She broke off, realizing she had no graceful way to end that sentiment.

"Whereas I'm churlish and intolerant?" He arched an eyebrow.

"Not exactly," she said. To her amazement, her cheeks were hot. She was comfortable enough with this man to stop checking her body's every reaction. "You're so matter-of-fact about it. It makes me feel that I'm doing fine."

He pulled her close for a kiss and she let herself go to him. "You are," he whispered into her hair.

"I know that this would all be easier if I didn't have my—predicament, if I could pack my bags and go with you. I know this is burdensome."

He held her chin steady and looked at her hard. "Nothing about you is burdensome," he said, his voice rough. "Do you hear me? You are clever and kind and"—he broke off to kiss her, clumsy and fierce—"you're sunshine. Meeting you is the best thing that's happened to me, and every time I see you I love you more. I'm going to take you on whatever terms I can get you. Separate houses, separate towns, marriage, no marriage." His arm tightened around her. "Just so you know."

She let herself imagine that he was right, and that what they had together—this honesty, this closeness—was strong enough to matter.

Chapter Twenty

Once Sydney discovered a problem, he had never been able to refrain from trying to solve it. This was why he did what he did—he found ways to build things that needed to be created, found ways to work around obstacles that couldn't be moved.

At the same time, when there was a rule, it was usually there for a reason. Don't build on quicksand. Don't store gunpowder in a hayloft. Don't attempt a lasting relationship with someone who lives fifty miles away. Don't leave children to be raised by eccentric aristocrats. But sometimes rules, however comforting and secure, stood in the way of something greater. So he refused to believe that there wasn't a way forward with Amelia. So what if they couldn't find their way towards anything as conventional as setting up house together, a tidy and easily understood coupling of one man and one woman under one roof. He had never had his heart set on any of that in the first place. Maybe there was some other way, something bigger and broader and messier. He spent his days building things a previous generation hadn't dared, traversing impassible gorges and working impossible bridges. He could figure out a way to span the distance between him and Amelia, between Crossbrook Cottage and Manchester. He could do that, and he would.

He returned to Pelham Hall in a state of determination. He needed to sit down with Lex and figure out how he and Leontine played into whatever plans Sydney was making. They needed to have this out, once and for all.

But when he walked through the front door he found the house deserted.

"Lex!" he called. There was no answer. "Leontine!" Nothing. Not stopping to drop his satchel, he walked through the house and out the terrace doors. The gate that led from the garden to the stables was ajar, so he went in that direction. As he approached, he heard sounds of confusion. A few lads who looked to be stable boys were running to and fro, and one of the nursemaids was sobbing into her pinafore. Lex stood on his own, one hand braced against a hitching post.

"Will someone tell me what is going on here?" Sydney demanded.

"Leontine fell off her pony," Lex said. "That's all I know."

Sydney's heart turned over in a way it hadn't since that day he had received the letter telling him of the fire and Andrew's death. "Where is she? Is she all right?"

"I don't know!" Lex said.

"What the devil was she even doing on a pony? She's six years old." Sydney's first, uncharitable thought was that he must have been delusional to think that Lex could make responsible decisions for a child. He nearly said so out loud, but caught the desolate look on Lex's face, and remembered what

Lex had said before Sydney left for Manchester. Lex needed him. "All right," he said, forcing his voice to sound calm. He put a hand on Lex's shoulder. "Tell me what you do know."

"A groom returned with the message that Leontine had fallen. Keating carried her to the nearest house. Miss Russell is with her as well."

"That's good," Sydney said, even though nothing about this was remotely good. "I'm going to have the carriage bring me to wherever Leontine is. Do you want to come with me or stay here?"

"I feel responsible," Lex said, his hand pressed over Sydney's. "It was my idea to get her the stupid animal."

And with that, any inclination Sydney might have had to blame Lex for the accident evaporated. "I know. You're wrong, but I know." His inclination was to rush out the door and head immediately for Leontine, but she already had two competent adults with her and didn't need him urgently. Lex, however, was plainly distraught. Lex, too, was family; Lex was the one who needed him now. The man had lost his entire family in the course of a few years, and God knew Sydney had been useless to him during that time; he could only imagine what nightmare scenarios Lex's mind was conjuring. "All right," Sydney said calmly, looping his arm into Lex's and guiding him towards the house. "I'm going to find out where Leontine is and check on her myself. I'll send word to you immediately, all right?"

He poured Lex some brandy and rang for Carter. Then, on impulse, he snapped his fingers for Fancy and put the dog onto the sofa beside Lex. He knew from experience that an animal snoring on one's lap was oddly soothing.

"That dog smells," Lex said. "Promise you'll let me know right away, regardless of—"

"Right away," Sydney said. Lex might think Sydney's sense of duty was a poor substitute for affection, but sometimes duty was just another word for love and friendship, another way to show people that they mattered to you. He bent to give Lex a quick embrace, then strode out to the stables.

Amelia sat in the wreckage of her writing room, regarding the papers that were strewn across the floor and the stacks of books that were toppled. Instead of trying to restore order, she curled up on the sofa. It still smelled of Sydney. None of what had passed between them was bad, she told herself. There was no reason for her to feel so cast down. She had known from the beginning that their parting was a foregone conclusion, and she thought she had made peace with that. Sydney's insistence that they could somehow continue despite everything shouldn't make her miserable. She watched the late afternoon sun stream through the window and tried to convince herself that she wasn't sad.

Then she sat at her desk and killed off a very annoying courtier, which proved to be a much more satisfactory way to spend an evening. She didn't know if you truly could kill a man by soaking his shirt in embalming fluid, but it sounded marvelous. This, she could do. She could write about jerkins and coronets and arcane methods of murder; she could describe a court and populate it with people who, she supposed, acted very much like normal people. People who did not need to hide away.

She put her pen down and frowned. Perhaps she had been thinking about this all backward: living this way didn't cut her off from the world, it let her live more fully than she would if she existed on the edge of panic. This way, she could have friendships and feelings; towards the end of her time in London she had been numb to everything but panic. She looked around her writing room, at the faded wallpaper and the dusty window. This was home. She might not get to see the people she loved as often as she wished, but seldom did a day pass without a letter. She didn't feel caged here anymore, only safe.

The sun had long since set, and was working by lamplight when she heard the door open downstairs. She glanced at her clock and saw that it was already past ten, so she sprinkled some sand on her last page and went downstairs. There she found Georgiana, her face pale, her riding habit muddy. Before Amelia could open her mouth to ask whether her friend was all right, Georgiana held up her hand to forestall any questions.

"I'm perfectly fine. Leontine fell off her pony and I've been with her." Georgiana proceeded to tell Amelia the rest of the story: she and Keating had been teaching Leontine to ride, the pony had bolted after seeing a hare, and the child had fallen. By then, they were some distance from Pelham Hall, so it made more sense to bring the child to the nearest house than it did to attempt to return her home.

"Who is with her now?" Amelia asked. "And where is she?"

"Mr. Goddard. And they're at Stanton House."

Amelia drew in a sharp breath of air, both because Stanton House was over two miles away from Pelham Hall, and because it was a stately home of some renown and the seat of the earls of Stafford. When she heard that Leontine had been taken to the nearest house, she had assumed that meant a tenant farmer's cottage or perhaps the vicarage.

"It turned out to be the best possible place for her, because Lord and Lady Stafford are having a house party and a physician was in attendance. He set the child's leg and now all that's left is waiting to see whether she wakes up."

Sydney had to be beside himself with worry. "I need to go to him."

"The house is crawling with people, some of whom you'll have met in London," Georgiana cautioned. "And, well, Mr. Goddard is not in the best of moods."

"I should think he wasn't," Amelia said, already stepping into her walking boots. "As for whoever is at Stanton House, that will be very bad, and I'm certain I'll feel terrible the entire time, but I'm not letting Sydney stay there by himself, uncertain of whether or not his niece will survive." And it would be bad—there was no question on that count. But this was her choice. Maybe part of her making peace with her constrained life was the knowledge that she could leave, and that it might be terrible, but it would also be temporary.

"Amelia. Wait. It's past ten. Keating can't bring you in the carriage, because he's at Pelham Hall. He feels terribly responsible for what happened, as he was the one who was teaching Leontine to ride. If you wait until the morning, I'll go with you."

"Fine," Amelia said, calculating how long it would take to get to Stanton House on foot. An hour? Two at the utmost.

"There's something else," Georgiana said. "There's been a development I ought to tell you about."

"Oh?"

"Hereford—Lex—asked me to marry him."

Amelia could not say she was surprised. Georgiana was spending increasingly long hours at Pelham Hall, and it had occurred to Amelia that they might be developing an attachment to one another. Perhaps not a romantic one, but an attachment nonetheless. "And what did you tell him?"

"That I had no interest in going to bed with anybody. He said that he doesn't have any interest in going to bed with women and wouldn't think to trouble me in that capacity, unless we agree to endure one another's company in that regard in order to beget a child."

"I assume he's proposing a marriage of convenience?" Amelia asked carefully.

"Not exactly," Georgiana said. "I don't think I could love anyone, not in the way most people mean when they talk about love matches. But we've become friends. I'm really frightfully fond of him. He wants to stay in the country for the most part, which suits me fine." She cast an arch look at Amelia. "And I'd make a very good duchess," she added.

"You'd make the best duchess," Amelia agreed.

Georgiana's cheeks were pink, not with embarrassment, Amelia guessed, but with happiness. Georgiana had found somebody she wanted to spend her life with. Amelia firmly tamped down an ugly swell of jealousy, and kissed her friend on the cheek. "You look very tired, Georgiana. Try to rest."

She waited until she no longer heard footsteps from Georgiana's bedroom above, and then slipped out the door towards Stanton House.

Chapter Twenty-One

Amelia knew exactly where Stanton House was, of course. For over a year, she had carefully avoided going anywhere near it or any of the other large homes in the area. Getting there wasn't the trouble. Making herself walk through the gate was where her mind kept snagging.

She had expected to find Stanton House closed up for the night. House party or no, it was past midnight. But carriages were lined up along the drive leading to the house's portico, and every window on the ground floor was bright with flickering candlelight.

A carriage passed them, its wheels crunching loudly on the gravel lane. Nan growled.

"My sentiments exactly," Amelia said. "They're having a ball." She counted the carriages. Where on earth had Lord and Lady Stafford even found ten families near enough to invite? And that wasn't even counting whoever was staying at the house. She straightened her spine. She had not come all this distance to quake in fear at the prospect of crashing a ball.

She stepped towards the front door, then thought better of it. The servants' entrance would be much more sensible. It was easy enough to find, with servants walking in and out, even at this hour. The door was propped open to let out some of the heat of the kitchens, so Amelia walked in.

"Excuse me," she said, approaching a woman who looked like a lady's maid. "An injured little girl was brought here earlier today. Her family sent for me to help nurse her, so would you please show me the way?" It wasn't the truth, but Amelia had always been a good liar.

"Oh ma'am," the maid said, getting to her feet. "I don't even work here. Bess!" she called. "This lady says there's a sick girl here?"

Bess cast a discerning eye over Amelia. Amelia followed the path of her gaze. By the light of the kitchen lamps, Amelia could see what she had not noticed outdoors in the dark: her skirts were muddy and covered up to the knee in nettles. Nan, not a prepossessing animal on the best of days, was in much the same condition as Amelia's skirts. Amelia did not even want to consider the state of her hair. Bess pursed her lips. "I'll have to ask Mrs. Powers," she said, then disappeared down a corridor.

If this Mrs. Powers was the housekeeper, there was no chance of her appearing in the kitchen on the night of a ball. She would have work to do upstairs, and a lot of it. And no lower servant would give Amelia, in her current bedraggled state, permission to venture further into the house. So Amelia had a choice: she could sit and wait and trust that eventually someone would get around to showing her the way to Sydney and Leontine, she could sneak upstairs when the servants weren't looking and prowl about until she found the way, or she could go to the front of the house, announce who she was, and demand to be helped.

Amelia sighed. "Come on, Nan. We have work to do." They retraced their steps back to the front of the house, past the line of carriages, directly to the front door. The night was fine, so the door stood open. Through it wafted a familiar scent: floor polish, lemon oil, beeswax candles, several varieties of perfume and eau de cologne, a faint undertone of sweat. It was the smell of a ballroom. Something deep within her filled with that old dread. She rubbed her arms. No matter what happened, it would be over soon, and she would never have to do it again. She scooped Nan up in her arms, both because acting like the animal was one of those tiny dogs ladies carried everywhere was the only way she could think of for getting Nan into the house, and because holding the dog close was at least slightly soothing.

She sailed through the door as if disheveled and mud-covered women bearing filthy dogs routinely presented themselves at all the best parties. "Good evening," she said to a man she assumed to be the butler. "I'm here to see the little girl who was injured earlier today."

"Who shall I tell Lady Stafford has called?"

"That won't be necessary," Amelia said, using her most clipped and polished accent. "There's no need to bother her in the middle of a ball. And as you see I met with some misadventures on my way. If you could whisk me away before one of your guests catches sight of me in this state, I'd be forever grateful."

Amelia would never know what finally convinced the butler—whether it was the dread of being discovered in conversation with a woman who looked like one of Macbeth's witches, or whether it was the prospect of rendering aid to a lady who might have deep pockets. But in any event, he ushered her to the servants' stairs and through a series of corridors until halting before a closed door. He tapped on the door and opened it without waiting for a response, then gestured for Amelia to enter.

"I told you, we don't need—" Sydney said, looking up from the bed where Leontine slept. "What the devil are you doing here?"

Amelia heard the door snick shut behind her. "You really are a bear when you're anxious." She put Nan down and stepped closer to the bed. "How is she?"

"She woke up an hour ago, asked about the pony, complained about her leg, and then went back to sleep. So her head is probably fine. I've already sent word to Lex. How the hell did you get here?" He looked at her dress. "Please tell me you didn't walk three miles in the middle of the night."

"All right. I flew. I tunneled beneath the hills."

"Amelia—"

"I turned myself into bats and—"

"Sit down," he growled. "Why are you here?"

Sitting in the chair beside his, Amelia cast him a doleful glance. "Oh, just happened to be in the neighborhood."

"You know what I mean."

"Almost everybody alive prefers to be worried with a friend by their side. So, here I am."

"Of course I'm worried," he said. "This should never have happened."

"I've fallen off a horse," Amelia said. "More than once. I'm not given to feats of athleticism, you see. One of my sisters broke her arm on a swing. The other twisted an ankle learning to waltz. Georgiana has a scar on her temple from crashing into a windowsill during a game of blindman's buff. Children get hurt. Sometimes it's because of a failure of supervision, but Leontine had a groom and Keating with her, not to mention Georgiana, who could ride almost as soon as she walked. Keating taught my niece and nephew to ride when they were four and I was there to watch him do it. I'd trust him with my life."

"There's no need for a child of six years to be on a horse."

"Indeed there isn't. There's no need for a lot of things, like books and dancing, or bridges and railways. You could keep her in a tower and she'd be perfectly safe and perfectly miserable. She's a spirited child and frankly I'm amazed she hasn't broken her leg before. While walking here I realized that she must have held onto the pony's neck for nearly a mile. Can you imagine? She'll be a fearless rider one day."

He opened his mouth to protest then snapped it shut again. Then he tipped his head back and banged it against the wall, his eyes squeezed shut. "There has to be a way to keep the people you love safe. If you follow all the rules and take all the proper precautions, it ought to be guaranteed."

She reached out and took his hand. "You'll get no argument from me."

They sat silently for a while. "I'm trying to be better. More broad-minded. But every time something goes wrong, my mind reverts to rules. If a bridge collapses, there's a reason. Somebody miscalculated or misjudged. I know that with people it's different, but my *mind* doesn't know that."

She squeezed his hand. "Well, you happen to be talking to the regional expert in minds that don't know what they're doing."

He sighed. "I keep thinking that there's a way for us to arrange things in a way that isn't quite so hidebound, but I'm afraid of what will happen if things go wrong. What if I were in Manchester and you were here, and you fell ill? What if I couldn't get to you in time?"

Amelia wanted to reassure him that this wouldn't happen, but that would be a lie, and not the sort of lie she could countenance. "It wouldn't be either of our faults," she said. "Leontine fell because her pony bolted, not because you weren't at hand."

For a few moments they sat in silence, hands clasped, Sydney's thumb tracing idle circles over the inside of Amelia's wrist. "Did you really climb over hill and dale in the dark of night only to tell me all these wise things?" he asked. "Did you—Amelia," he said, turning to her abruptly, his eyes wide, "you walked into a house in the middle of a ball. Thank you."

"I hope never to do so again, but it seemed the most reasonable course of action at the time. And you're welcome." She felt anxious but sane, sitting in this strange house far away from any place she wanted to be. It was good to know that she could test the boundaries of her world and see exactly where her limits were.

"I'd never have asked you to come," he said, bringing their joined hands to his mouth to kiss her knuckles. "Never in a million years."

"I know. I think it's the same as when Nan bit you—maybe worry over other people shakes my own worry out of my head temporarily. What do you mean, you're trying to arrange things in a way that's less hidebound?"

"Well, I love you and I want to have you in my life," he said as if this were the most obvious thing in the world. "And if you're at Crossbrook Cottage and I'm knee deep in muck halfway between Liverpool and Manchester, that won't make me love you less. If the best we can do is sporadic visits, would that be acceptable to you?"

"Yes, it would be acceptable to me," she said, trying not to laugh. "But is it acceptable to you? It seems you're the one being done out of a proper wife and hostess and all those things people seem to want."

"Are those things terribly important to you?"

"No," Amelia said. "Not in the least."

"Then to hell with all of it." He drew her close and kissed the top of her head.

It was still dark out when Sydney woke, stiff and bleary-eyed in the hard-backed chair. Amelia slept, her head in his lap. He brushed a few strands of hair off her temple. Leontine's eyes were shut, but he could see the steady rise and fall of her chest.

If anything ever happened to either of them, he didn't

know how he'd pick himself up and carry on. He also had the distinct impression that at some point this past summer, coincident with the moments Amelia and Leontine entered his life, his entire world had been tipped onto its side. Everything he thought he knew and believed seemed a lot hazier than it had two months ago, but in exchange he had something vaster and more sprawling. The fact that he was pleased by this was frankly terrifying.

Amelia stirred and turned her head up to face him.

"I've been thinking about something," she said sleepily. "I very much enjoyed your mother's book."

"Good morning to you, too," he said, smoothing her hair back. She was going to have a devil of a job trying to get the brambles out later.

"I especially enjoyed the story of Hannah and Mary, who share a house. It put me in mind of friends who have found their own happiness in unconventional domestic arrangements. If I were a man, or you were a woman, we wouldn't count ourselves unlucky if we didn't share a house, would we?"

"No," he acknowledged, while marveling that he was going to have a lifetime with a woman who spoke in complete paragraphs at unconscionable hours in the morning.

"I don't know how persuasive this will be, but my parents weren't married and only lived together sometimes. It was still a family. You know, Georgiana and Hereford are getting married, and that'll be a family too. The rules as we know them might work wonderfully for most people, but they're absolute rubbish for anyone who's a little different. We don't need to twist ourselves around to fit the conventions of marriage and love, conventions that maybe weren't meant to suit us anyway. And then there's the other matter. We've somehow surrounded ourselves with other people who share our, shall we say, capacity for those unconventional arrangements. It's safer for us all, but also it's good to know that one can be oneself."

He remained silent for the space of two breaths. "Yes. That is something I've found as well," he said. His eyes were stinging and he thought he might cry from relief, but he didn't know why. Amelia knew him, knew who he really was, and that was something he hadn't even known he needed.

When the first rays of sunlight had barely started to shine through the lace curtains, the door was thrown open. Georgiana stood on the threshold, bearing a stack of books and briskly ordering Sydney and Amelia to go home and get changed. "And that dog! Take it away. I don't know whether to be appalled that you brought that flea-bitten mongrel into Stanton House or relieved that you had some protection on your insane midnight ramble. I cannot believe you, Amelia. I nearly had a heart attack." As she spoke she readjusted Leontine's quilt, lay a hand on the sleeping child's forehead, and pulled the cord for a servant. "You and Amelia take the carriage back to Pelham Hall, then send Lex and Carter back here in it. The carriage can ferry us back and forth in shifts until Leontine can be moved. Lady Stafford has offered us the use of her own carriages but I took it upon myself to explain that the child is the Duke of Hereford's ward and that the duke obviously has his own carriage. Now go."

"Your Georgiana has two modes," Sydney said when he and Amelia were seated in the carriage. "Absolute indolence and . . . whatever that just was."

"She'll be a splendid duchess," Amelia said, suppressing a yawn.

Sydney muttered something anarchical but forbore from any more pointed remarks. When the carriage stopped in front of Crossbrook Cottage, he wrapped his hand around the back of her neck and pulled her close for a kiss. "Later," he said. "Get some rest."

Upon entering Pelham Hall, Sydney found Lex lying on the sofa in the great hall, Fancy asleep in his lap. "She's all right," Sydney said as soon as he walked through the door. "Also it wasn't your fault Leontine was injured. I'm going to repeat that to you until you believe it."

Lex raised an eyebrow. "Thank you. I reserve the right to blame myself forevermore. Keating persuaded me not to have the horse shot. I hope I don't regret it," he said darkly. "I expect you'll be whisking Leontine off to Manchester as soon as she's healed."

"No," Sydney said. "You're quite right that this is her home and I ought to have realized that weeks ago. With me, she'd be in the care of maids and governesses around the clock. Here, she has you all the time. I'll visit as often as I can. I believe I've persuaded Amelia to marry me or at least to live in sin with me periodically so I'll have even more of an incentive for frequent visits." Lex had gone perfectly still as he listened. "So it would seem that my entire family will be in one convenient corner of Derbyshire."

If there was perhaps a slight glistening about Lex's eyes, it quickly passed. "That, you imbecile, is what I've been trying to tell you for over a month. I don't even want to know what Miss Allenby had to do in order to persuade you of it. Never tell me. By the way, I'm marrying Georgiana. We're never going to bed together and we'll be raiding an orphanage at the earliest opportunity. Wish me happy."

Sydney was not a man overly given to displays of affection, but he leaned down and wrapped his arms around his friend, holding him close until Lex finally pushed him away. "You disgust me. Take a bath."

The sound of Lex's cackle followed Sydney all the way to his bedroom.

Amelia had barely managed to wash and change before she heard the sound of carriage wheels below. She assumed it was someone from Pelham Hall come to fetch Keating, but then she heard a familiar voice.

"Where the devil is everybody?" somebody shouted. "Keating? Place is as empty as a plague village."

"Robin!" Amelia called, and ran down the stairs and out the front door.

Robin—excessively dusty and wearing breeches, top boots, and a bottle-blue riding coat—dismounted the horse. "Did you murder the whole lot of them?"

"No," Amelia laughed, embracing her friend. "They've all forsaken me for the Duke of Hereford. When did you get back from France?"

"A week ago," Robin said. "Is the Duke of Hereford really in Derbyshire? We heard that he left town in the most secretive and thrilling manner. Alistair will be hideously jealous if I see him first."

"Does Alistair know the duke?"

"They were at Eton together. Are we quite alone? I suspect they"—she lowered her voice—"were at Eton *together* if you understand my meaning. Alistair went to Eton with a shocking number of people, I'll have you know. Is he handsome? I've never met him."

"Very," Amelia said, struggling to keep up with Robin's train of thought, and distracted by a realization of her own: she and Robin were able to discuss this sort of thing without any fear of judgment or exposure. She had known that for years, of course, but now it occurred to her that it *mattered*: she could be open and honest with Robin and other friends who shared similar secrets in a way that she could not with anyone else. It was the same with Georgiana, Sydney, and Hereford. They were safe together in a way that bound them, and the result was something like family.

Robin laughed. "Figures Keating would find the nearest aristocrat with a handsome face."

"I can't imagine he'd have time, what with the curate and the butcher's apprentice and heaven knows who else." That would, however, explain Keating's mysterious absences and several consecutive days of a decent mood.

"Where there's a will," Robin said lightly. "I suppose I'll have to put up the horse myself. Come on, Jess," she said, patting the animal on the rump. "Let's get you watered."

"It seems the entire county has paired off in the most egregious manner," Amelia said. "If you're correct about Keating and the duke, that's one. Also Georgiana and Hereford are thick as thieves."

Robin looked up. "That's only two, which hardly seems a rash of couplings, especially since Hereford figures in two of the pairings." Then Robin looked more closely at Amelia— possibly lingering on a bruise where Sydney had kissed her neck. "Oh, I see. Are we happy or sad? What's their name?"

This was why Amelia loved Robin. There was no beating around the bush, no asking about intentions, no exaggerated concern. Robin let Amelia define her own emotions and then follow Amelia's lead.

"His name is Sydney Goddard. And we're happy," Amelia said. "He works in Manchester but I'm staying here."

"Good for you!"

"You don't think it's odd that we'd have separate homes?"

Robin looked at her carefully. "It's a bit out of the ordinary, but so are a lot of things I happen to like very much. Heaven save me from the ordinary."

"You don't think it's unfair of me to saddle him with a life that's probably very different from what he expected?"

"No, you ninny, and neither do you or you wouldn't be asking *me*. You'd ask the vicar or someone else who sets any stock in ordinary things. We don't decide whether we're inconveniences or beloved additions to the lives of our partners. I tore myself up about whether Alistair ought to make a proper marriage. Marrying me *did* tear up his peace quite thoroughly. But at the end he didn't mind, and I realized that my minding only rained on his parade."

"I suppose," Amelia said.

"Oh, Amelia. Sweetheart. Is your Sydney *very* stupid?"

Amelia laughed. "No, quite the contrary."

"Then give him some credit. By all means, spell out your limitations to him, if you haven't already done so. But chances are they mean more to you than they ever will to him."

"That's almost exactly what he said."

They were interrupted by footsteps on the lane.

"Keating!" Robin called. "You randy old goat, where have you been?"

"Living an honest and decent hardworking life, unlike some yellow-haired imps I know. Amelia, how's Miss Leontine?"

Amelia decided not to ask how Keating already knew that she had been at Leontine's bedside, just like she decided not to ask why, at this early hour, Keating was coming down the lane from Pelham Hall rather than from the carriage house. "Much better. Was Mr. Goddard abrupt with you yesterday?"

"Goddard? He thanked me for carrying the child to Stanton Hall, tried to give me five shillings, and then muttered under his breath about horseback riding being worldly nonsense and something about perdition and Babylon." He turned his attention to the horse Robin was currying. "What's this hack you're riding? Tell me you didn't buy her."

"God no. She's a mare I hired in Cromford when I couldn't

stand the prospect of another mile in that bloody nuisance of a curricle."

"Aw, your arse too fine now to be jostled on the road?"

And that was a pretty characteristic reunion between Keating and Robin, Amelia reflected. A couple of insults, maybe a gruff hullo. Whereas the last time Amelia's mother and sisters had visited, they all stood in the drawing room and cried from happiness. Amelia suspected that if more than a week passed between Amelia's letters, her mother would drape the house in black crepe. Amelia had given those near and dear to her plenty to worry about over the years. And yet, they did love her. She had never doubted it. There were different kinds of love and different ways to express it, and what she had with Sydney was as valid as anything else. Even if they never shared a home, even if they never actually married—that didn't mean their love was worth less than anybody else's. For the first time in years, maybe, Amelia realized that she didn't fear loneliness and isolation; she had built a life for herself that let her have friendship and love.

Sydney was not shocked to discover that a bedridden Leontine was even more of a handful than usual. At the end of a week she had beaten Sydney at chess, cajoled one of Lady Stafford's maids into bringing contraband sweetmeats, poured her medicine onto the floor, and told Lex to summon the magistrates because she was being held hostage by miscreants. Once word had gotten out that she was the Duke of Hereford's ward, Lord and Lady Stafford insisted that her caretakers join the family at meals and treat the house as their home.

Sydney refused on principle. Lex and Georgiana accepted on principle. Amelia graciously declined and then all but barricaded herself in Leontine's room. "There is a limit," she announced to Sydney, her back against the door, her face slightly flushed. "And I think I have crossed it." He went to her and told her she was brave and good and kind and reminded her that she never had to come back. And so she didn't. Instead they exchanged letters over the course of that week, and everything felt wonderfully, impossibly simple.

After they finally brought Leontine back to Pelham Hall and got her settled in a bedroom on the ground floor, Sydney walked to Crossbrook Cottage. It was far too late for social calls, but he and Amelia had done everything backward and improperly from the start.

There was a light in her writing room, so he decided to take a chance. He picked up a small pebble and tossed it from hand to hand. He had never thrown a rock at someone's window in the hope of getting their attention, and wasn't certain how gently he could throw the stone to make sure it didn't break the window. Perhaps he could aim for the wall beside the window?

Before he could puzzle that out, a dog started barking. It was Nan, and she was not pleased to see him. Mortified, he passed a hand over his beard. Likely Keating would come out and threaten him with firearms. But it wasn't Keating who opened the door, but Amelia herself. And she wasn't carrying a firearm, but a frying pan.

"Sydney?" she asked.

He was grateful that the moon was full enough for her to recognize him. At least he wasn't going to be bludgeoned tonight.

"It's me," he said.

"Heel, Nan. Good girl. What are you doing here?" Her hair was in a plait and she wore a dressing gown.

"It took hours to get Leontine to sleep," he said. "And at some point in the past week, half Lex's household has moved to Pelham Hall. His secretary seems to be sleeping in my bedroom, and I can't tell if this is due to confusion or if Lex is trying give me an excuse to spend the night here. As if I'd need the excuse. I missed you."

She kissed him, and he could feel the promise in it. The feel of her hips under his fingers and the scent of her hair almost brought tears to his eyes. She was warm and solid in his arms and he didn't want to step away, not now or ever. She pulled back enough to speak. "I love you. We'll make this work."

"We already are."

She tugged on his sleeve, and he let himself be led inside. He let himself be led right up the stairs.

"You don't mean to tell me you mean to do this in a bed," he asked when she had shut the door behind them. "Although if you intend to keep holding that frying pan, I suppose it'll add a bit of a frisson."

She pantomimed hitting him in the shoulder with the pan, then put it aside on a table.

"Oh well. Guess we'll do without the—"

She kissed him. "When did you become funny?" she asked. "You used to be so stern. All eyebrows and jaw and shoulders."

"I still have all those things."

"But they aren't always cross." She unwound his neck cloth and dropped it to the floor.

"It's probably you. Don't let it go to your head."

"Oh, I already did."

There went Sydney's coat. He held still while she untucked his shirt and lifted the hem.

"Get it off," she said, already applying her mouth to his chest. She bit his collarbone as she began unbuttoning the fall of his trousers.

The previous times they had been together, they had hardly removed any clothing at all, only loosened this and pushed aside that. Now, in the moonlight, he wanted to see her. So when he kicked off his boots and stepped out of his trousers, he took hold of the cord of her dressing gown. He raised a questioning eyebrow.

She hesitated. Not, he conjectured, from shyness; she had stripped him naked and currently had one pale hand wrapped around his cock. Under no circumstances would he think of her as bashful. He had seen that hesitation before, when she was deciding whether to be honest.

"I'm confident we can make do with your wrapper on," he said. She could wear three dressing gowns and a riding cloak and he'd find a way to make her feel good.

She let the dressing gown fall. Her night rail, or chemise, or whatever it was called, was nothing more than a spiderweb of fine cotton lawn. With her back to the window, she was silhouetted by moonlight and he could make out the lush curve of her hip and the softness of her waist, the heavy fullness of her breasts and her plump arms. And that was through the gown—his mouth watered.

He put a hand at the small of her back and pulled her close, relishing the feel of her with nothing between them but that gossamer-fine cotton. He bent his head to kiss her throat, loosening the drawstring around the neckline, then skimming his hands over her breasts. He ran his hands over her nipples, heard her catch her breath, and then dropped to his knees. He slid his hand up her leg, then lifted the hem of her chemise and pressed a kiss to her stomach. He raised his eyes to make sure she liked what he was doing, and only saw hunger in response. He brought his mouth lower, kissing her thigh before seeking out the place where she would want his full attention. She let out a gasping, needy sound. "Sit on the bed," he said softly, and she did so. He pushed her legs apart, putting one of her knees on his shoulder, and then kissed her. She let her legs fall open further as he tasted and explored her.

She sighed and weaved her fingers through his hair, then gave his hair a tug. That was what did him in. She wanted his mouth exactly where it was and was letting him know about it. Her thumb stroked over his cheekbone and he almost whimpered against her soft, wet skin. He looked up and saw that her shift was rucked up to her chin, and one of her hands was cupped over a breast, working a nipple between thumb and forefinger. His hips bucked helplessly with nothing to grind against, and he was afraid he was going to come right there, his cock untouched, his entire body alight with her desire. When she came, soft and gasping, he worked her through it, then hauled her up to the top of the bed. She grasped his hips and pulled him towards her, wrapping her legs around him, arching up to meet him.

They were being carefully quiet, so when he entered her and felt her clench around him, he buried his face in the pillow to muffle his moan. He braced himself on one forearm and looked down at her, her lips parted in pleasure. She stroked a hand down his bicep, and then her hands were everywhere, exploring the contours of his shoulders and the planes of his back. He gripped one of her hands, pressing it into the mattress, holding onto it like a lifeline. He was being undone, coming apart.

She came again, his name on her lips, and he felt like a genius, like he had done something cleverer than build bridges and dig through granite. He pulled out—there was no handkerchief, damn it, he looked around frantically. "Your sheets," he said, and it was probably the least erotic thing anyone had ever whispered in the throes of passion, but his cock was aching in his hand and his ability to articulate himself had taken leave some minutes earlier.

"Here." She patted her stomach. His brain exploded. He hardly needed that last stroke to bring himself off. Only the thought of it, and he was lost to his climax.

After, he looked down at her, trying to catch his breath, trying to process the image of her with his seed on her belly, her *breasts*. She wriggled the rest of the way out of her shift, then used it to clean herself up.

He wasn't sure if he collapsed onto her or if she pulled him down, but either way they wound up in a tangle of limbs. "I'm crushing you," he said.

"I like it," she answered. "I like how big and heavy you are."

His cock twitched at her words. "You'll kill me," he said into her hair. "You ruined your chemise. I was trying to spare your laundry."

That must have been very droll because she laughed, and he felt very clever again.

It was Sydney's last day in Derbyshire before starting work on the railway. It would be a fortnight or more before he was able to return, so he bid farewell to Lex and Leontine and waited for Amelia at the gatepost where he had met her so many times.

"Where will you take me today?" he asked when she approached him. He touched her sleeve, the feel of her plain cotton dress so familiar under his fingers, the scent of her soap nothing less than a relief. She was warm and soft and he couldn't believe he had a lifetime of her to look forward to.

"You'll see," she answered.

They climbed to the top of the nearest peak in relative silence, he occasionally putting a hand to the small of her back to steady her as she made her way over some unstable rocks, she directing his attention to a fluffy owlet in a nearby tree.

"Look," Amelia said when they had reached the apex. "You can see the river from here."

And sure enough, you could: the River Wye was laid out like a silver crescent beneath them, its valley a deep green. In a few weeks, days even, the green would fade and the leaves of the trees that shadowed the valley would begin to turn. The summer was nearly over, and with it would go the sense of holiday unreality that Sydney had allowed to take over his life this past month. He turned from the river valley to the woman beside him, her bright hair loose in the wind, her skirts gathered in one hand to make climbing easier, and his heart stuttered in his chest with love for her. And when she turned to look at him, as if sensing his gaze on her, he saw the same thing reflected back at him.

"I love you," he said.

She kissed him again, needier and deeper this time.

Through the gaps in the trees, he could see part of Pelham Hall. It was just a house. A home, for some of the people who he had lost and then found, for a family he hadn't known was possible. It was filled with the past, but also with the promise of the future. He turned to Amelia, made sure her shawl was tied securely around her shoulders, and walked with her down the mountain.

Don't miss any of Cat Sebastian's Regency Impostors!

UNMASKED BY THE MARQUESS

The one you love . . .

Robert Selby is determined to see his sister make an advantageous match. But he has two problems: the Selbys have no connections or money and Robert is really a housemaid named Charity Church. She's enjoyed every minute of her masquerade over the past six years, but she knows her pretense is nearing an end. Charity needs to see her beloved friend married well and then Robert Selby will disappear . . . forever.

May not be who you think . . .

Alistair, Marquess of Pembroke, has spent years repairing the estate ruined by his wastrel father, and nothing is more important than protecting his fortune and name. He shouldn't be so beguiled by the charming young man who shows up on his doorstep asking for favors. And he certainly shouldn't be thinking of all the disreputable things he'd like to do to the impertinent scamp.

But is who you need . . .

When Charity's true nature is revealed, Alistair knows he can't marry a scandalous woman in breeches, and Charity isn't about to lace herself into a corset and play a respectable miss. Can these stubborn souls learn to sacrifice what they've always wanted for a love that is more than they could have imagined?

Available now from Avon Impulse

A DUKE IN DISGUISE

One reluctant heir

If anyone else had asked for his help publishing a naughty novel, Ash would have had the sense to say no. But he's never been able to deny Verity Plum. Now he has his hands full illustrating a book and trying his damnedest not to fall in love with his best friend. The last thing he needs is to discover he's a duke's lost heir. Without a family or a proper education, he's had to fight for his place in the world, and the idea of it— and Verity—being taken away from him chills him to the bone.

One radical bookseller

All Verity wants is to keep her brother out of prison, her business afloat, and her hands off Ash. Lately it seems she's not getting anything she wants. She knows from bitter experience that she isn't cut out for romance, but the more time she spends with Ash, the more she wonders if maybe she's been wrong about herself.

One disaster waiting to happen

Ash has a month before his identity is exposed, and he plans to spend it with Verity. As they explore their long-buried passion, it becomes harder for Ash to face the music. Can Verity accept who Ash must become or will he turn away the only woman he's ever loved?

Available Now from Avon Impulse

CAT SEBASTIAN lives in a swampy part of the South with her husband, three kids, and two dogs. Before her kids were born, she practiced law and taught high school and college writing. When she isn't reading or writing, she's doing crossword puzzles, bird watching, and wondering where she put her coffee cup.

Discover great authors, exclusive offers, and more at hc.com.